Ascendant

The Bright Heritage Chronicles

(Book One)

A. M. Aguilera

The Bright Heritage Company—Modesto, CA
Paperback ISBN: 979-8-8691-4204-7
eBook ISBN: 979-8-8691-4210-8
Title: *Ascendant | The Bright Heritage Chronicles (Book One)*
Author: A.M. Aguilera
Available formats: eBook
Paperback distribution

Any resemblance to persons living or dead, as well as any location, event, or entity is purely coincidental. This novel is a work of fiction.

Dedication

iii

To the Kid-lets: Miranda, Isaac, and Audrina. For all the bedtime stories we were forced to miss.

Acknowledgments

v

Thanks to Darlene Isaacs for the endless support and belief in me and in whatever I choose to take on as well as the countless hours spent on her original artwork for the illustrations throughout the book.

Raquel Aguilera, for contributing your fair share so I could finish this work and inspiring so much of its content!

Rebecca Aguilera, for coming through at a most critical time. I couldn't have crossed the finish line without you.

Mike Aguilera, for showing me how to fight to the very end, no matter the odds.

Preface

I started writing this series for my kids in 2015 — by hand — and it became an everyday joy to discover where the story would lead. Then, in December 2016, I suffered a nearly fatal brain injury. I woke from a coma months later with the complete loss of my dominant side, including my writing hand.

The completion of this series was never in question, even as I relearned to speak, function mentally, and walk again. It's been a fundamental part of my rehabilitation. My stubborn morning ritual: typewriter, coffee, and desk in the early morning hours before physical therapy.

As the story's characters progressed, grew, and overcame their travails, so did I. Many scenes were written from within the darkest imaginable dungeons of mind and body. Yet "we" battled on.

I credit inspiration, drawn from an inherited fighter spirit and the best — and absolute worst! —examples of people and events in the world around me.

Each character has become a dear friend, and they've taken over the story long ago. I'm their scribe, rendering it as accurately as I can. They will always hold a special place in my heart, and I hope they will live in yours. Enjoy!

A.M. Aguilera

Prologue

A pinpoint of green energy flickered in an achromatic abyss, stirring a slumbering host, a sigh of waking thought.

A tinier thought asked, without echo or sound, "Are you there?"

Like rushing wind through leaves, a throng of whispered consciousness responded, "Yes, we are here."

"Yes, we are here."

"Is this how it will be then, forever?"

"No, it too will pass."

"But I can't see, move, feel…or breathe!"

"Be still and sleep; with us."

"Are we dead?"

"No, child, not yet."

"What are we now?"

"We are what is left. Soon we will be less and then gone."

"Is there anything we can do?"

"Not us."

At this, the pinpoint of energy flickered frustration. The little thought ceased trying to reason with the collective. She tried with all her power to feel her limbs beyond space. To pry open her eyes, but if they existed, they were far away. All she had was awareness in utter blank space.

"Are you there, little one?"

The 'blankness' wasn't dark or light; it was without color. Then, the pinpoint tumbled into oblivion, aware of being amid nothingness and overwhelmed with vertigo.

"Are you there?" The host whispered with concern. She tried to respond but couldn't. Spinning, tumbling, she gave in to panic and screamed, "HELP MEEEE!!!"

She tried to thrash, feeling nothing, hearing nothing, seeing noth—

"Do you understand now? We are gone from the world. The void only remains. Now sleep."

"NO!"

"Yes, little one. Sleep now. Sleep and wait for this to pass."

The speck of green energy wanted to scream but didn't. So, instead, she tried to conjure the first thoughts she could remember. The spinning eased. Memories flickered green. She didn't know if they were dreams of reality or illusion, only that she was sure there was much more to existence than this. She thought of colors and textures, the wet of cool liquid, and the warm kiss of golden light on her skin.

She became vaguely aware that her corporeal body lived but was disconnected somehow. She felt sad and grieved silently. Instinctively she tried to breathe, and when she couldn't, she panicked and thrashed again, "HELP MEEEEEEE!!!"

***

Horace woke, gasping for air. He waved a hand and his room lit up with a gentle glow. He rubbed his crepe-wrinkled eyes and scratched an itch while trying to grasp at the fleeting dream. Such dreams held meaning, so failing to catch it, he sat up to meditate. A heavy growl inquired outside his door as his guardian familiar sensed his distress. The beams of the door groaned under her weight.

He ignored her, already settling into a patterned breathing rhythm.

His inner being began giving over impressions of the dream sense: suffocation, nothingness—a great wrong in the land.

It was the location of the land that piqued his interest. Could it be? After all this time, a stirring remnant of light in the tainted wilds?

It was time for him to make his rounds. He conjured a water blob, dipping his head in and scrubbing it with aged hands. He dispelled the globe and swung his legs off the bed.

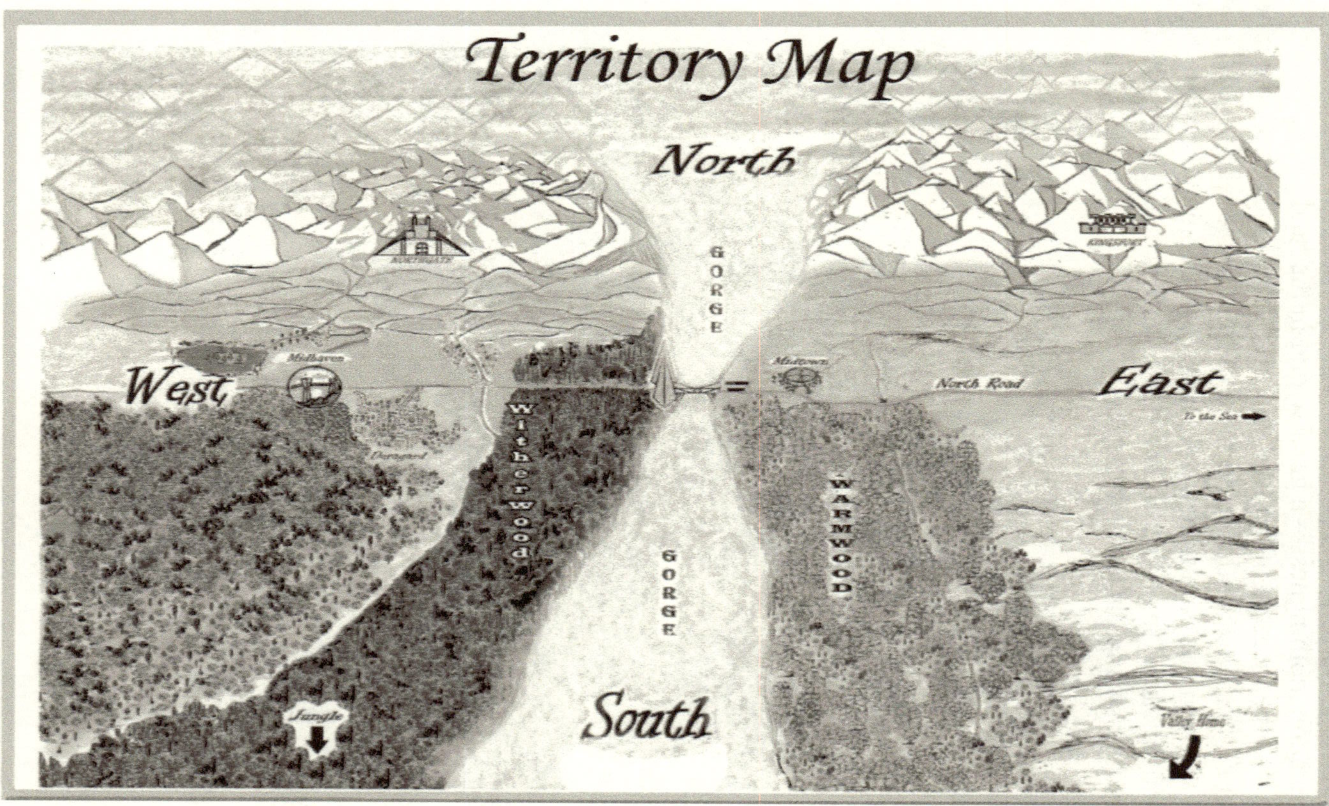
Territory Map
North
South
East
West
GORGE
GORGE
Witherwood
Warmwood
North Road
To the Sea
Jungle
Valley Home

MIDHAVEN

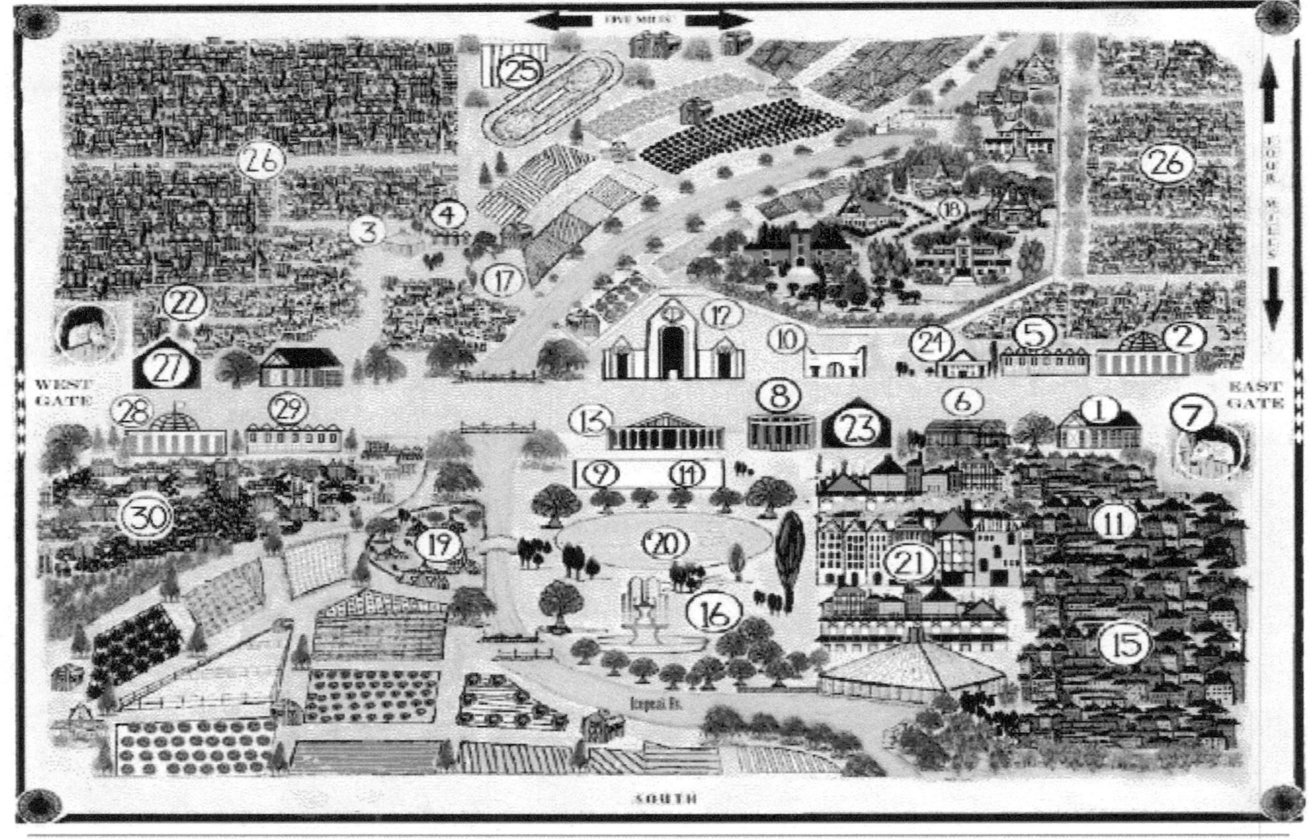

MIDHAVEN MAP LEGEND

1. Midways – East End Tavern and Inn
2. East Guildhall – Fighters Guild
3. Weapons
4. Armor
5. East End Weaponry/Armory
6. Wholesale Supplies
7. Liz's East End Stables
8. Town Portal
9. Fighter Training
10. Sorcerer
11. Thief Training
12. Temple
13. Legion Headquarters
14. Legion Barracks
15. Slums
16. Plaza and fountain
17. Merchant District
18. Mansion District
19. Farmers Market
20. Central Park
21. Warehouse/Industrial District
22. Entertainment District
23. Cartography
24. Magus Pedagogy – Ed's Shop
25. Racetrack
26. Residential District
27. Maps and Guides/Information
28. West guildhall – Mages Guild
29. West End Weaponry/Armory
30. Education/Higher Learning Centers

CHAPTER ONE

Muck. The curious combination of mud and manure. Detectable slightly by appearance, yet distinct in aroma. Two days of trudging through the stuff brought the traveler this profound insight. The downpour turned the road to muck. With his head bent against the gale, his hood drawn, there was nothing else he could see. It had been a rough passage through the hills, now separating him from the valley he'd lived in his entire life. He'd left it once at ten years old when his father took him to Midhaven to trade. The trip impacted him, altering his view of the world and his place in it forever.

He was drenched. Soaked through coat, shirt, and leather breeks. He couldn't tell if the moisture within his new leather boots was from condensation, sweat, or rain. As far as he knew, his feet were no more than twin chunks of frozen meat. Yet, he relished in it. Not even this storm could sway him from the freedom of his course. Nothing could repress the thrill of leaving the valley.

All his gear was new. He'd saved and collected everything for this journey, beginning a year ago.

Mom and Dad would be okay. They'd owned the local tavern since before he was born. Between the two, they'd done well in the valley of small villages and farmsteads. He'd never wanted for anything, with only fond memories of growing up there.

Thunder rumbled in the distance. The shower's tempo increased. He looked west, spotting the last remnant of the sun's amber glow diminishing, leaving everything dark gray and black. Above, roiling thunderclouds poured in from the east, over the gorge and wilds, chasing the light from the realm. He couldn't recall a scene as dark and menacing. Sinister black smoke billowed across the sky.

Hitching up his sword belt, he continued slogging up the North Road to Midtown. As with all towns near the entrance to the wilds, the gates would be closed at dusk. However, he knew he would need to find a place to pass the night before crossing the gorge. There'd been a homestead, inn, or trading post every few miles, so he decided he could continue until forced to stop.

He looked up again and found the scene had transformed into a landscape devoid of color or warmth. To his right were fields of waist-high grass, precluding the foothills that rose south nearer home. To the left extended the Warmwood forest, beyond which lie the gorge: a mile-wide abyss dividing the land. Some say it's possible to see the infamous Witherwood on the far side on a clear day, even through the mists that linger there. People believe even looking upon the Witherwood is terrible luck if only to avoid enticing its inhabitants. Yet, while he didn't doubt that evil lurked there, he felt nothing restrain his desire to explore them and the wilds beyond.

Right hand on the hilt, he pulled his sword from the scabbard an inch or so to ensure it was free. There hadn't been any reports of attacks on the North Road in ages, not by darkspawn, but it was best to stay vigilant. After all, a well-known species of the human variety was known to plague a traveler.

Just then, the deluge let up and ceased abruptly. The silence was deafening in its wake. Though drenched, his coat cleaved through the wind, retaining enough body heat to keep the traveler from shivering.

He heard creaking ahead long before he saw a sign swinging violently. Once in range, his hand shot out, interrupting its trajectory with a steady grip. The weathered insignia of a foaming mug, food, and bed was painted on the board attached to a one-mile marker.

Adjusting his travel pack and hitching his sword belt, Aven continued north, spurred by the expectation of drink, hot food, and a warm fire. Somewhere near the gorge, the keening of some unknown creature pierced the night.

***

Raliel stared into her wooden mug. The bright sparkle of firelight reflecting off her beer did nothing to cool her temper. How could he? She thought, 'self-centered, moronic jerk.' To take off, leave his friends, his family! She brooded over the thought of his Ma n' Pa. With nobody to help around the shop. And with no more than a day's notice for his closest friends. Friends who had been there for him all his life.

"Are you feeling well, miss?"

Thoughts interrupted, she realized she'd been growling.

"Yeah," she responded, "another beer, please."

"Pay for that one, and I'll be happy to oblige, miss."

The inn's owner was a kindly, rotund man of middle age. He'd seen his share of travelers, the hardened and even harder, over the years, and for the latter, his favored cudgel 'beater' always excelled in quelling any trouble. His left hand rubbed his bald pate, then scratched his black beard, dark eyes narrowing. His right hand slid below the bar to unconsciously stroke Beater's old ironwood, darkened with action.

"Of course," Raliel replied, a gleam of steel in her green cat eyes while she retrieved the appropriate coinage with equal feline speed and precision.

He knew a fighter when he saw one, but rarely with such beauty. What a waste, he thought. With that lifestyle, her looks would be battered away soon enough.

Finishing her current mug, she let down the hood of her fur cape, revealing flaxen waves of hair like spring sunshine. Noticing Balik's look, she also adjusted the ties of her cloak, exposing the gleam of chain-mail and an array of weaponry on her belt, one of which was a wickedly shaped, slender but lethal hand-and-a-half fighting axe.

"Real nice axe you've got here. Old?" asked Balik, the barkeep.

"A family heirloom. How about that beer, then."

3

Startled back into action, Balik hurried off to comply.

Turning her back to the bar, Raliel surveyed the inn's taproom. There were a few more heads since she'd arrived, but no more than ten men divided up in groups of two or three. A red-haired barmaid bustled to and fro, dispensing and retrieving beer or food. Raliel watched her, trying to imagine her life as she navigated rough-made tables and chairs across a sodden, rush-dusted floor. Next to a large stone hearth, two men well into their cups were slurring in animated conversation near the crackling fire. She heard Balik deposit her beer and retrieve the two coins. If he stayed to further any conversation, he would have to direct it to the back of her head. She was not feeling sociable. She rarely did on a good day. Hoping the beer would serve to ease or fuel her anger, she turned back to the bar, her drink, and her thoughts, relieved to find no Balik spoiling her view.

She could hardly wait to run into Aven so she could give him a good tongue-lashing. She'd made good time, taking a longer route through the hills by horse. She wanted to surprise him. Smiling wickedly, she lifted her mug in grim satisfaction at the thought. She was suddenly feeling much better.

***

Ahead Aven could vaguely discern the glow of firelight from what he hoped was the inn's windows. He'd been fooled twice already. The absence of sun and rain had left a chilling cold, and once the wind eased, the mist began to rise from muck and mud alike. The fog made everything indistinct, softening everything beyond twenty feet into a haze of shapeless shadow. His boots were caked in layers of filth. He was cold, hungry, and weary. Yes, he thought, definitely firelight ahead. This realization settled into fact as a building seemed to materialize before him. Smiling with relief, Aven angled to the front entrance.

***

Raliel smelled sour breath and decaying teeth before she heard the words,

"Ey there shweety, mine ifsh I haf a sheet?" Without waiting for a response, the sot sat uncomfortably close to her left. His reeking brown beard was matted with food and filth, and his bulbous nose was speckled with ruptured blood vessels. She could see his partner slithering onto a stool on her right from her peripheral. Snatching a look, she met leering eyes, cold and reptilian. Righty had a wicked scar running from the left eyebrow to the right cheek.

"Hey there, honey," he greeted lewdly, reaching a hand to her thigh.

"Wouldn't do that if I were you," she growled with genuine menace. Righty retracted his hand with a slimy chuckle. Raliel whipped to her left, addressing the beard in the act of touching her golden hair.

"Back up, both of you," she ordered.

"Or wath, hnnnnn? Wath a preddy lil fing like you gon' do?"

To her right, Scarface was flicking his tongue obscenely, reaching again. Back turned and occupied, Balik was too far away to hear the lout's rude remarks. Raliel sneered viciously for the second time this night. She began to finish her beer.

Gulp.

"That's more like it, honey."

Gulp. A hand on Raliel's hair.

Gulp. A hand on Raliel's thigh.

"Let's see what's under that cloa—" Scarface never finished, wondering how he ended up on his back with the angle of the room all wrong.

Her mug had done the job leaving a broken handle in her right fist, shattered ends sticking forward like the horns of a Balor.

"You shorry bi—" Brown beard reached with both hands for Raliel's neck. "I'll kill you, wench!"

Raliel's left hand delivered a jarring back-fist across the bridge of his nose even as her right came swinging her body off the stool. Then, with a gory 'pop,' it connected squarely in the nose again. Brown Beard fell back on his seat with a crash.

"Hey!" Balik yelled. He quick-stepped around the bar, Beater in hand.

Reacting to the movement, Raliel spun, her fur cape flowing, to find scar face scrambling up, spitting blood and teeth, and holding a sharp stone knife. Raliel's axe came high in a puff of singed blood.

"My hand! Oh, Gawd!!"

Still in motion, Raliel's axe whirred in a blur catching a blow from Beater and resting against Brown Beard's neck before he could rise, her mug's handle embedded across the bridge of his shattered nose.

Rivulets of blood, snot, and saliva oozed from his face.

The taproom's patrons had backed against the walls or fled to their rooms. Silence hung heavy, broken only by the gasps and whimpers around her.

Raliel maintained her deadly stance, eyeing Balik, the nub of a once stout cudgel in his hand. "Who are you?" he stammered. "What blade could do that?"

Scanning the room and finding no further threat, Raliel relaxed gradually.

"I warned them to leave me alone," she offered.

The tavern door banged open, and Raliel heard a gasp, coupled with the unmistakable hiss of iron parting scabbard. Then, still eyeing Balik, she grinned, body coiling for another vicious whirl.

"Raliel?!"

Spinning away from Balik, Raliel hung her axe from a peg on her belt, pausing only to say, "Put that away; let's go," before stomping out into the night.

Aven, travel-worn, cold, and muddy took a second to absorb the scene: two men lay low, one squirming, holding out a smoking stump, one trembling on his knees with a red welt on his neck and a piece of wood sticking from his face. The stunned barkeep was already beginning to upend the fallen stools with a wary eye. Yet, most memorable was the look on the barmaid's face as he left; she was beaming.

***

Aven found Raliel sitting on a large stone facing the dark woods. The moon had emerged, turning the nightscape from gray to silver. Raliel's hair shone pale and beautiful. She must have heard his approach because she spoke first, "I was waiting for you."

"What happened in there, Rali? Are you OK?" Aven heard her stifle a sound that could have been the beginning of a laugh.

"They asked for it," she explained.

"Rali, what are you doing here?" he asked but realized he already knew.

"Didn't you think, at least once, that you weren't the only one wanting to leave? We're the same age, one year apart, and…."

As he circled, Aven could see tears streaming down her face, somewhere between grief and rage. Possibly more to the latter, he warned himself. But, as always, he was amazed at the strength of her feelings. She was trembling, fists rigid, when they locked eyes.

"How could you just leave us like that? Do you not think, at least, about your friends?" Her eyes glowed silver in the moonbeams, distracting him. She shook her head, composing herself, and looked again to the woods.

"My parents will be fine, you know that, and you know the most difficult part was leaving you and Vic, my best friends, behind." He took a breath to steady himself. "Knowing you both would be safe helped."

"And what about us, Aven? What about Vic and I, left to worry about your safety? You, to become an 'adventurer'?" she snorted, "We're not kids anymore. Haven't you been listening to the stories from across the gorge?"

"That's why I want to go! To do my bit! What is there to live on this side of the gorge? To become complacent and soft? Living a 'safe' life?" Aven scowled now, crossing his arms, "Out there is an adventure, a story in the making." He looked past the Warmwood. "My story."

"And if your story ends, not in 'glory' but death? What then?" Raliel wondered what he saw out there beyond the gorge.

"Better to die a hero than to live a coward."

"Whoa—ho now! So your father's a coward? So my father's a coward?"

"No! Dad's looking after mom, and they both sacrificed a lot to raise me. If it weren't for me, they'd probably still live in Midhaven. And you know, as well as the whole valley, that your Pa is a hero many times over!" Aven turned his scowl on Raliel, "Both our fathers have traveled and made their fortunes; now it's my turn." He finished with a definitive nod.

Who's he trying to convince, Raliel thought, himself or me? "Well, then it's my turn too," she said.

"WHAT? Fargar will never let y—" he blurted. And he had been doing so well.

"Let me?! Nobody 'lets' me do a damn thing. I make my path, and I've made my decision."

For the first time, Aven noticed her appearance. She wore her mother's fur cape, mail, steel boots, spurs, and Fargar's weapons belt. But, most significantly, she carried an antique axe from her father's wall. Aven had seen it only once off that wall when Fargar killed a crazed hill-boar. The most significant anyone had ever seen, just under eight hundred pounds, and insane with blood-lust.

"He knows you're here?" he asked skeptically, and when she hesitated, Aven fought a strong urge to look over his shoulder.

"Well, yes and no. I told Fargar I mean to accompany you to Midhaven." When he didn't seem convinced, she added, "It was he that outfitted me, not without a good measure of cursing though." She sat, smiling at the memory, then, "I told him that if he didn't let me go, I'd run away as you did."

"You threatened Fargar?" Aven asked, amazed, and they both burst into laughter.

"I'm going with you, Aven, wherever you go."

"Well, who am I to stop what mighty Fargar could not?" more laughter.

As they wiped their eyes, Aven added, "I'd be honored by your company Rali. I know no one better with an axe and no better friend, equal only to Vic."

"That'll do. So, you ready to go?" Raliel asked.

"Raliel, I'm exhausted and pretty hungry," he replied.

"Well, I'm not staying in that dump. Probably flea-infested anyway. You can sleep as we go." She grinned at his disbelief and continued, "If we start now, we can reach Midhaven by dawn."

"How? You going to carry me?" he grumbled, becoming grouchy.

"Not me," she replied, placing her fingers to her lips and whistling a distinctive trill.

***

Hidden by the mists and brush of the woods, the Watcher silently observed the travelers. Although he was across the North Road, his keen hearing could pick up bits of the conversation. His exceptional night vision could easily make out their expressions and, in the moonlight, near thoroughly read their lips. With amusement, he decided to wait before he made his move, enjoying the stalking of his prey. He had first caught sight of the male coming out of the hills to the south and shadowed him, careful to stay within the cover of the Warmwood.

His leather stealth suit, oiled dark brown, looked black in the night. What raindrops that made it through the dark canopy above beaded off of him without penetrating to his warm under-wool. Formfitting, his stealth suit allowed swift and agile movement without sound. He flexed his hands, admiring the supple leather enclosing his hands and feet seamlessly by design. The fully masked helmet, sealed tight with thinly stretched leather, exposed nothing but the glint of gray eyes. Two sets of imperceptible air-ducts, hidden under the nose and jaw, allowed for comfortable breathing. Cleverly fitted apertures over each flattened ear directed hearing forward, sideways, and behind.

The Watcher stiffened. The female was staring directly at him. She had done this repeatedly, each time her eyes flashed with moonlight like white-hot embers. It was a bit unsettling. The Watcher quietly retracted further into shadow. He would have to be careful with that one; he admonished himself.

The pair had patched up their differences as far as he could tell. Their tone and body language smoothed. Then, suddenly, the female whistled an eerily melodic trill. In seeming response an instant racket of thumping, snapping branches, and splintering brush erupted from behind the Watcher. With honed reflexes, he, as quick and silent as a spider, skittered safely to the upper reaches of his tree, just as an enormous orange monster smashed violently underway, barreling straight for the young travelers.

***

Aven was startled by the commotion in the woods. Thoughts of a half-ton hill-boar flashed through his mind, chilling his blood. Instinctively, he pulled on his sword to ensure the catch was free. The thrashing reached a crescendo of cracking and thumping before breaking free of the trees into a rolling thunder of pounding tread. Mists swirled, Aven's bones vibrated his guts to jelly, and an enormous and majestic horse burst from the fog.

"Hoover!" she called. "To me!"

With puppy-like love in the horse's big eyes, all vestige of danger vanished; Hoover rumbled to a stop before Raliel and nudged her with its massive head. "Good boy," she cooed, "Yes, I missed you too!"

"Is that the foal birthed last season?" Aven asked, impressed.

"The same," she replied, rubbing Hoover's nose.

"He's massive! He can't be old enough to be full-grown!"

"Oh, he's not, but he can carry us just fine," she assured. Aven stepped back for a better look at Raliel's mount, and step back he must, he mused; the young draft horse's back was at least two inches above

9

his six-foot frame. Hoover's winter coat was a coarse golden orange, highlighted by a thick flaxen mane, hooves, and tail, all like spun gold. Above a pale tan muzzle, his eyes were light amber, large and expressive.

The beauty of the pair struck Aven. Both seem straight from one of the legends told them as children. Raliel's eyes met his, catching the look. She smiled. Aven's face flushed with embarrassment. He tried, unsuccessfully, to shut his drooping jaw with dignity.

"His eyes remind me of yours," he said, putting on his best doe-eyed expression, batting his eyelashes to dramatic effect.

"Oh, that's my expression, you say? You haven't changed since we were small," she scolded. Hoover snorted and rolled his eyes in a peculiar human-like gesture.

"Hoover?" Aven asked, cocking an eyebrow her way. He followed her deliberate look down to the horse's massive hooves, large even for his size, "I see," he agreed.

Looking fondly at her mount, Raliel again cooed, "You have yet to grow into them, don't you, boy?" Hoover responded with impatient pawing.

"You're right. We should get going." Raliel leaped upon the mighty Hoover's back in a blink, one hand gripping his mane, and one held out to Aven below. He was surprised, more than usual when taking her hand, by the grip and ease of her strength. Of course, growing up the only girl among seven brothers, not to mention the rigorous farm work she had been born into, was to blame. Yet, anyone who knew Raliel could vouch that she possessed an intensity in all she did, but her temper had honed a strength beyond her deceptively delicate body.

"I'm glad you came, Rali." He felt her relax against him, for just a moment, before spurring Hoover north at a charge.

***

The Watcher bolted, weaving swiftly between branch and bush alike, leaping from root to rock or sprinting at a dead run when possible. He enjoyed the test of agility and stamina, executing hurtles and dives, keeping pace. Shadowing.

CHAPTER TWO

Aven woke long before he opened his eyes. He didn't remember falling asleep. Aven allowed himself to absorb the telling details swirling around as he surfaced from the depths of sleep. He was warm, covered by the back of Raliel's fur cape. He felt his knees regularly nudge her thighs and rump with movement. His back and head reclined upon Hoover's massive back. The grace and power of the animal was soothing. The occasional clop of hoof was rhythmic. Hypnotic. He held onto the restful state in the motion, feeling the warmth radiate from below his legs and shoulders, which ached from his two-day hike. Finally, he opened his eyes a crack, and his mind began chattering thoughts in restless curiosity.

The sky to the east showed the first hues of lavender in the midnight blue sky. To the west —scattered here and there— were the last twinkling stars. As he rolled his head back to the right, his eyes latched onto a single white luminous star, fading reluctantly with the predawn. Mist rolled through the Warmwood, receding down the gorge, far from sight. Above, lazy dark puffs of cloud moved west over the woods and canyon. For a moment, he let himself fall into the depths of the sky, staring into the abyss.

Raliel's rump shifted between his knees. The fading memory of a dream fluttered illusively to the deepest parts of his brain—something to do with talking with his parents as they prepared to open shop.

During the day, the tavern served more than food and drink—a place one could procure all manner of staple or one of the horses Fargar rented out. At least two of his sons attended a small stable around the back. There were no rooms for rent, but a small inn just across the way, run by an elderly couple—whose numerous kids had grown up, leaving several empty beds—were available.

Aven's home was farther up the hill, by way of a path that cut through a small grove behind the tavern. He'd miss feeling proud as his friends gawked at the many artifacts and collectibles decorating the taproom that his parents had gathered from their travels. Mother was from farther south, near the ocean, tan and blond with the sea-green eyes of her people. Father, a dark olive skin tone, with irises of ebony and gold flakes. They had feared Aven leaving, but he could see their understanding. They knew the desire for adventure better than most, even if it conflicted with their commitment to protecting their child. They had given up so much for him; his conception froze their lives in a place, plying their trade and business sense in order to settle.

One day, he planned to visit with tales and wealth of his own. The pain they could endure motivated him not to fail.

***

Raliel felt Aven stir behind her. That last marker meant they were less than a mile from Midtown. Hearing Aven fumble with her cape, and the pack he had used as a pillow, she was relieved he was finally getting up.

He had slept when she'd slowed to walk Hoover a bit, so she had kept the going slow for the past few hours. She wasn't hungry after the jerky and dried fruit they had shared earlier, and she wasn't tired from the long ride. Instead, she was content to enjoy this crisp early morning moment, yet aware of Hoover's anxiousness to increase the pace.

Hoover's ears flicked back with each rustle from Aven, followed by a deep impatient sigh. She smiled.

Raliel's father trained all their horses to return, even after being fed and rested. No one was foolish enough to try and tamper with these fiercely intelligent giants. Still, an occasional fool tried his luck, only to be hooted and hollered about in the taverns that night.

They were an unusual breed, only seen in her father's stables. Raliel's father claimed a foal he had found stuck in a mud pit on his journeys into the wilds sired the entire line. Fargar spoke of an endless plain where the most magnificent beasts were believed to exist, but he had never seen them all himself. His foal grew to live up to the legend, siring a line that remained in their family's care. Many had tried to purchase or trade for them, but Fargar would have none of it, conceding only to rent the services of his brood, keeping them engaged and practiced. No more extraordinary draft horses existed, no work too hard for Fargar's towering steeds.

Ahead, the road forked into three: the right lane to the coast, various villages and small towns. Continuing north would lead to 'Kingsfort' with, as the name implied, the King's home fortress overlooking a tree-filled vale and the Greenwood villages. Raliel had visited Greenwood with her family many times for the holidays while Fargar conducted business. She took the left lane for Midtown, the guardian of the gorge. She felt Aven shift again. "You awake yet?"

"Yeah. I think, anyway," Aven mumbled.

"Good. Sit up; Hoover needs a stretch before we get there."

"How far?" he asked, yawning.

"Aven, look yourself," she said.

Forcing a sit-up, Aven managed to get upright to peer over Raliel's furred shoulder. Through stray strands of gold hair, he spotted inclining terrain. A mound of earth rose to meet the horizons, upon which rested the walled village of Midtown. The remaining storm clouds spread far above and beyond its profile.

"Just as I remember it. It's like Midtown is teetering on the edge of the world." Raliel's hair drifted back with the breeze, tickling his nose.

"Father says it's because the world beyond the gorge's swell declines for a way," he said.

"As the only stop this side of the gorge, it is the world's end," she agreed.

"Yup," Aven said, wrapping his arms around her waist, smiling.

Then, he said over her shoulder, "Ready when you are."

Responding to a squeeze of her legs, Hoover reared into a mighty lunge, powering a violent gallop. Aven's eyes watered as he wondered at the sheer force of acceleration. His ability to hold on demanded more and more of his concentration. More than ever, he felt giddy at striking out on his own. No, not on his own anymore, he thought. Now, he was as responsible for Raliel as well as himself. He would do well to remember that. She had not questioned his path or leadership, not once, and he knew he must carefully consider her wellbeing under such trust. A faint flicker of dread responded to the notion of anything terrible happening to her because of him. A sample of what carrying the burden of leadership would mean—balancing a tightrope of exhilaration and fear into the unknown. Speeding on a thundering mountain of springing muscle, tendon, and bone, Aven had never felt so alive. He squeezed Raliel tighter and felt her press back, steady in his arms.

***

The watcher observed the friends enter below the east wall overlooking Midtown's open portcullis. From this height, the teens seemed small children atop the colossal mount. With his helmet removed, his hair and face remained hidden within the shadowed confines of a dark gray hooded cloak. Then, in a swirl, he spun, leaning his forearms upon the inner ledge, and watched the pair dismount at the rental stables to turn in their horse and adjust equipment.

From this vantage, he also watched as the town came to life. Already, people scurried about their chores—smoke plumed from hearths inside dozens of chimneys of various shapes and sizes. Women swept the front steps of their homes, kissing their men goodbye for the day, some with babe resting on the hip. Finally, the town guards' night shift settled into their traditional taverns for breakfast, and a beer or two, before heading home.

The Watcher's attention returned to observe the friends' progress. After a farewell to a young stable lad, they too headed off to an inn, he assumed.

Their slowed pace earlier had allowed him to cut ahead, knowing their destination. When the pair settled, he would be sure to do

14

likewise. Focused on the two, he sided to the left of the gate, then swung over and down an iron ladder. Wrapping his cloak about his body, he blended into the foot traffic. Soon he would find a place to rest. The time was coming soon to reveal himself…and he would be ready.

***

They decided to split up. Raliel to secure rooms and dinner, he to investigate the local shops.

Aven's parents had, separately and secretly, fortified his pockets with a few items of value and the most gold he'd ever owned—five gold royals. It was enough for a person to live comfortably for a few years back home, a sum, and he reminded himself, could easily be squandered in cities near the wilds if one didn't know what they were doing. But, disdain for the simple life of a merchant back home aside, he was no fool regarding the value of mercantile prowess. Both to make and save coin.

Hidden bells tinkled as Aven entered a shop displaying a sign with two universal symbols: a bubbling potion and a scroll. The shop contained a tiny foyer area with benches and a square room with a long wooden counter at the back. Behind the counter was a wall with a grid of shelves that stored scrolls and potions to the ceiling. Glass displays under the counter boasted a variety of goods from vials of colored liquids and strange talismans to plain unidentifiable items.

A tall, fair-haired, fair-complexioned man stepped through hanging beads, partitioning a back room full of bubbling concoctions and tinkling glass sounds. His long angular face, height, and delicate but strong features hinted at possible Elden ancestry. He quietly observed Aven inspect his wares and politely left him to it while waiting to be of service.

The shop was peaceful and quiet, a place that radiated solemn respect for powerful items of specialty coupled with scents of exotic spices. Aven looked up in greeting, "Good morning, a fine selection you've got here."

In a surprisingly deep voice the half-eld replied,

"Good morning to you as well, young master. Anything in particular I might help you find, or just browsing?"

Knowing well the pleasures and peeves of keeping shop, dealing

15

with customers day-in and day-out, and for no other particular reason, Aven decided to make a good impression by getting straight to business. After all, his reputation with the merchant class started here. A reputation among dealers was worth his weight in gold.

"I've come to stock up on travel items before crossing to Midhaven. I've heard prices tend to increase that side of the gorge."

"You've heard right, master," he replied.

"I've prepared a list," Aven said and handed over a small scroll, "to make things simple and efficient, as I'm sure you're a busy man."

The man replied, "Very kind, sir."

He bowed slightly and began scanning the list. Aven resumed browsing. After a few moments, the shopkeeper broke the silence, again with resonating bass, "Very good, young master. I can have all these items prepared and ready for you by tomorrow morning. Will that do?"

"Yes, that would be ideal."

"Can I interest you in anything else?" he asked with a slight lift at the corner of his mouth.

"Such as?"

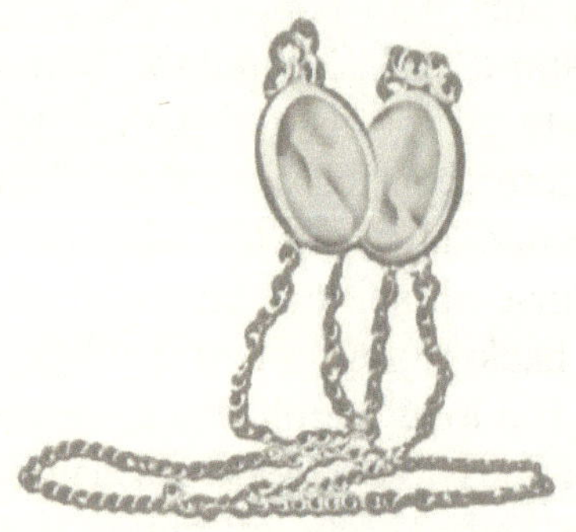

Aven had given her a whole silver royal to break into change and cover the cost of room and board for the night. Raliel did not feel obliged to inform him that she was capable of paying herself. Whatever Raliel didn't spend could be saved for future use, possibly an emergency. Yes, she thought, that would do.

She secured one room with two small beds, meal accommodations, and the use of a heated bathtub, all for only twenty-six silver pieces. That left seventy-four silver, which she would not volunteer unless asked.

She used the tub while she waited for Aven to finish his errands. The water had cooled while she soaked, so she reached out and tapped a rune located on the side of the tub once and twice, and it began to glow orange. Soon, the water was steaming at a comfortably hot temperature. She deactivated the glyph. She had washed her underclothes and anything that wasn't chain, leather, or fur, by hand and hung to dry on the bed board nearest the open window. Body scrubbed, hair washed and twisted in a bun, Raliel allowed herself to drift in a state of content reverie. She thought this might be the last chance to relax for a while, so why not make the most of it?

The door rattled as a key fumbled for the lock. Raliel's hand glided over the handle of her axe, leaning discreetly against the side of the tub. The door opened.

"Raliel?" Aven called. Other voices mumbled from the hall.

"Back here behind the curtain." There was no bathroom, only a corner space large enough for the tub with a curtain hanging from brass rings in the ceiling.

"Oh. Are you decent?" Aven asked.

"If you mean am I naked, yes, but I'm not sure that has any bearing upon my character," she purred.

"Um…OK, well, our food is ready." Aven directed his voice to the mumbling in the hall, "Come on in."

Raliel's eyes bulged; she sank self-consciously below the tub's rim. Steaming water moved dangerously close to the edge. Apprehensive cat eyes peered as footfalls accompanied the scent of food. In a short time, the commotion receded to silence, punctuated by the click of the closed door. Only the pleasant aroma of hot food remained. Her stomach acknowledged this with a grumble of longing. Quiet filled the room.

"Aven?"

"Yeah, right here on my bed, just waiting for you to finish. No rush."

"Uh, could you please hand me my clothes and the towel on my bed?"

That done, the friends eventually joined each other at a small table, their dinner between them. The sun shone to their left through the small window despite the haze of fragrant chimney smoke. A breeze stirred an open curtain as they filled up on roasted beef in gravy, coarse dark brown bread with walnut bits, a bowl of black olives, and a bottle of wine.

Silence ensued as they ate. Finally, after a generous second helping and refilling the wine, Aven settled back, observing Raliel leaning back in her chair casually eating olives and sipping wine from a wooden cup.

"So here's my plan," he began, measuring her interest. "Once we get to Midhaven, I'll register as a contractor with the Quest Guild's main office."

"Wouldn't it be easier to sign up with an existing company?" she asked.

Good, Aven thought. Aven enjoyed her company but didn't want overt interference with his goals. "Well, sure, that's what I thought at first, but that was before you arrived. I've got the money for the license, enough for supplies and expenses for a while, and I think if we work hard, with a bit of luck…" Aven paused, waiting for input.

"OK. Sounds good to me."

"Yeah?"

"You bet," she assured, and they smiled.

"OK, supplies are the hardest part, and that's covered for now. If we gotta hire help, for certain jobs, their cut can come with the job's completion and…." Raliel's attention wandered a bit, thinking. Aven got his business sense from his father and his mother's propensity for organization and detail. She smiled, nodding encouragement as he talked, "…on a fixed budget per week…." He was at his best when discussing such things. She studied him intently, over the rim of her cup, careful to nod and interject the proper response here and there. The wine had left both their faces flushed, sanguine, and she found herself enchanted by his brown-gold eyes. Reading her fixation as close attention, Aven became more animated, "…as long as we're careful not to exceed expense we'll save enough…." Looking at him, one would never guess at the intellect behind his well-muscled neck and shoulders. Although, like his father, he had always been 'built,' naturally emanating strength and command without effort. He made you want to agree with him. Her eyes traveled over his dark brown hair and large brown-gold eyes to the definition of his chest muscles, straining his shirt as he gestured with his hands.

"Uh, Rali, are you feeling OK?" he asked, head tilting to the side.

"What? Oh! Yeah, just tired," she yawned.

"Well, let's get some sleep. We need to head out early."

"OK," she said.

"Oh! I almost forgot." Aven reached into a pocket and presented her with a heavy silver-colored necklace.

"Ooh, Aven, its beautiful!" she squealed. Puzzlement flashed across his face, followed instantly by a deep blush.

"Um…well yeah, there's two of them," he said, pulling down his shirt to expose its twin. Only then did she notice a small rune dangling from each chain.

"Here, let me put it on you to see how well they work," he said as he rose and walked behind her. She lifted her hair. When he clasped the necklace, she felt a slight pulse from the rune. She noted a visceral yet distinct awareness of Aven's presence, akin to the spatial proprioception of one's body position.

Back in sight, Aven spoke, "Neat, right? The man at the shop gave me a deal. They gotta be rare, artifacts even. He said they were likely Elden-prehistoric!" He shrugged. "They'd been sitting for years with no takers. He claimed that they 'called' to me," Aven chuckled. "Not a bad sales pitch; it worked. Unfortunately, the guy said that they were unsaleable items; they were waiting to choose their next host." Aven's excitement cooled as he reflected, "Took my coin all the same. I was kinda worried they wouldn't work, but…"

"They're amazing, Aven, a smart investment," she offered, studying the eldish rune. The metal was unlike any she'd see; no, the tempered edge of her axe blade matched the silver-like gleam.

"Mythrallum," he said, reading her thoughts, "the chain too. Mythrallum is very light, near-indestructible, and toxic to darker beings, as the story goes. Never saw the stuff either; I thought it was no more than a myth. But, if it truly is the stuff, we got the better end of the bargain."

"How much did you pay?" she had to ask. When Aven didn't answer, she whistled, "That much, eh?"

"Worth it," he said, tucking it back under his shirt with a pat, "I would've paid double, maybe more, for such an advantage. With these, we never need to worry about losing each other."

"How far do they reach?" she asked.

"Not sure yet, as they've been inactive for so long, but he told me that charms like these tend to personalize and grow in strength the longer they stay with an owner."

He looked weary.

"We really should get some rest now," Raliel told him.

Had their leisurely meal stretched so long? The sun was all but gone.

"I'm thinking a bath would be in order before joining you," he yawned.

"I'll check the beds for bugs again," she shuddered off.

CHAPTER THREE

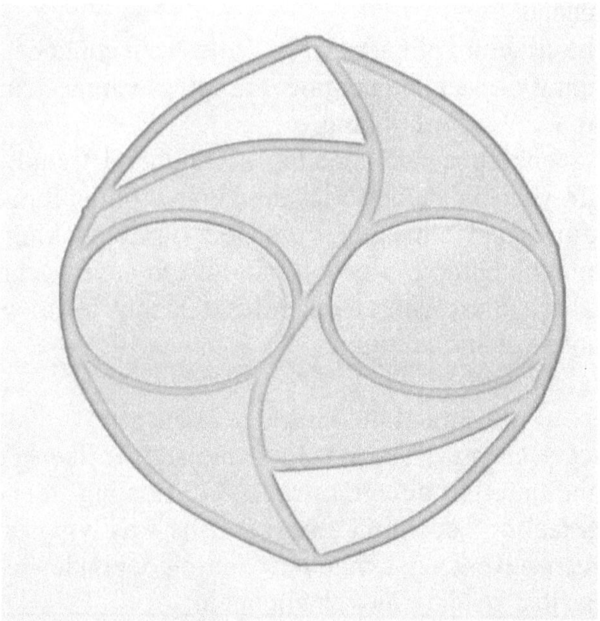

"Where we goin', dad?" A miniature Aven asked.

"I want to introduce you to an old friend," his father answered.

"More birthday presents?" little Aven asked hopefully. His father squeezed his tiny hand. Aven took the opportunity to swing through the air, giggling, all brown curls and big brown-gold eyes.

"Yes, a gift related to your age. You know how mom and I teach you lessons?"

"Uh-huh, like my numbers? And Stories!"

"Yes, I'm taking you to meet a teacher of a sort."

"Why?"

His father, Mikel, chuckled at the typical question for most kids his son's age. "Well, that's a good question, son. Your mother and I want you to grow up wise, of course, but also strong," he explained.

"I am strong; wanna see my muscles?" Aven flexed a little bicep with a fierce effort and scrunched up his face.

Fighting through mirth, Mikel said, "Very impressive, son, but there is more to learn about being strong. And, there exist people, even creatures in this world that you'll need to be stronger than, in specialized ways, to survive. Here we are." They approached a strange-looking building. "Remember to be respectful and obedient to your new teacher."

Within the structure of paper walls, little Aven could hear the sound of steel ringing on steel…clanging…dinging. Chimes ringing? That wasn't right. Clinking…clinking.

Another scene appeared: meeting a childhood friend. A serious-looking eight-year-old named Vic, already in training for a year. Vic's aquiline features and demeanor, eyes alert, darting, taking everything into account, calculating, was intimidating to seven-year-old Aven. Puffing his little chest with courage, little Aven tried to speak to Vic but could not sway his attention.

(Clinking, a rustle)

Aven sensed movement, a whisper without words that Raliel was near. The scene changed again; colors ran together like an oil painting left out in the rain. His attention wandered, floating serenely back to a conscious reality, becoming aware that he was lying in bed, in an inn. Not seven, seventeen, a man now setting out on his own.

There was that stealthy movement again.

Aven opened his eyes to find the window faintly lit with the early dawn. He found Raliel, fully dressed, sans fur cape, rolling to the left, lacing her steel-plated boots. Her chain mail shirt jingled softly. Her hair was fixed back tight in a long ponytail. She adjusted her belt last with quiet concentration.

"You don't have to be quiet anymore; I'm awake," he whispered.

"Did I wake you? Sorry, I couldn't sleep. Anxious," she explained.

"No. It's fine. I need to get ready too."

He stretched his arms out wide, enjoying the sensation, as was his habit since age seven; while his tendons, joints, and muscles were still stiff, he rolled to the floor to press out a hundred controlled push-ups, all at once. By 70 reps, the pain and protest from his body became excruciating, spiking his heart rate, waking him, and pumping him up. Then, feeling exhilarated and eager for physical activity, as Raliel indeed was, he started for his things.

Daily training was routine to them, and his muscles yearned to strain.

"I dreamed of my first day at Master Nazar's when I met Vic. I'm gonna miss him most now that you're here." Aven felt nostalgic over the dream. "Dad was walking me there. It was so real."

Raliel finished with her belt and stood, looking fierce and beautiful. Her mouth twitched into a smile, "Well, one thing's for sure, if not for Nazar, none of us would've met. Kinda makes up for all Nazar's 'lessons.'"

That got him thinking again about Vic, and the ache in his chest intensified.

"I'll head downstairs," Raliel informed, "check us out and see about breakfast."

Then, seeing Aven lost in thought, she huffed, "Meet me when you're ready," and she was gone.

As Aven dressed, he wondered if they would ever see Vic again.

As kids, Nazar had trained them according to their ability. Raliel was quick, fierce, and uncompromising; he, solid and calculating. Master Nazar helped them hone these skills and taught them to harmonize as a team. Vic was something else altogether. A few months before Aven's seventeenth birthday, Nazar confirmed their long-held suspicions on Vic's eighteenth by offering Vic the honor of ascension to master and possibly succeeding Nazar himself.

Fighting prowess was revered, even in their small village, and everyone was proud to have produced a possible master. Of course, Aven was proud, and he and Raliel did enjoy some notoriety as his friends.

Aven, dressed, fastened his leather chest piece and greaves, buckled on his iron broadsword in its wooden sheath, and went through his mental checklist. That done, coat rolled tight and strapped to his pack, he slung it all over a shoulder and followed after Raliel.

Vic had found his calling and already made a name and place in the community worthy of him. Seeing this had only propelled Aven more in his decision to leave to achieve something worthy of himself. The prospect cheered him.

Aven shut the door and headed down the hall. At the top of the stairs, he could hear activity throughout the building. It felt empowering to be acting toward achieving a better life. This feeling, coupled with Raliel's company, eased the sting of leaving everything he knew.

The bottom step brought him to the back of the inn's small taproom. The tables were half-capacity with working-class men and women, primarily miners breaking their fasts before work. A waving hand caught his eye. Raliel was at a table by a far window.

They fortified themselves for the journey from big wooden bowls filled with steaming eggs, bacon, potatoes, and herbs. It was delicious, and they left in good spirits.

Midtown was founded as a mining community. The gorge's cliffs nearby were rich in ore. The sheer face of the cliffs contained caverns and mines that led deep under the east shelf.

War had decimated the races beyond the gorge three hundred years ago. Today, the former kingdoms of the once-powerful Elden and Massifae were overrun by wild creatures otherwise held back. Some were ancient and very powerful. Humankind, faced with growing hordes of nightmarish creatures, slowly lost ground, forced back to the fortress of Midhaven. Many Midtown residents were pressed into service, by royal decree, as defenders of the pass. Midtown was the final defense should the gorge fail to hold the hordes at bay. Miraculously, Midhaven had survived, and no action was ever seen in Midtown. A garrison of troops was constantly maintained. Now, more of a tradition, the community youth received training and served a short term of duty, afterward taking jobs in the mines.

Midtown life was hardy and straightforward. This morning the streets were crowded with miners heading out in long columns. Picks, helmets, and lunch pails swinging as they headed to the south and north gates and out to work.

Part of the preparations of long ago was the building of a 30-foot circular wall of stone around the town, contrasting wildly with the log homes of the original village within.

Aven cleaved a path through traffic for the items shop. Bells twinkled as they entered, and the tall glass door swung shut, sealing off outside noises. The shop was quiet. Drowsy burbling in the back and the scent of spices compounded its peace.

"Wow." Aven reacted to Raliel's comment, finding her head tilted back, eyes cast above. Following her gaze, he, too, couldn't resist voicing his wonder.

"Whoa." Not sure how he had missed it before, they silently studied skeletons and loose bones from various creatures, suspended and dangling four feet above their heads, specimens that varied in luster, from bleached white to aged-dark patina. A complete skeleton of an unlucky biped, boglin, judging by its four-foot frame, large round skull, and feet too large in proportion to the rest. Other miscellaneous animals abounded, but fronting all, nearest the entrance and themselves, was a large preserved reptilian head. Within shiny scale encrusted skin, yellow slit irises stared down on them. A menacing display of serrated teeth as long as Aven's fingers filled its long snout.

"Drakar," a deep voice hummed helpfully as the imposing shopkeeper entered. They hadn't noticed the beads in their wonder.

Even now, the clicking of the settling strands confirmed his recent entry.

"Pardon the wait, young master; I had to deal with a complicated concoction." He bowed his head to them, saying, "I expect you two haven't been across the chasm to see the Drakar yet. You can find them in the great plains of the southwestern wilds, so I've heard," he clarified.

"I've never seen a live specimen myself," he continued, sensing their curiosity, "they hunt in pairs, sometimes whole packs, and are said to be swift, running on their hind legs.

"Carnivorous — they eat only meat — and not too picky," he clucked his tongue. "This unlucky Drakar was found as-is, a victim of his kind, you see, the Drakar never consume the head of their prey. I had this one magically preserved. A worthy addition to any collection."

Curiosity sated, Aven and Raliel exchanged a look, sobered by the prospect of meeting such terrifying denizens of the wilds.

"Care for a demonstration?" the shopkeeper asked, then barked an indecipherable reptilian sound that made Aven's hackles rise. The thick chains securing the head to ceiling began to rattle, followed by the hiss of pressurized vapor. The Drakar's yellow eyes flicked back and forth between them. Its long mouth widened, letting loose a bloodcurdling screech, like the rending of tortured steel. Then its snout slackened to its original toothy grin. The head, inanimate once again, swayed on a clinking chain.

"Neat!" Raliel expressed, unperturbed.

On the other hand, Aven worked to suppress any terror from his face and forcefully extracted each finger from the hilt of his sword. Raliel's face was flushed, her eyes alight with fascination as she reached a hand to poke at the head.

"Are you displeased, young master?" the shopkeeper inquired.

"No, not at all. Just," Aven hesitated, "surprised." Aven forced a smile to corroborate this even as the ache of wasted adrenaline flooded his system. Raliel had already wandered off to inspect other curiosities around the shop.

"Your supplies are ready. All that remains is the settling of accounts." If he doubted Aven's ability to pay, he did not show it. Aven wouldn't have been offended, considering the expensive nature of the list. Aven had ordered a large stock of minor spell scrolls that were lightweight and would double in price once they crossed the gorge. Father's advice, of course. All other money concealed, Aven dug into his visible coin pouch and extracted an amount previously calculated to be fair. Palming these coins, he asked, "How much then?"

"Ninety silver pieces, including the extra pack you requested."

Aven found this favorable. He had expected a hundred-twenty and would turn a good profit. So he decided to reward the excellent business and handed over a silver royal worth a hundred silver. "Keep the change."

"Why, thank you, young master." The shopkeeper smiled, reached under the counter, and lifted a linen travel pack swollen with goods, which Aven swung over his shoulder to join his much smaller one until he could redistribute supplies. As Aven turned to go, the shopkeeper called out, "Young master?"

"Yes?"

"You've done reputable business here. If you would be so kind as to supply your name, I will inform my associates abroad. My name is Raphu the Collector," he finished with a wave at the dangling bones above.

"Well met, Raphu, my name's Avenderan, the…er…adventurer, but my friends call me Aven," he said, feeling a little foolish.

"Excellent! Safe travels, Aven, and remember to mention 'Raphu' whenever you do business in items."

Raliel was waiting by the door, yawning, "Done?"

Aven nodded.

"Good."

Back on the street, Aven saw that traffic had dwindled drastically. The roads were clear. They headed west at a nod from Raliel for the gorge's only pass and whatever lay beyond.

***

Beads clicked and clacked in passing; fluids percolated as Raphu the

Collector entered his workshop. He made straight for the far wall and pressed a stone brick, identical to the others, and it made an audible 'click' initiating a sequence of muffled sounds. Finally, a door-sized wall-length slid into a recess in the floor to reveal Raphu's private sanctum. Retrieving a velvet pouch from one of many intricate chests along the right wall, he crossed to a small table and plush chair just as the collapsed wall returned to its original upright position.

Magic-infused runes glowed across the ceiling in the darkness, like pulsing green constellations in a night sky. Raphu reached into the pouch and pulled free a sky-blue orb. He set the skull-sized sphere in a depression on the table. He sat, breathed deep, and recited a brief incantation. The pulsing blue ball cleared in seconds and revealed a face he knew and respected.

"Has the boy departed?" the man in the orb inquired coolly.

"Oh, yes, only moments ago," Raphu reported.

"Were you able to place a beacon?"

"Better, I sold them pairing runes, to which I'm attuned. So they're much less likely to lose or dispose of them," informed the collector.

"Where were you able to find such rare items?"

"They belonged to my parents," Raphu said.

"I'll reimburse you for them immediately."

"No need, Esteemed One."

The man in the orb silently considered the report. "Excellent, Raphu. Please keep me informed of their location daily until I see you in person."

"Understood."

"Oh, and Raphu?"

"Yes, Venerable One?"

"Spread the word through the network in the port city, with their names and descriptions."

"And how should I instruct our people to proceed? Shall we detain them until you arrive?" Raphu asked.

"No, just watch and report."

"As you wish," the collector assured.

"Thank you, brother."

***

Midtown itself was in the midst of a dusty barren plain. Home to rock, brush, and a sparse tree here and there. The friends passed through the west portcullis. Ahead, the dusty road split into three paths. Their course lay west to the gorge's crossing: a giant steel cable bridge, barely two horse-drawn carts in width. Not like Aven had ever seen it. However, he might as well have, the bridge being the starting point in many of his father's detailed stories as well as every adult who had seen it, so he knew it was a feat of Massifae-inspired human ingenuity. A marvel that Aven was excited about crossing: just by this accomplishment, he would have gone farther than most people he knew back home.

They stopped to redistribute supplies, and he managed to get everything divided well. His new larger pack remained, the smaller inside; Raliel took almost half the scrolls, and they got her fur cape rolled and bound tight on her pack like his jacket was on his.

The day warmed, the sky was bright and clear. The sun negated an occasional chill breeze.

Aven judged it to be mid-morning by the sun, with time to reach the wall and daylight to spare.

They trekked in silence for an hour or so, concentrating on covering more ground while the sun cast their shadows before them. Then, leaning into a gust, using the weight of his pack, it was his silhouette that Aven contemplated when Raliel informed, "We've got company."

The only other person they had seen today was a very old man with a ponderous backpack, matching another upon an equally ancient mule. He had passed them earlier at a brisk march, at odds with his advanced age. Nevertheless, he managed a "G'day" in passing, followed by, in the distance ahead, "Will ye hurreh ye ole' hinny? We've na got the whole day ta be waitin' for ye," which the mule responded to with a very UN-mule-like titter, that induced both friends into a bout of quiet snickering of their own.

The 'company' referred to a couple of rough-looking men, apparently having words with the old traveler. The conversation was beyond ear-shot, on the horizon. Here and there, the wind carried the tone of confrontation, if not the actual words.

Aven and Raliel quickened their pace when they saw the taller of the two ruffians shove the older man, causing him to topple. The friends broke into a run. Spotting their approach, the thugs squared up to receive them, drawing crude weapons: a small knife and cudgel glittering at the end with broken glass.

The young duo responded with singing iron and the whir of spinning axe. Then, with a hoot and flinch, both thugs bolted, scrambling and tripping in their haste to escape.

They were long gone when Aven and Raliel found the grayed and grizzled old man wriggling supine upon his overlarge pack. Like a river turtle trying to gain purchase on the ground just out of reach.

"Are you hurt?" Aven said, sheathing his weapon. It took both of them to right the man properly. His pack was heavier than it looked and appeared even more ridiculous up close. Back on his feet, the man studied them from behind leathery folds of wrinkled brown skin and two great silver eyebrows. They reminded Aven of bushy mustaches, twitching as he analyzed them.

"Ye two," he mumbled, "uh, thank ye kindly for the help. Ye needn't have bothered yerselves, me n' Jenny had the matter well in hand." He stamped his feet, shedding dust from his pack, then again stuck out that gnarled hand.

"Name's Hori, by the way," his grip was surprisingly firm, and the muscles of his brown forearm rippled.

"Aven."

"Raliel."

"This here's is Jenny," and to the mule, Hori added sternly, "Mind yer manners ole' hinny."

'Jenny' stepped to his side, offering a huff before turning her head west with a deep sigh. If Aven didn't know any better, he would say she looked worried.

"Mind telling us what that was all about?" Aven asked.

"Ye mind if we get ta stepppin while I do?" Hori started before Aven could reply. He shared an amused expression with Raliel, one that she banished with a solemn nod, communicating wariness. The ruffians could return.

"I'll take point," Raliel informed, jogging past Hori and his trailing pack mule. Aven quick-stepped around Jenny to Hori's side. Raliel set a swift march ahead, axe flashing sunlight, as she twirled the blade, handle resting on a shoulder

"I would'na worry ta much about those two," Hori began. His bowed legs added a gait that swayed his towering pack perilously left and right. Then, from somewhere over his left shoulder, he slid out a four-foot-tall staff, thick aged wood that came to his shoulders.

"They have'na been at highway robbery long, an ye and yer lady warrior may've helped 'em decide the mines an' quarries ain' so bad, eh?" he grinned, revealing a gleaming pair of gold fronts, amid surprisingly strong-looking teeth.

"What'd they want anyway?" Aven asked, eyes scanning the horizon for a sign of the troublemakers.

Hori adjusted his grip higher, right beneath the staff's top, which had a lethal-looking petrified wood knot.

"The same ye can expect from such as them, demandin' coin ta pass their bridge ahead." He nodded to where Raliel approached two posts, at the crest of a swell in the ground they had been ascending.

"Their bridge?" Aven asked, adjusting the strap of his pack as he walked.

"The ol' quarry bridge. Not much of a large quarry more n' the remains of the spot where the army dug stone for the town. Folk still manage ta retrieve good enough stone, for this n' that. Enough ta make a small living from." He paused in thought, then added, "Not as much work as minin', though."

The bridge looked sturdy, clearly kept in good repair. The actual quarry was no more than a deep excavated trench, long enough to be a delay to bypass and about thirty feet across. The bridge didn't even creak as they crossed.

From this vantage, Aven could see the land decline into fields of tall yellow grass, undulating in the wind. Then, again, this plain swelled up in the distance, where the road disappeared on the horizon.

"The gorge is right over that crest there, Aven friend."

They took a short break at the base before the fields sharing some travel jerky with their new friend Hori. He explained to them how he'd been a traveling merchant for a'hunnerd plus years and was well known. The farthest he liked to go was a few other ports beyond Midhaven, but only then via town portals avoiding the wilds. Boglin raiders, an occasional Heena pack, or Grawl were among the inhabitants of the wild areas near Midhaven.

"Not that ye'd know much about such things, bein' from this side o' the gorge."

He wasn't wrong. The worst any had heard this side was the rare robber or two, but rarely more than the ill-conceived attempt they'd just disrupted.

The sun had climbed overhead as they traversed the hard-packed road through grassy fields.

"So you probably know Raphu, the Collector," Aven asked.

"Yer correct in that supposition. He informed me that ye were of the friendly ilk." He nodded. "We merchants need ta watch each other's backs, eh? It was ta his advice that I travel today, while ye n' yer lady warrior also made yer way. I'll be owin' him a 'thank ye' when I get back." Hori continued to nod quietly, then added, "Perhaps give 'em a discount on them bones he fancies so much."

Hori continued talking about himself. A minor portion of his profit came from hauling supplies others felt profitable, which he took to places no one else would go or could without a cart. "The profit is enough ta keep me in business ye see, but the true riches are in the people. In doin' a service ta the communities far in the ranges or villages out o' the way. I only get ta Midhaven for customer demands for items only available there."

Aven decided that he liked the older man. Hori continued to regale them with stories and descriptions of his travels, from the waterfalls and majestic mountain vales north of Kingsfort to the coastal pearl divers where Aven's mother was born.

Hori seemed a man who enjoyed the journey over the destination, doing good where he could, lending help to those in need more than profiting off of them.

"Was quite the scrapper in my youth, an' can still hold me own, with tha proper support." He turned a disapproving eye to Jenny, who remained aloof.

"These roads have ne'er been as dangerous as now, ever since that king's proclamation. Many men and women." He nodded respectfully to Raliel. "That would regularly encourage peace, are determined to venture west an' claim a share o' land an' fortune."

Perhaps that explained the grubby teens seeking to bully an old merchant. But, unfortunately, if Hori's assertion were correct, things would only worsen.

They learned many things from Hori by the time they reached the final summit shortly after noon.

At the lip of the gorge, they encountered two structures: a guard station and a barracks farther north. The station was just right from the bridge. Two royal sentries, lounging under the eaves of the post, came to attention as they neared.

"Halt!"

Stopping as instructed, Aven noticed Hori rummaging through a pouch at his side.

"State your names and business for the record, please," said one sentry holding quill and writing board. The other remained at attention, blocking access to the bridge.

"Avenderan Amoniel, seeking work in Midhaven."

"Raliel Merari, for the same," she chimed in. Wondering at the delay, she looked to Hori.

"Just a moment, just a moment, aha! Here ye go, young Mort," he said, handing the sentry a tattered leather scroll. "How's yer Da?"

'Mort' scanned the document, adding details to the board. "Er, he's fine, Hori," he muttered. But, "the toll is ten silver apiece for you two," he eyed their outfits and weaponry in a much more official tone.

"Twenty silver? Ha! Ye don't expect anyone ta pay that, do ye?" Hori asked incredulously.

Mort turned to Hori exasperated, explaining in a hushed tone, "It's true! We just received royal command, doubling the toll for the cost of policing the roads!"

Raliel scoffed openly, rolling her eyes.

As Aven made to retrieve the funds, Hori stayed his hand with a swat.

"Not this time Mort. These are me hired guards, and well worth it considering the job yer boys are doin' policing the roads," Hori arched an eyebrow at the guards lounging near the barracks. "If ye look closely at me royal pass ye'll see me guards are covered, under 'contracted help.'"

Mort reexamined the scroll and nodded when he found the related script. "Very well, all seems in order; you may pass." Duty fulfilled, Mort returned to the shade, followed by his silent partner. Mort then gave a boyish wave to Hori.

Hori began checking and adjusting Jenny's pack straps in preparation for the crossing. The friends followed suit, checking each other. When done, they waited patiently for Hori, both staring off over the gorge, contemplating their futures. They locked eyes, and they were kids again, nervous and unsure, but only for a moment. Then both as one came to understand that together they could do this. They were capable of success. Their confidence fed off each other's, bled together, supporting one another. Aven nodded and said, "No turning back?"

Without breaking eye contact, unhesitating, she nodded. "No turning back."

It struck Aven, not for the first time, just how much Raliel meant to him and although he didn't understand how to express it yet, he was glad she had chosen to come. His respect for her and their friendship had grown unfathomably because of it. He wanted her to know but couldn't find the words. The silence grew awkward.

"A-hem!" coughed Hori.

They broke eye contact.

"If ye two wan'ta stand there gazing in each other's eyes all day, then kindly step aside so Jenny n' I can get goin', eh?"

Aven took point this time, and Raliel stayed back conversing with old Hori.

The bridge was a marvel of engineering and colossal construction. A scaled-up wood and rope bridge, but with planks of thick steel and twisted cable as thick as a man, running parallel across the chasm. The smaller version striated from the massive cables —thick as Aven's wrist—over each other, suspending wide and tightly lined planks for a mile across the gorge. Those main supporting cables were stretched tight, held on each side by massive iron frames and anchors riveted deep into the granite cliffs. The result of all this manipulated steel and iron was a corridor wide enough for two carts abreast leading off into space.

To Aven's despair, a little afraid of heights, this 'corridor' never held straight but swayed left, right, up, and down, so distant points came in and out of sight. Like peering down the throat of an enormous roiling serpent. This movement increased the farther out they got.

Aven noticed that Hori had fitted blinders on Jenny. Lucky her, he thought. Raliel appeared unafraid as ever, staring in awe, all around at once. Hori continued chattering unabated of the many facts and wonders he had discovered in crossing many times.

Twenty feet elapsed from the steel planks underfoot to the massive cables overhead, affording an expansive view of the tremendous gorge on each side. Then, very quickly, the cliff face that stretched beyond sight with its many pockets, scaffolding, crags, and rubble, faded from view. It seemed they were suspended in the sky. Below, perpetual mists obscured all detail, swirling eerily and adding to the illusion of walking in the clouds. Nobody claimed to know what the bottom of the chasm held; if there was a bottom, it was a mystery.

The moving state of the bridge, while logically secure, did require a slow and careful pace for a variety of reasons. There was that instinctual rein tugging on nerves, the breathtaking view to consider, perhaps even appreciation for design, but mostly because it was like walking on top of a swelling ever-moving sea. At least Aven imagined so. He could be walking up a slight incline applying added effort when suddenly it became a decline, jolting his poor heart, forcing him to lean back and fight to slow his descent. It was nerve-wracking. The constant shifting and balancing demanded the concentration of a drunk struggling to walk normally. Something he might have an easier time imagining after this experience. Running or walking swiftly, while possible, probably would not end well.

Aven's muscles strained from the exertion of maintaining balance, speed, and composure. He thought this place would be ideal for martial training because if he could fight under these circumstances… he nearly tripped and shook silly thoughts from his mind.

With the pace what it was, it took fifteen minutes to reach the bridge's mid-point. Marked by a network of locking mechanisms joining cable and plank. Aven noticed how everything seemed tied into a vast rune symbol apparatus here. He stood in its middle, looking down at the symbol when Hori's voice, much nearer than expected, caused his heart to skip a beat.

"Legend says that the rune will'na suffer the pass o' evil. Though I've seen many o' rotten scoundrels crossin' back n' forth without a hitch."

Beneath the glyph, the swirling sea of fog lent an air of solemnity that rested on their shoulders.

"OK, kids, gather 'round the symbol for a bit." Hori's voice was grave and authoritative, "Now, I hav'na spoken about, an' I'm na' sure anyone has yet. Bein' we're here, it's all the more appropriate, as this is a place of oaths and binding magic." Hori paused, big gray brows fluttering in the wind as he formed words.

"Ye are headed ta a place of danger an' death, where horrors have ruled for centuries, as ye know. As soon as ye cross an' leave this bridge, yer lives will be in danger, ne'er will they not. If ye underestimate the peril, yer as good as dead.

"Now, I see yer both of a mind ta put yerselves in danger's way, which is liable ta get ye killed. More have died doin' what ye plan than not, an' I want ye ta let that sink deep into yer hearts n' minds because only a healthy fear will keep ye humble enough ta stay alive. Try yer hardest ta avoid gettin' out in the night, if ye hav'na heard yet, that's when the worst comes a crawlin' out, and in numbers, ye could ne'er survive. I want ye both ta promise right now, over this glyph, an' before me ol' bones that ye'll ne'er become too proud or arrogant to look out for each other or let the other slip. Ye'll not be able ta trust humans much more n' beasties. Ye'll be the only ones on who ye can rely. So, promise me ye'll not disservice each other for any reason or allow anything ta distracts ye from yer oath to protect each other. Until ye cross this glyph to return home or renew yer promise." He made eye contact with them and looked above when he said, "Now swear it."

"I swear, Raliel, to put your life before mine."

"As I swear, to put your safety above myself, Aven."

With that, any building tension vanished. Aven felt a vibration radiate from the center of the big rune, rattling his bones in passing, and continue out along the bridge. He and Raliel shared a look and turned to Hori, who smiled cheerfully and said, "That'll do fine, just fine."

"Now," Hori continued, "if ye'll step away from the glyph, I must be on me way."

Looking puzzled, Raliel stepped around Hori to Aven's side, and they both retreated from the huge rune mechanism.

"Come now, Jenny; we've gotta hurreh." The mule and Hori fit well within the symbol, with room to spare. Hori lifted his staff, which began to glow blue from the center of the knotted wood atop. "Take care ye two, an' I hope ta find ye well on the other side!" A flash of blue lightning engulfed Hori and Jenny, and they were gone, leaving the crackling of tiny blue bolts to scatter and dissipate.

"He sure knows how to exit," Aven said.

"He could've shown us how to operate the thing," Raliel complained, "he'll probably be far from here, snug as a bug by the time we finish crossing." Her brow furrowed as she studied the spot where Hori had disappeared.

"I'm sure he had his reasons. We should be going."

Raliel blinked, not seeming to hear him, lost in thought.

From their position, it would be easy to confuse direction in the center of the bridge. The last thing Aven wanted was to head back instead of forward accidentally. He looked up to the sun for surety.

They walked west in comfortable silence, digesting all they had experienced this day, knowing it was far from over.

***

A shadow lay flat atop a massive cable and observed the oath and dramatic exit. He had taken an oath himself and was startled when a visceral vibration nearly shook him from the perch. Hori's speech carried loud and clear, and though he couldn't be sure, he thought that the older man had spotted him above the two friends just before the oath. It was highly improbable but not impossible, he thought.

Perhaps he was becoming lax in the pursuit of such easily stalked prey. He would meditate on this and Hori's words. The shadow was nothing if not open to improvement. He was honing his skills as a lifetime commitment; he would never allow stagnation. He knew that he could sharpen his ability beyond any bladed edge. That was the essence of a master; a lifetime dedicated to training, an open mind to perfecting his art: the administration of instant and certain death.

That should be a good enough lead, he thought, as the companions began to disappear ahead in the swells and twists of the flexing bridge.

Springing from a prone position to his hands and feet, once again the hunter, he followed swiftly—a spider in a web of steel, prey in sight.

CHAPTER FOUR

The west end of the bridge was a testament to the dangers beyond. Awaiting the friends was a militaristic stronghold filled with solemn warriors. Guardians of the pass. What first caught the eye were enormous twin pyramids of natural rock jutting 300 feet high on each side of a wall. Each mini-mountain had sharp-pointed peaks slanting down to squat bases a hundred yards in width. These pyramid-shaped granite horns marked the pass, visible for miles around. Aven could appreciate the advantage these formations gave the defenders. There is little doubt, he thought, why the guardians chose this spot. The squared bases were angled so that their points met the cliffside, providing a clearing some 300 yards wide that narrowed as the two mountains met, creating a small gap on the far side of the wall. Aven knew from the latter he'd heard that the pyramid's shapes were not wholly natural but carved by design while mining stone for the wall.

The wall was a hundred feet tall, built just 40 yards within the narrow strait. Atop was an assortment of heavy ballistae used to rain destruction upon the small space below.

Inside the wall was a great use of the triangular area betwixt gorge, wall, and granite pyramids. On the northern point was a three-story barracks for the renowned '300' soldiers tasked with defending the wall. No less than a hundred remained present on it, ready to man boiling pitch, bows, and catapults day and night. Next to the northern pyramid, a thick circular commander's tower stood between the barracks and wall, rising over the border to afford a clear view beyond. The same granite of the pyramids formed the tower building and barracks. All bespoke entrenchment is capable of holding another 300 years or more as it had since the Great Divide.

The works on the south end of the clearing were most remarkable by far—diagonal lines of furrows of growing crops of various colors and sizes. From the base of the granite slope, nearest the wall, burbled a freshwater fountain. Additionally, the positioning of the camp meant that the sun shone all day at the defender's backs, in the eyes of enemies, and on the crops, as it arched overhead from east to west.

Night fell before they could embark beyond. Hori had warned not to travel at night. But, even if they had wanted to, the guardians wouldn't open the gate or allow access near the wall after sunset.

Comfortable yet spartan, rooms were available for rent in the barracks; for a price, the commander's tower offered more palatial accommodations within. Anyone else was free to camp out under the stars, which the friends chose. The weather had cleared during the day, and the evening was mild. They chose a spot next to a roaring communal bonfire centering the grounds.

After a quick wash by the fountain, they refilled their canteens and settled by the fire to a humble meal of traveler's tack Aven had bought in Midtown.

"These are horrible," Raliel commented, trying to take a bite out of one of the small, hard biscuits.

"They're like rock," he agreed, "I think we're supposed to let 'em soak in water."

Raliel just shrugged, having decided to leave hers in her mouth. Instead, she poured in a bit of water, smiling at her ingenuity. Aven laughed and followed suit. After a few minutes, they could get the things down without choking.

That's when the howling began. At first, they thought someone was hurt or crying, but as it neared, it became clear that it was not a single creature. Instead, many agonizing cries joined into a great howl beyond the wall.

The initial attack was over in minutes, assailants repelled for the moment, but the soldiers' work-frenzy continued. They repaired and reloaded equipment as if expecting an immediate attack. But, instead, it came within the hour and held all night.

As shifts changed and fresh troops rotated, those relieved sought respite before heading to their beds. Some shared the bonfire to thaw the chill left in their bones from their grim work. But, for the icy dread that no fire could cure, some chose to talk, hoping to prevent the nightmares almost assured.

"It's the undead that curses the night these days," said a grizzled old veteran sitting next to a young recruit. The older was training the other, his nephew, to take his place. The younger was a sturdy-looking lad in his trade's shiny new steel helmet, breastplate, and boots. But, as his uncle spoke steadily, he stared blankly at the wall, fire reflecting in his glossy eyes.

"You get...hardened to the sights, learn to trust in our defenses...but never really to the dead come a-knockin' every night." He chuckled darkly, "The lad's holding up well." Then to his nephew, "Hear that Stanis? You're doin' better than most."

Stanis blinked, nodded slowly, and then resumed his trance-like state. But, the older warrior continued, "As I recall, I was a blubbering mess myself when my father brought me to the wall."

At the wall were ones of honor, passed down through families from the first defenders to the present. One could serve five years to life but could only be relieved from duty when they provided a worthy replacement, usually from their line.

"What are they like?" Aven asked.

"They come in all shapes. From my time, I've learned much on this evil." Then, with a glance at young Stanis to ensure he was paying attention, he resigned himself to relaying what he knew:

"As was passed down from the first defenders, who served during the Great Divide and subsequent war, the first undead were fresh-fallen Elden and Massifae, and I do mean fresh," he emphasized with a wide grin, "blood still scabbing, wounds still weeping. Nobody knows how or why the dead rose but never before had such a horde of abominations existed. You can still see these original dead, as marked by their ancient armor and weapons, which, I'm warning you, may still carry powerful enchantments.

"It doesn't matter to them that their flesh and sinews have long passed. Their bones are preserved and animated by magical green fire flaring from the recesses of their skulls or whatever they've got left. Nothing short of fire or acid can destroy these old ones. If even a finger remains, it will seek the living. So much as a scratch from these ancient fiends will turn the host within hours. Their screams of pain easily identify victims as the cold spreads, putrefying flesh and life from the cut. Today's hordes consist of dead animals, humans of all sizes and ages, and even more extraordinary creatures of the realm. Fresh and old.

"We know they fear the light of day, retreating to darkness. There are tales of old ones caught in the trenches and rendered to dust by the sun's rays, but the fresher dead will stir again when darkness falls. Sun for them is uncomfortable, at most. Perhaps it has something to do with age, time in undeath, or maybe the original magic of the curse within the old ones; I know not. Only by severing the head from the body or destroying it can these young ones be stopped. However, it doesn't hurt to burn them just to be sure.

"Be wary of the moon. It seems to have an effect upon their strength and frenzy to kill. The brighter it gets, the more deadly. Be warned! These old ones become supernaturally strong, capable of incredible feats of strength and speed. The freshly turned not so much, besides their usual mania to extinguish life.

"The moon-cycle is especially important to note if you are traveling the wilds because while charms to repel the dead do exist, they're rendered weak or useless by the moon's power. Nevertheless, we've got such charms working here." The veteran scratched his gray whiskered chin. "Don't mistake them for ghouls, the undead hunger not for flesh, or anything else except extinguishing life…um…also, you can tell if there's a full moon if you can see the old ones glowing green, with a like-colored luminous mist among them. Just one of these horrors presents a formidable threat, even here." He lapsed into his respite, leaning back against one of many thick logs placed around the fire.

"Thank you for your knowledge," Raliel offered.

"Think nothing of it, for if it helps you survive to kill more of 'em, then it serves us all. Only by destroying as many as possible can we ever hope to be free of the fiends."

A short period of silence was broken by the 'thwack' of a catapult launching a freshly lit pitch pot beyond the wall, followed by a handful of shrieks. After that, gaps of silence grew, interrupted only by the random crackling or pop of the fire.

"Well, Stanis, my boy, I believe it's time we turned in. Goodnight, you two, and good luck on your journeys." And they were gone.

CHAPTER FIVE

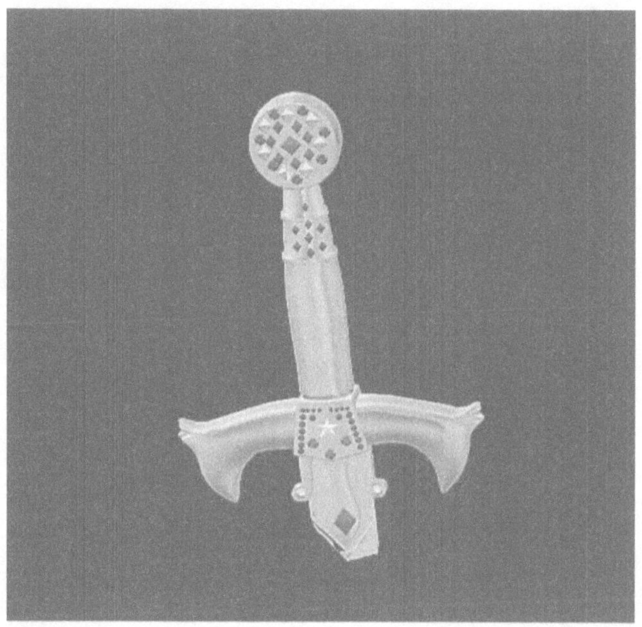

Raliel was floating serenely in mist, neither hot nor cold. At peace. She found herself in Master Nazar's garden. Legs folded beneath her, hands resting on her knees. She felt the familiar cushy moss underneath her, which carpeted the small islet used for meditation studies. A well-manicured garden surrounded the tiny island, filled with a variety of colorful flowers and trees. Pink cherry blossoms floated through the air, some settling upon the creek's waters that split to encompass this unique isle.

She breathed through her nose all the sweet fragrances of flora, fresh cool water, and rich black soil. Then, breathing deeply, she contemplated silencing her mind, immersing herself in a trance, as Master Nazar had shown her.

Among the quiet gurgle of water and wispy breeze, she heard the customary creak of weight upon the small cherry wood bridge that led off the isle. Opening her eyes, she observed Aven, watching their Master approach in like position.

Nazar was clothed in simple tan, loose-fitting muslin smock, and pants he wore while tending his magnificent garden. Feet bare, hands covered in a pocket fronting the smock, Master Nazar's long straight beard, of delicate white, trailed in the breeze, matching his eyebrows and hair, the latter in a neat, fist-size bun atop his head. He took his place upon a flat stone before them to commence the day's lesson.

"Vic," he began, "name for me three virtues of inner strength."

To Raliel's left, also with legs folded, hands upon knees, nine-year-old Vic replied smoothly,

"Yes, Master, among many are justice, mercy, and honesty."

"Very good," Nazar agreed. But, he continued, "Aven, what have you learned from your inner observer today?"

Aven's little face scrunched up in concentration. He then relaxed and, with a nod, replied, "Silencing the chatter of my mind is hard, yet for a moment, from deep down, I felt not frustration but amusement at the effort and peace. I felt stronger by this presence. I don't know if I can explain it better than that, master."

Nazar's eyebrows raised in a rare expression of approval. "Very, very good Aven, you're becoming acquainted. Great progress."

Aven beamed. Raliel, the youngest of the group, thought it all well and nice to relax in the garden but was ever anxious to partake in training like the older boys. Before Nazar could speak, she asked, "Master, when will you teach me to fight like the boys?"

At this, the boys' poorly suppressed giggles made her scowl. Master Nazar's curiously young, unwrinkled brown face smiled benevolently and spoke, "Peace, young Raliel. The first and most potent battle we must wage is within ourselves. There is war within everyone, a fight for your attention between various forces. We first must become aware of this struggle and learn to identify these forces. Only then can we tap into our true strength. The strength of a warrior starts from within. Anyone can know to fight, but the power and endurance of the will to fight well stand upon this inner knowledge. A great warrior must first conquer the distraction of the fettered mind and flesh. Only by silencing these can one come to perceive their inner witness: The Divine Spirit awareness unique to them. A gift of the gods for those wise enough to listen. What deity or attributes lie latent are unknown to all but your spirit. Anyone can receive proper guidance through their spirit. What is the correct measure of fighting prowess? One can achieve true power by unlocking a well of will. What is the accurate measurement of battle prowess? Is it not when a warrior has been stripped of every physical advantage? When she has nothing but her will to continue fighting? Only then is true strength measured by an indomitable will. At this moment, we are as the gods created us to be. Reflections of the personal image are achieved with greater clarity through communion with the great observer within our hearts—one who rallies for the cause of good or ill and unleashes the powers of the divine.

"Once you have mastered this, once you have united with your essence, then you will be ready to learn to wield the lesser martial weapons of the body and steel. Which, are only extensions of your will."

Raliel's mind twisted and coiled with the effort to understand these words. But, for her, it was only a necessary step to begin her ascendancy to physical training. Rising, Master Nazar excused his students for the day.

***

"Aven? Where are you going? Don't go too far," his mother called as he burst past her and out the back door, doing his best to pretend he didn't hear, as kids often do. He couldn't afford to get held up with any random chores. He had to meet up with Vic and Raliel. Jogging past the backyard to the hard-packed dirt trail amid a grove of trees, Aven hoisted his wooden shield over a shoulder. It was one of many groves planted throughout the village, shading the areas between each house, orchard, and square.

In a predusk sky, the sun gleamed through red and orange leaves. The air was fresh and cold; Aven enjoyed how the cold numbed his face and kept him from sweating, even under his heavy jacket and two pairs of heavy work pants. He and his partners had a quest to do, and he was excited.

He was glad to find Raliel and Vic already waiting at farmer Reck's well, on the outskirts of his yard. Then, he saw the huge barn, with all of its sinister glory and promise of adventure. Vic sat on the well's edge in his work leathers, twirling a throwing spike in each hand with ease. "There you are, care to tell us what we're up against, fearless leader?" he whispered, casual and relaxed.

Raliel chimed in, "Let's go check it out before it gets too late," agitated, as she often was before conflict, though it never seemed to affect her ability. Aven squared his shoulders and studied her weapon, a stout club held firm in her fist.

Aven explained, "Farmer Reck claims something has been scaring the livestock and waking him every night."

"What could it be?" Raliel asked.

Aven shrugged, "Every time he gets to the barn, it's gone, sometimes returning as soon as he gets back to bed."

"Any tracks?" Vic whispered.

"Nope. It's a mystery, a nuisance that we're gonna resolve," Aven grinned, "If we do this, Reck says he'll reward us."

"With what?" Raliel asked.

"He didn't get into specifics; guess it depends on how well we do."

"What's the plan?" Vic asked without looking up from his spinning darts.

"We take the position and wait. Then, depending on what it is, we'll handle it."

"Sounds like a solid plan," Raliel commented.

"That's not all of it, smart girl; we've gotta check out the area first."

Having done so, Aven set Raliel in the hayloft, the open door facing the back. Vic was on perimeter re-con by choice, leaving Aven to wander between the two before settling in a hastily constructed blind of hay bales, viewing the barn's side and back.

The air chilled further, and his choice to remain squatted changed to taking a knee. Cold and dampness seeped through. An orange moon hung low, leering, casting a nightmarish tint over the barn. A chill scurried between Aven's shoulder blades. He tried to stay focused and not give in to his morbid imagination. Inky shadows extended from the barn, and at this angle, he couldn't look into the open hayloft to see Raliel. Then, just as he thought to head in to check on her, a shadow dimmed the moonlight. Aven's heart leaped. He looked behind, but nothing was there, worried he had let something sneak upon him. He shifted his angle so he could include a frequent glance back. Probably no more than an owl or bat, he thought.

Without a hoot or squeak? He doubted it. The silence was oppressive; not even the animals in the barn stirred. Again, the shadow swept the nightscape. This time Aven looked up and was startled to see how near the movement was. He raised his arms, flinching against the bales before realizing it wasn't as near as it seemed. It was big! Then it vanished back into the starless void.

Feeling foolish for not having done so earlier, he strapped his shield to his arm and drew a wooden sword. He peered over shield into the night with a vision of himself heroically battling a fairytale dragon, fantasizing over how he would accomplish it with wooden equipment. Before the fantasy could play out, with scenes of adulation from his peers, a whistle signaled Vic's approach.

Holding a heroic pose, Aven whistled in response to guide his friend to his hiding spot. Vic's shadow flickered this time. "Did you see it?"

"Not very well," Aven admitted, "what was it?"

"You wouldn't believe me if I didn't have this." Vic produced a feather.

"That's the biggest feather I've ever seen," Aven hissed, "are you sure it's' from 'it'?"

"Saw it fall with my own eyes. Flew within feet of my position in that big tree," Aven pointed to a tree tall enough to brush the belly of the orange moon, "Aven, it looked like a ghost, the biggest white owl I've ever seen, the biggest thing I've ever seen, it had to have come here recently. Something that big would've caught plenty of attention pretty quick."

"From across the gorge."

"That's what I hear, bro; nothing good comes from across the gorge." Aven knew what he meant; everything that crossed, the only examples from lore or otherwise, spoke of creatures crazed and tainted by darkness. "Aven, we should probably report what we've seen and get the village militia involved."

Aven knew this too. These encroachments had become more frequent in recent years, and the memory of Fargar's fight with a giant boar was still fresh enough to inspire caution. "You're right, let's lock up the barn, get Rali, and get outta here."

A scream of rage and terror pierced the night as they stood. "Raliel!"

Vic moved fast; it seemed impossible to keep up. Nothing was more dire than getting to the loft for the next successive few heartbeats. Once there, there was no time to think of what they intended to do. All that mattered was getting there in time.

While Vic scrambled up the outside wall, Aven took the ladder on the side. Nothing could've prepared them for what they found.

Through sheer ferocity—in a blur of blows—Raliel kept at bay a horror of snapping teeth and whirring claws. Without hesitation, Vic fell upon one of the creatures, a four-foot-tall 'possum. Rank gray fur flew, darts made a hundred punctures, as claws raked leather. Wooden sword, honed sharp bit the back of the other, surprising both it and Raliel, but only for a moment before it whirled on Aven and rushed. It stopped short, its thick grayish pink tail trapped beneath Raliel's work boots. Aven plunged forward with the tip of his weapon, puncturing its hide with a satisfying 'pop.' The skin slid aside without further purchase. Beady crimson eyes flicked between targets. By now, the livestock was causing a racket.

In a ball of fur and fangs, the monstrous possum tore free its tail and shot through the opening into the night.

"Damn!" Raliel covered her nose.

The stench of death saturated the loft. An unmoving animal lay at Vic's feet, joined by a thickening pool of blood, seeping from uncountable wounds. The trio met eyes in unspoken agreement and rushed after the fleeing creature.

"There!" Raliel yelled.

The monster had taken cover in Aven's fort. They spread out to overtake the possum out of sight but heard it digging for shelter. Already beyond, Vic closed in. Aven, the nearest, waited for Raliel to block off her end. All readied themselves. The sound of digging continued.

A shadow fell, and 200 pounds of silent predator slammed in the center of the hay bales. The impact resounded through Aven's feet, where he crouched. His shield raised reflexively. Vic was halfway through a dive, hanging in seeming slow motion. Raliel just stood still, amazed. The fort exploded, bird and prey shot skyward, and a gust of wind buffeted the trio. Aven looked up, spotting a shrinking silhouette against a reddening moon. A majestic giant departed—a limp form dangled from its talons.

***

Aven sensed a shift in Raliel's consciousness next to him, an effect of the amulets they shared. They'd risen before dawn's first light and joined each other on the green grass near the gurgling spring. Aven was drawn from his meditation by the sudden light and warmth of true dawn. The inside of his eyelids turned from dark red to bright orange. A spectacular gold/red majestic sight rewarded him upon opening his eyes. The immense mist-filled gorge stretched to meet the sun beyond. One side of the silver bridge shone like a mirror, disappearing into the haze of frothing brume. Red, orange, pink, and gold: the rising sun highlighted all before him.

"Beautiful isn't it," Raliel said.

"Yes, it is," agreed Aven.

There had been movement and constant activity all through the night, yet with the coming of day, Aven sensed a tangible release at the wall. A subtle relief, as day banished the horrors of the night.

Feeling refreshed and focused, more from his reverie than sleep, Aven roused himself and stretched in anticipation of their journey to Midhaven.

"Had a vision of us as kids, back in Nazar's garden; it was so real," Raliel remarked as she extended her arms, arching her back. They were both dressed for travel, with cape and coat rolled tight on the packs at their feet.

"I like when that happens," Aven said as he hefted her pack and helped her strap it on.

"Me too. I always feel more refreshed after a vision," Raliel said.

He made adjustments to compensate for her mail. Raliel wore a quilted vest over a linen shirt under her chainmail shirt. The mail hung to her knees, where her steel-plated boots began. She buckled her weapons belt tight around her waist, creating a skirt of steel ringlets. Her leather breeks, almost unseen, were tucked into her boots, the toes capped with steel spikes. The sight made Aven's shins hurt. He'd never seen her so appareled, but it suited her.

"Looks like you're all set," he said.

The head of her axe was fastened to a steel peg on her belt, leaving three feet of red leather handle hanging within easy reach of her right hand. Such pegs meant that she could free her weapon with a twist. He only just realized that the belt was of the same dark red leather bound to the slim grip of her axe.

Aven fastened his pack. His leather armor was tan and lightweight, almost two inches thick in places, protecting back, shoulders, chest, stomach, and thighs with hardened hide. It was of good quality and sculpted to imitate muscle tone but wouldn't do much against a direct stab or cleave from a steel blade. He planned to upgrade soon, as his arms were too exposed. He slid out his broadsword with a rasp, continuing his inspection. He had bought the sword secondhand from the local blacksmith. A hefty iron weapon, four-foot blade, plain crosspiece, and pommel with a hand-and-a-half black leather handle. The most expensive single item in his inventory spoke of brutal, if cumbersome, lethality. He slid it back in its wooden scabbard just as Raliel finished her inspection.

"Shall we?" he asked.

They found the iron portcullis already raised. Up close, the wall was enormous. Once through, it was easy to see the futility of any mob attempting to scale it. A broad passage tunneled through the first barrier with several murder holes to the sides and above. The rounded tunnel eliminated blind spots and an efficient gauntlet should the outer door be breached.

Focused on their task, soldiers came and went in small groups offering brief nods, some carrying tools, outfitted for battle in chest plates and helmets. The only defining characteristic was their choice of spear, mace, axe, sword, or flail.

The opening ahead showed gray in the wall's shadow as they exited beneath a two-foot thick iron drop door; they slowed to study the pocket of death and destruction between wall and granite choke point.

An even smaller path led out by way of two trenches dug on each side, filled with sharpened stakes and debris, including the remains of would-be invaders. Siding the narrow path, soldiers prepared to ignite the remaining dead still tangled in the stakes and serrated iron tines.

The young adventurers trod along, hands covering their mouths and noses. Against the stench of decaying flesh, many, on clean-up, wore linen masks. Then, just as they escaped to the clearing beyond, they heard the 'thwump' of blooming flame.

Outside, they got their first glimpse of the lesser wilds and the northern edge of the Witherwood forest. To the north of the road, the forest petered out. To the south, it thickened, spanning several miles along the gorge, as far as the eye could see. The dirt road cut through the north-most portion of the wood to the west. On Aven's previous trip, he and his father had taken the town portal from Midtown, an expensive yet safer way to travel. So although Aven understood the terrain, this was as new for him as for his partner. Aven had purchased a decent map from Raphu. He and Raliel had taken turns studying it last night to familiarize themselves.

"Hey!" a small wall-man called, hailing from among a crew tending a large burning pit. Oily smoke billowed black overhead. With massive iron rakes, the team dragged wriggling creatures to the hole. The wall-man jogged over from north of the road and stopped, pulling down his blackened mask.

"Oh, hello, Stanis. You're looking well today," Aven greeted.

"Yeah, thanks, uh…Uncle Reginald wanted me to give you this," he said and fumbled under his breastplate to retrieve a waxed brown package. He nodded for Aven to grab it.

"Well, thanks to you both. Hope to find you well next time we come through," Aven reached out, and they shook hands goodbye. It dawned on Aven that they were about the same age. As they parted, he wondered in what ways they would be changed if they should meet again. From the map, Aven estimated the trip to Midhaven would take about seven hours on foot. He judged there to be about ten solid hours of sunlight by looking at the sun—plenty of leeway. The broad, even road allowed a brisk pace as he studied.

"So it looks like we have a few hours of Witherwood, then about six miles to the river crossing. That's a little more'n halfway, but the map suggests hills between there and Midhaven. We should make the city with sunlight to spare," he said, rolled the map, and stuffed it into his pack.

"I think that's a little too optimistic, Aven," Raliel observed, "Hey, take a look at the package Stanis gave us," she suggested, chainmail jingling.

Aven dug it out and tossed it to her. "You check it out while I watch the road." He heard the heavy wax paper crumple and rip.

"It's a small book but most of the pages are blank." She flipped through pages as Aven studied the gnarled trees of the Witherwood. They weren't dead since they still bore leaves but looked sick, unlike any trees he'd seen. Their bark was grayer than brown, and the leaves were black and shiny; they were trees, of course, just changed somehow. The floor of the wood, not so bad this far north, was barren with patches of gray and black brush. Further south, where the trees thickened, the forest floor spawned a strange hazy mist, obscuring his ability to see beyond. He shook his head—a foul place.

"Oh, wait!" Raliel interrupted his musing.

"You almost gave me a heart attack!" Aven complained. He checked to make sure his sword was free.

Snorting in dismissal of his weak nerves, she continued, "There's writing on the front pages; I'll read it."

'Aven and Raliel,

A broad and dangerous world awaits you, but also wondrous. Most of which remains shrouded in mystery.

Any adventurer worthy of the title should record what they learn such as the strange creatures and places they encounter. Such information is valuable to many who can't or haven't traveled abroad. I wish I'd done just as you are, but duty called. I fear I'm much too old for all that now.

This journal was to be my record, but I never left to journey, as I've said. Meeting you both has brought it all back, that spark in your eyes, and I envy you.

There are sparse notes that may be of use. I hadn't the time to recall and share them in our brief time together. It's my gift to you, with one condition: that next we meet, you share the knowledge, just as I have here.

Luck and fortune to you, and may Crom strengthen your sword (and axe!) arm.

Your friend,
Reginald Wallace'

"Following this are a bunch of old entries for the next several pages." Raliel shut the book and let out a squeak upon further inspection, again raising Aven's hackles.

"What now?" he asked, trying to suppress the strain in his tone.

"There's a small stick held in the binding. Some sort of writing instrument, how clever!" Raliel carefully tucked the book beneath her shirts and mail. It settled, safe in the space above her belt.

"I'll study it later after we get out of these woods," she said, scanning their surroundings.

The road extended beyond sight. Thin haze cutting down visibility. It was easy to imagine movement within the dark reaches of the shadowed wood to the south. Waist-high mist clung to the trunks of the gnarled trees.

Mountainous clouds had gathered above and threatened to shut out the sun. Just then, a large cloud cast its shadow. The world dimmed.

Aven surveyed the landscape. His ears pricked at the sound of a branch snapping. Then another. Undeniable movement in the trees to the south.

"Let's jog," Aven ordered, and they both picked up the pace. The shifting continued, central with them.

Then from the south, two dark figures exploded from the mist, smashing through the brush with no apparent regard for injury. One paused, its long white hair hung in thick tangled ropes, leaned its head back to let loose a bone-chilling howl. Its body shuddered, hands clenched, and limbs contorted awkwardly. Its partner ran crouched, it's back hunched over, head upended, feet stumbling as it tore their way: twenty yards and closing.

"Damn!" Aven cursed, ripping his sword free and skidding to a halt, braced to engage. Just one scratch, Reginald had said. Damn it, he thought. To his right, Raliel also stopped, axe in both hands, far enough away for them to maneuver appropriately. Then all thought ceased.

The leading fiend closed the remaining gap with a leap and landed between them. Aven hopped to and swung down with both hands. The iron sword bit into its humpback, crumpling it like a stack of kindling. Its clawed arms raked furiously at the ground from its ruined torso. Its legs scrambled in a senseless frenzy.

The second fiend jumped high, its long wispy hair trailing, yellow teeth, and dead eyes intent on Raliel. Its hands and feet clawed simultaneously to slash her. She neatly thrust the top spike of her axe devastatingly into its chest, leaving it tottering over her head for a second before bringing both axe and creature slamming down upon its teammate with a crash of knocking skulls and bone. Thus pinned together, the blade of her axe began to glow bright red, like steel fresh from the forge. Their tattered shrouds started to smoke. They viciously attacked each other, trying to separate their entangled bodies. Then, flame bloomed with a 'whoosh' of heat, quickly consuming them. In seconds, their thrashing ceased, leaving a smoldering pile of embers. Raliel's' axe pulled away free and clean, sparks trailing as the glow ebbed and returned to normal, leaving a red razor edge. "Handy," she said with a grin, admiring her handiwork.

Just then, a cacophony of movement and howling erupted from the south. As more figures materialized and froze, Aven's gut fluttered,

"There must be fifty of them! Run, Rali, I'll hold them."

"I'm not going anywhere without you."

"What are they waiting for?" he asked.

Undead responded, charging in a hail of shrieks and howls. Then that heavy cloud, all but forgotten, passed. Golden sunshine returned to bathe all in its radiant warmth, and light rushed to meet the advancing line. Dark met light. Smoke billowed amid the undead, and they slowed. Obvious discomfort forced them to retreat under the dark canopy of the Witherwood and out of sight. Movement and haze minimized with the sun's return until only the eerie silence remained. A silence Aven now knew to be a deadly illusion.

"Run from here on out?" he suggested.

"That'd be wise," Raliel agreed.

Weapons out, they fled westward, with only the occasional glance behind. However, the feel of watching eyes never left their backs.

***

The hunter was relieved to see the friends flee, knowing that he'd be last out of the dreaded wood if he wanted to remain unseen. But, unfortunately, he couldn't shadow from the trees to the north as planned. He'd meant to cut ahead to take advantage of their leisurely pace and so had taken the thicker wood to the south. The shadows had appealed to his need for stealth; it had nearly cost him his life.

Just south of his targets, he stumbled upon an unexpected clearing clotted with moss and stones, pacing their progress. Countless bones, damp and dark. An ancient battle site, perhaps. He felt he was intruding upon a slumbering evil, and his gut, as usual, was correct.

He heard stirring immediately and slowly and quietly inched back out how he'd come. He became transfixed upon a horrible sight: a mound of bodies, bones, and rags collectively thrashed once, then fell silent. Step by step, he continued to edge back. Under the mossy overhang and haze, it seemed a mass burial chamber, walled and roofed by petrified wood and mold, but he knew better. The pile quivered again, freezing his retreat. Ahead, a gleam caught his eye to his right, and he noticed a small stone marker.

Curiosity overrode caution, and using all the stealth he could muster, he slowly crept to the right, warily circumventing the tangle of undead. Another rustle from the pile. Step by silent step, he was in total control of his pulse, enjoying the rush, using it to hone his awareness instead of allowing it to panic his system. His heart slowed its pace as he slowed to enhance his stealth. He was breathing through his nose quietly and smoothly. Step. Step. Rustle. Step. Step. Step. Step. Rustle. He made it to the tiny grave, which appeared to be an ancient shrine. A single ray of sunlight, through the canopy, bathed the stone.

On closer inspection, he found it an ancient tombstone, which he had approached from behind. Finally, he discovered the probable cause of the flash from the front that had caught his attention. He carefully blew the dust from a gem-encrusted dagger hilt. He lifted it and despairingly realized that the blade was missing; the slender hilt and pommel fashioned of heavy gold, the grip wired in bronze. On the pommel was a semi-transparent gemstone that sparkled brilliantly in the sun.

He felt an odd sensation as he held the blade-less dagger, almost like a tug toward the shallow cairn below the grave marker. Then, just as he was about to investigate, the ray of sunlight went dark. Cold mist plumed, corpses thrashed. A body rose. He bolted westward from the clearing as fast as possible, forgetting his prey for now. The newfound treasure was tight in his fist.

Thinking back, now from a hiding place among the tall grass, he was relieved to find this recent misadventure hadn't interfered with the pair he was shadowing. Instead, they were just then exiting the Witherwood at a swift pace. Were they fleeing?

The sun had come back out a while ago, and he didn't think the undead were much of a threat in light of day, although now he knew they could be just within the mark of their domain—nesting.

The hunter rolled on his side and observed large billowing clouds creeping in from the west, though the sky was open around the sun. He hoped the travelers and himself could make enough headway from that cursed forest before they arrived.

He was tired of the game and began plotting its end. He rolled onto his chest, concealed and observing the two. He grinned beneath his leather mask. If it were possible to see, it showed the glint of calculating iron-gray eyes.

CHAPTER SIX

Far afield, lower in the plain, Aven could see the sparkle of the river 'Veld' mentioned on his map. They had stopped jogging, and he knew they must. His legs were cramping, and a couple of new side stitches made it difficult to breathe. But, on the other hand, he was in his rhythm, his body could handle the abuse, and it felt better the farther they got from the wood.

It was Raliel who convinced him to slow. Not by any complaint on her part; quite the opposite. Not only was she armored more heavily than he, but he knew she could press on, chainmail jingling until she died from exhaustion. He had to think of her, he reasoned. They were both breathing heavy, and his sword drooped. "Let's stop a moment," he gasped, sliding his sword home in its sheath.

"I'm not tired, Aven. We should press on if we can," she growled, still holding her axe.

"There's no sense in exhausting ourselves when other dangers may be ahead. So we rest for a few minutes, catch our breath, and walk from here on out."

She conceded with a grim nod and with obvious irritation but left her axe resting on a shoulder.

Raliel scanned the sky and turned to face the now distant forest to the east. A west wind lifted her golden ponytail over her shoulder, flicking toward the dark woods as if warding against evil with sun-colored locks.

Aven was starting to wonder if she was bluffing about pressing on. As he gasped, shook off cramps, and wiped the sweat from his face, she stood, hardly fatigued, as still as a statue; this had never been the case before. She was no weakling but so vastly superior? Something had changed.

"Is it the axe?" he asked, finally catching his breath.

"What?" She looked back, eyebrows raised quizzically.

"You're not even winded, Rali, and you're in steel with a pack," he added, his tone a little more acidic than intended. He wasn't feeling patient at the moment.

"Oh, it's the belt," she replied offhandedly, "strength enhancement and control of the axe."

"I see," he said, remembering how she viciously skewered and slammed the undead creatures earlier.

Raliel continued, "Its attributes will…personalize and enhance endurance with time. Father explained." She turned, green eyes focusing on him, axe on her right shoulder, ponytail billowing behind.

"Handy," Aven said smiling.

Raliel smiled back.

"We should get going," he thought aloud, looking to the river then to the sky. The wind was strengthening, and rain seemed possible by nightfall. They still had a distance to go, and he wondered if his estimated arrival time had been realistic.

They began to steadily walk down the slope into the grassy lowland between them and the lumpy hill country in the miles to come. To the far right of the hills, Aven could see the beginnings of a mountain ridge, growing larger and more imposing until clouds obscured the north peaks. The hills' southern expanse grew thick with green. Mounds blanketed by forest beyond sight.

The pair continued, clear of any more danger. Eventually, Aven heard the metallic click as Raliel fastened her axe to the peg on her belt.

Without breaking stride, he consulted the map. Soon they could see for a mile around in knee-high grass that had changed gradually from yellow to lush green. A lone tree, thicket, or protruding gray boulder contrasted the uniform green.

The map confirmed the existence of a forest that edged Midhaven's south wall and spread along the road to the south end and beyond. Once they reached that tree line, they would be within four miles of the city.

"Listen to this," Raliel said, interrupting his thoughts.

Aven glanced over to see that she had the journal out.

"'Witherwood' isn't a place as much as a condition. There are various instances of Witherwood plagued by undead and other evil infestations. There is much mystery regarding such woods, enhanced by the fact that nobody has been able to explore or compare them due to the concentration of deadly enemies. Still, we know that inhabitants specific to a withered wood don't normally travel far beyond its boundaries.' It goes on to explain the spreading and nature of these boundaries. Blighted appearance and such, but do you know what this means?" she asked, looking to Aven.

"That we should be safe from the Witherwood?"

"Yup." Both visibly relaxed, though the remaining tension had until now gone unnoticed.

"That's good to know; what else is in there?"

"Several notes that don't make sense to me yet. Some mention shops of good reports, hmm, which look like journal entries. The name Witherwood just happened to grab my attention. I'm gonna have to read this straight through because, if I'm right, there may even be some quest notes, referring to some crude maps an' stuff." She finished.

"Sounds worth the time." Aven finished with the map, rolled it tightly, and lodged it back into his pack.

Raliel's curiosity kept her nose in the journal. Aven was also curious to see what she found next.

It was an hour later when they met other travelers. Aven knew that Midhaven relied heavily upon imported goods while trading in goods not found west of the gorge. He was surprised that it had taken this long to see some kind of transport. Town portal capabilities were expensive, profit draining, and only capable of moving so much at a time. When it came to large quantities of food or staples, the only option was freight wagons. They encountered four such wagons rumbling east on the road. Unlike any freight wagon they'd seen back home, the first three resembled rolling fortresses with a six-horse team apiece. Each had a heavily armed and armored driver, crossbowman, and four spearmen overlooking the lip of the steel siding. The wagons' walled tops reached a minimum of twelve feet high and looked sturdy enough to hold through a siege. They thundered past without pause, forcing the pair to retreat to the edge of the wide road. Each guard looked ready to launch a bolt or spear at the first provocation.

Then, a fourth vehicle: a steel-plated stagecoach built for speed approached. The driver reined in four horses with a "whoa!" its trailing dust clouds blew northeast with the wind and dissipated over the sea of grass.

"Hullo!" greeted the driver. He was a burly man heavily armed and armored with a black beard, blue eyes, and a conical steel cap atop his head.

"Hello!" Aven replied. It struck him then that although the vehicle was small and a little more rugged, it was identical to the armed coach his father had described using in years past.

"Pardon my askin', but what brings you kids walkin' about in the wilds? In need of a lift?"

"We're headed west to Midhaven," Aven answered.

"By yourselves then?"

"Well…yeah."

"Then you must be formidable warriors." He engaged his carriage brake, sprang nimbly off his seat and landed in a clamor of black armor, he offered a beefy hand, "Names' Corban. If you're travelin' the roads of the wilds, we'll be seein' a lot of each other." They each shook his hand and offered their names. Corban removed his helmet and mopped the dust from his face with an equally dusty and sweat-streaked cloth. Once finished, he continued, "Pleased to meet you both. I'm on my way to meet a customer at the Wall. We spotted some Grawl tracks in the hills, and word is bandits have hit a few travelers. Not that we've seen any," he chuckled, "or that they'd want to be seen by our group. They tend to stick to the easier marks." With raised eyebrows, he cast a knowing look to each of them. Raliel explained their earlier encounter with the residents of the Witherwood.

"In broad day, you say?" He seemed genuinely concerned, "Ain't never heard of that happenin', clouds or not!"

Corban looked in his mid-thirties, a man of girth, under six feet tall, but very broad in the shoulders with muscled arms and two long, thick braids hanging from the back of his leather insulated steel cap. He seemed to think their incident deserved significant concern and asked several serious and intelligent questions about it. "Well, undead beasties aside, I wish you luck. Keep your guard up, especially past the bridge," he said as he hopped back in his seat. "I'd better warn the others before we get to those woods. Thanks for the warning, and you would do well to heed mine." He was off with a tip of his cap and crack of the reins; the racket of hooves, spring-shocks, and grinding gravel trailed his swift departure.

"An interesting fella," Aven said and rolled his eyes toward Raliel. She smiled and shook her head.

They continued at a quick rate, all downhill. Aven broke out some travel rations, which consisted of hard biscuits and some gamey jerky. They ate as they marched.

They got to the bridge a little after midday. The bridge, an ancient stone arch, spanned the south-flowing Veld, swollen with recent rains. They were both anxious to reach Midhaven before nightfall and didn't pause—the path inclined at this point. The terrain rose ahead and to the right with a limited field of vision. Just past the river, to the left was a significant downslope into a more incredible grassy expanse, allowing them a clear view of the vast ruins about a mile away.

"Deragard," Raliel volunteered. Everyone knew the story of Deragard. A thriving city before the dark times. It boasted several miles of remarkable architecture and beautiful monuments to civilization and peace in its day. It was the seat of the Tribunal, where elected representatives from each race would hold court, ensuring peace and prosperity for a millennium. After the Great Divide and subsequent desolation of Elden and Massifae populations, the remaining neutral, humanoid races had tried to maintain the city. First, to salvage the colossal economic empire.

Deragard lacked two things crucial to the changing world for all its magnificence, something it had never needed before and had never expected to require. Something that would only degrade the beauty of its parks, ponds, and carefully sculpted landscapes, theaters, mansions, and markets: There were no battlements or city walls. Even during a state of foreign war, as a neutral city, expecting no threat, what guardians existed were minimal.

The first horde of dark creatures came as a surprise to all, but none more than the civilization of Deragard. It was the first coalition of beasts known in history at that broad scale. Evil had waited patiently for the opportunity, and the pinnacle of good civilization was the primary target. Everyone could hear Deragard's cries for leagues as dark waves fell upon its peaceful men, women, and children. The cruelty of the horde was inhuman; it knew no bounds. With the evil scourge pushed back into the southland, human and halfkin retaliation was swift but ineffective. The once-great city was never repopulated and left in ruins—a memorial to the horrendous atrocities there, hundreds of thousands perished, were captured, or worse. No one knew.

The pair silently observed this fallen city with somber reflection, for what was, what was lost, and what was learned.

The clouds had thickened and chilled the air around them. They paused to don jacket and cape, the warmth more comforting than necessary. After the glacial effect of witnessing Deragard's ruins, it was hard not to feel frail and vulnerable, so near to such a humbling blow to the goodly races. More than anything, this heightened their sudden awareness of the drop in temperature.

As they progressed, the colossal city ruins spread out below for miles, over an increasingly distant and broadening view. As they neared the end of this spectacle, they discovered Deragard's main road, which curved wide around the old city expanse. The road down was barely discernible as they passed, so choked with weeds and wild grass. Aven supposed that superstition and the pain of memory kept most people away, but there was a very narrow dirt path down the center. Animal, or possibly those brave enough to salvage whatever was left. It seemed that secrets and the possibility of treasure lured treasure seekers for centuries after its fall. They felt the tug.

Gradually the way became more inclined. Finally, they crested the first hill to the last portion of their journey. The road swayed between growing northern hills and the beginning of a new forest to the south. It would be a few more hours, with about an hour of daylight to spare by the time they reached the city.

"Do you see that tree line far ahead, just before the road disappears around that hill?" Aven asked, breaking the long silence.

"I do," Raliel confirmed.

"Midhaven should be visible once we get there."

Raliel sighed wistfully, "I want to bathe, eat, and sleep as soon as we arrive."

"You'n' I both," he agreed.

The lumpier terrain of rock and grass grew more densely populated with bushes and trees. The ground south had flattened and inclined slightly, while the north side rose dramatically each time the road cut through hillock and knoll, transforming the north view, from rock wall to dirt ledge, to grassy slope.

The sun had begun its descent before them; shadow reached from beneath each bend and cleft. Aven felt grateful for Raliel's company and took a moment to express it.

"Hey, Rali?"

"Yeah?"

He went for honesty, not caring if it came out mushy since there was no one there but them, "I know I've said it a lot lately, but thank you for coming." Saying it now breathed life to something more inside of him. He was more than glad. His heart warmed at the feeling.

"Didn't have many choices, did I? Although, I couldn't just let you get your fool-self killed," she stated, "at least you have a chance with me."

They exchanged smiles, and there was a warmth between them that he could not describe, an intimacy that he all at once cherished and feared losing. Aven realized then that he had always known, even expected, her to come. When she appeared and stayed, he never felt more secure in their relationship. Knowing she didn't hesitate to leave everything behind for him. That seemed selfish.

"Why the scowl Aven?" she studied his expression.

"I was just feeling terrible for causing you so much trouble, for making you leave home for me." Aven was startled when she exploded in a roar of laughter.

"Hahahaha! That's how you see it?!" she held out a hand to stay any response from his bewildered face. "Get over yourself! You've always believed everyone is some character in the book of Aven! Well, here's a wakeup call buster that should alleviate any guilt: I came for my reasons more than yours, fool boy."

"Oh?" Aven asked skeptically, pride stinging just a little, "like what? If you don't mind me asking."

"I do, 'cause it's none of your business," she said with enough disdain to wound him and that earlier feeling.

They walked on in silence, and Aven made little effort to hide his irritation. She made no secret that she was equally peeved. Aven wanted to tell her that she had a hard heart, that she had permanently hurt his feelings, but couldn't will it so. Which only made him angrier. She had that effect on him, and he'd forgotten how insensitive she could be for a moment. He didn't know why her opinion mattered so much to him when she'd always done this. Nobody could make him as angry as Raliel could. She had that power over him; she could inflame him with just a word or a look that to him spoke volumes. They were stewing to a vigorous boil, and he succeeded in getting a handle on his when she next said.

"I don't know why you're always so sensitive." She emphasized 'always' with a roll of her eyes. It was all Aven could take; he exploded.

"I'm sensitive? I was thanking you! And for that, you insult me!"

"Insult you?! How's that? You're the one who insulted me, talking like I'm your lackey! Is that how you see me, as your dog?!"

"SHUT UP!" he yelled.

"You shut up!" she shouted back.

"No, seriously, Raliel, shut up!" he said, raising a hand.

"How dare you...."

"Listen! Be quiet and listen!" he whispered hoarsely.

"What??" Raliel whispered back.

It sounded like a rustling in the grass behind a large boulder about ten yards to their left. Aven drew his sword and prepared to investigate.

"That's far enough!" came a growl from behind another group of boulders fifteen yards to the right of the road. Perfect spot for an ambush, Aven's guts fluttered in warning. At the voice's instruction, Aven proceeded no further and instead edged back to Raliel, who stood, axe in hand facing north while Aven kept an eye on the southern rock, the source of the original rustling. Ambush foiled, two men stepped from behind Aven's rock, wearing grimy leather armor. One held a spear, and the other a short sword and leather shield.

"Aven..." he looked. Three more men spread from the northern rocks. The largest angled ahead with a giant crossbow leveled their way. The other two—one wielding a hatchet and a small buckler, one an enormous battle-axe—mirrored the two on the south as they closed on the friends in a rough circle just out of weapons range and held their ground.

Axe-man growled, "Lookie here, boys, a fine lady it is. We'll be having some fun tonight."

Spearman, swordsman, and hatchet man snickered approval. All four maintained their positions poised to strike. Raliel and Aven were back to back, focused on those closest. They could do nothing about the crossbow wielder—but hope he missed—as he was some thirty yards up the road. When crossbow spoke, the friend's eyes never left their targets.

"You not been rob before?" crossbow snarled. His size and tenor betrayed his half-bogran heritage. Crossbow continued in a wet, guttural voice, "Woman, drop clothes too; I think I reward you with quick death...after." He issued a deep chortle joined by his fellow marauders.

The sun was behind 'crossbow,' so he was now a hulking shadow, but Aven felt the aim of the crossbow bolt gliding over his side and braced himself, feet spread, ready for a chance. As for his orders, Aven and Raliel made no move to comply, and for what? If death was assured, their only shot was to fight. They knew that and trained for it.

Calm, cool, they waited for the opportunity. But, instead, Aven's earlier anger over their argument was fully transferred, bubbling into a barely restrained rage. He fought to control the urge to commit reckless violence.

"Enough!" Aven challenged and lunged at the spearman— succeeding in getting too close for the long weapon to be effective— and stabbed forward, broadsword taking the robber in the right shoulder. Then, without pause, Aven spun toward the other, lashing back blindly with right hand extended, his heavy broadsword quickly knocking aside the anticipated short sword. Aven could hear Raliel grunting and shuffling and knew their survival depended upon how fast this ended.

Spearman had dropped his weapon, right arm hanging limp as he hesitated, snatching it up with his left, now wary of Aven's speed. A glance revealed crossbowman reloading. Aven turned full force upon the short sword. He began a figure-eight slashing pattern with his heavier sword while rushing his opponent, building momentum with each impact on short sword and shield-arm, increasing in fury until the robber was overwhelmed and focused solely on blocking the barrage. Aven chased him back into the grass. As Aven had hoped, the change to soft soil took the robber's balance and forced him to thrust his shield to intercept the anticipated hit, realizing too late that

Aven had changed course. Aven crushed his skull right into his shoulders with a heavy overhead chop in an explosion of brain matter.

A war horn sounded from the direction of the half-bogran. Reinforcements could be near; this needed to end quickly. Aven scolded himself, resisting the urge to wipe his face. Instead, he began evasive maneuvers while spying his surroundings, zigzagging to get his bearings.

Spearman was out of the fight. He'd regained his weapon but was sitting down, pale from blood loss; Raliel fought toe to toe with the battle-axe wielder, whose partner, hatchet man, ran shrieking, shield-arm severed neatly through the cleaved shield and smoking bone. Raliel grunted as she swatted away the heavier axe, out-sized but not overwhelmed, to the axe man's dismay. There was a crossbow bolt pinning her cape to her pack. The half-bogran!

Aven turned just in time to catch a twelve-inch steel bolt in the chest. The world pivoted awkwardly, and Aven found himself staring up at the sky. It was suddenly a challenge to breathe.

CHAPTER SEVEN

Raliel sensed Aven's pounce moments before he engaged his opponents. Years of training together will do that. Thus, she could strike almost simultaneously, taking advantage of her enemy's surprise. The hatchet and buckler bearer winced. In a normal situation, Raliel knew that when facing more than one foe, you should engage the shield-less or less armored opponent first, but her ancestral axe was an unknown variable, one she was counting on to gain the advantage. The length of her axe was another, so she thrust straight, axe tip forcing the nearest bandit to raise his wooden buckler to intercept. Raliel pulled back short, legs kicking out in sidespin, axe trailing in a vicious arch toward buckler. He readied to absorb the flow, hatchet cocked back for the counter strike. She expected to destroy the small shield. Instead, his amazement surpassed her shock as the glowing axe melted straight through without a hitch. It was all she could do to keep her balance. She wheeled a right kick into the injured arm to stop her tumbling forward, and leaped back in time to avoid a heavy axe swing from his partner, who she spied from her peripheral. She heard the twang of the crossbow and spun in time to catch the bolt in her travel pack. She had a small amount of time to dispatch the axeman before the next projectile flew.

She saw that Aven had downed one enemy and was raining a flurry of hits on the second.

She maneuvered, blocking the reloading crossbowman's next shot with her combatant. Then, she focused on the axeman with a huff—this was a veteran, short, squat, and well-muscled. Likewise, he took stock of her as he worked his fists on the double grip of his axe. She heard the half-bogran sound a horn from behind her opponent. They didn't have time to play.

She tried a quick forward jab. It was viciously swiped aside, coming dangerously close to disarming her. Something she was sure would've happened had she not been endowed with enhanced strength. The axeman's counter-attack: two quick chops, right, left, and then his own lunging jab. He was trying to get close. She fended both chops with two-handed parries in a shower of sparks from her molten axe. She sidestepped her opponent's thrust, locking weapons, as the axeman altered the jab to a sideswipe for her shoulder. Weapons tangled; with Raliel's lighter body whirled airborne by the axeman, it became a contest to try and topple one another. Instead, she held on to her axe with unnatural strength.

Feet again planted, she attempted to wrest her axe free, both struggling to upend the other, hoping to maintain their grips, holding on for their very lives. Axeman again pivoted, using weight to whirl her through the air, but she was ready for it this time. Using the Axeman's momentum, she swung her legs with it, velocity and supernatural strength enabling her to fling her opponent through the air, his stubby legs swung wide. Unable to keep his grip, a hand slipped free. Raliel wasted no time delivering a jaw-crushing blow to the wide-eyed veteran with her axe pommel. He tumbled away, his weapon still tangled with her own. Discarding the cruder axe, Raliel checked on the crossbowman to find him aiming for Aven.

"Aven!" she tried to warn him. But, to her horror, the crossbow let loose with a THWAK! It was followed by a sickening 'thunk' as it took her childhood friend fatally in the chest, from his feet, and flat on his back. "Aven!"

Her vision tunneled on his murderer. She cut her pack's straps without breaking eye contact, letting it and her cape fall as she rushed. In response, the half-bogran cast aside his spent crossbow, drawing a monstrous great-sword from his back. Molten axe and heavy iron clashed. Glowing particles of ruined iron sprang from each bite of her weapon. Rage engulfed her, and she allowed herself to sweep into the dance of death she'd been practicing all her life.

Chop, spinning backhand, kick, parry, sidestep, and lunge. She traded blows with an enemy twice her height and thrice her weight. It mattered little. All she knew was a fire of blood-lust, an aching appetite for vengeance. Perspiration shone from her face and arms as she worked her opponent's defenses, looking for an opening to which she could exact swift and deadly justice. Yet, for every move, the great-sword was there.

The half-bogran more than made up for what he lacked in skill with sheer ferocity. Blood-lust lit up his pinkish pig-eyes. He, too, relished in violence. But, try as she might, she couldn't finish this powerful foe. His reach exceeded hers; she had no advantage over him. Her superior armament and skills only kept her in the fight. She tried another forward feint planning to execute another version of her spinning kicks and arching axe maneuvers when she noticed something very wrong.

Her axe became heavier. Every movement required more effort, as her enchanted strength dwindled to nothing. She had never considered it before. But, she had come to rely upon it, the setting sun a reminder that she had used it heavily all day. The half-bogran noticed and launched a mighty flurry of bone-jarring strikes with a roar. It was all she could do to hold onto her weapon as she weakly blocked and parried, knocked back with each blow. Sweat streaks soaked her face. Her arms ached. She was very conscious of the weight of her chainmail, slowing each increasingly exhausted maneuver. She couldn't last another second.

Her heart thrummed with rage at that moment, strengthening her resolve. She would fight with every ounce of her being. Instinctively, she roared, a war cry of her ancestors. She bellowed from the very depth of her soul. Wary, the half-bogran hopped back. Raliel let loose an ear-piercing scream, causing him to cover his ears in pain. Her fatigue forgotten; she was lost to her rage. Her muscles began to swell as she convulsed with unleashed power. Still screaming, she raised her ancestral weapon, and it took fire. She lunged into a devastating kill-frenzy.

They began trading blows, and crazed Raliel wasted no time or strength in blocking, soon dripping blood from a dozen minor wounds. Her opponent was worse for wear, singed flesh hanging in ribbons, flesh scorched and blistered by magical flame. Finally, Raliel's axe shattered the great-sword in a hundred glowing embers just as she expended her lungs on the frenzy-inducing screech.

Resigned to his fate, brownish half-bogran blood poured from his sides and arms; the murderer, exhausted, fell on his knees before his supernatural executioner. Raliel's axe extinguished. Drooping. Her muscles slackened as she swayed, stumbling back three strides before landing hard on her rear.

Ten yards from each other, the combatants stared, gasping and spent, both unable to make a move. Finally, the half-bogran settled to his seat, flesh hanging loose from his heavily jowled bogranish face.

"Raliel…" Aven's voice! His appearance tempered her momentary elation. He lay on his side, left arm cradled in his right, right elbow supporting his wheezing form.

"Aven," she said weakly, her blood painting the ground in fat droplets. Aven looked like he was about to say something, but all that came out was bright red blood. His head drooped; her heart sank.

The half-bogran, taking this momentary reprieve, had begun crawling for his crossbow. He was halfway to it. A groan to Raliel's right reminded her of the knocked-out axeman. He stirred and rolled onto his stomach, slowly raising himself on hands and knees. His jaw, deformed by massive swelling, gushed blood over purple flesh.

She swooned, catching herself with the palm of one hand. Sharp gravel jabbed mercilessly. She tried to lift herself again, and darkness swept in from the edges of her vision, dissipating as she relaxed. She knew any more of that would steal her consciousness, and she didn't want that. If she died now, she couldn't witness all of it.

She stole another look at Aven, whose head still hung limp, strings of bloody saliva pooling in the dirt. Yet, he stubbornly wheezed on though also out of the fight.

The half-bogran reached his weapon but had difficulty drawing back the heavy cable. He had it almost engaged when a gory blade sprouted from his throat, steel throwing-handle visible as his head smacked the gravel road.

Too dizzy to care. Raliel watched this new threat make an

appearance. A specter materialized from the shadows up the hill on swift and silent leather-padded feet—no more than an inky shadow against the setting sun. The figure retrieved the heavy throwing knife and sent the missile whistling upon hearing the garbled groan to her right. The specter was already in pursuit before the knife could land, marked by a pitiful shriek—having drawn a long slender blade. Axe man's gurgling abruptly silenced. She no longer possessed the energy to look or care.

She made to rest on her elbows, knowing she could never defend them from this phantom. She was tired, and the silence was so serene. A gentle breeze stirred the grassland in the now fading light. She heard a groaning protest from Aven. This spiked her heart rate, threatening another swoon. Her head lolled in Aven's direction. She saw the specter crouching over him, blade in hand. Again, she swooned into a void, spiraling deep into oblivion.

***

"Drink this," a voice called to Aven in his dreams. He'd been swimming through the cool waters of a beautiful river when it began to get too cold. He tried to make it to the shore where, strangely, Raliel lay. His feet slipped on cold mossy stones below, and he plunged deeper into the frigid waters. He needed air.

"Drink" Aven gagged on fiery liquid, sputtering, swallowing some, inhaling most, and thinking he would drown. But it somehow served to clear his head and make breathing easier. He wasn't underwater but could see Raliel still lying on the shore, asleep. No, he remembered....

"Raliel!" he choked, feeling the broken pieces of his left side jabbing, poking, and stinging softer innards. He could taste blood streaming from his mouth.

"Drink; we've not much time." The voice was strangely familiar, though he was too delirious to wonder how or why. Aven managed a generous swallow of the blazing liquor and felt markedly better. Clearer. He could feel the bones of his shattered ribcage knitting. A potion of healing; he made to drink more. "Not yet. Brace yourself."

Before he could respond, a foot-long spike was ripped unceremoniously from his left pectoral in a crimson spray of blood, which filled his left lung heavily.

"Now! Drink deep!" This time, Aven did, quaffing the stone bottle contents, every drop. A powerful healing potion. He felt his wounds sealing from within and without. The source of the voice turned him over, beating on his back. He began hacking up globs of ocher until his lungs were mainly clear.

"You'll be fine, but you've lost a lot of blood. You'll be weak for a while. Lie here and rest while I tend Rali." The voice was male but muffled and hollow behind an armored mask of indeterminate material. His eyes were the only visible feature, and he turned before Aven could study them. Aven sat up and tested his body movement. He felt itchy and weak; the motion tickled in a way that reminded him of removing a splint from a newly healed broken bone. Also, that anxious unfamiliarity tinged with the fear that the bone would re-break from the smallest jarring. Uncomfortably whole. He got to his feet with great effort, found his sword, and sheathed it. He looked up, felt incredibly dizzy and nearly stumbled, hands on the knees of his greaves. Nauseated, he watched multiple pastel-colored spots burst on the edges of his vision. Closing his eyes almost sent him tumbling headfirst into the gravel. It was all he could do to remain conscious, staring at the rock, mouth salty and stomach sour. The pale spots continued to crackle and pop.

"Uhhhhh," Aven groaned. He wondered how long this feeling would last. Then something wet blocked his airway triggering a series of racking coughs. Finally, rewarded with a view of his newly blooded boots, globules of thick coagulating plasma that recently arrived at the party, he cracked open his scrunched-up eyes. On top of that, he had a splitting headache, garnished with an extra helping of dizziness.

In short, he was a mess. Finally, he cocked his head up, hands still on his knees for balance, and scanned around through blurry vision; he found the form of his savior, although the lowering sun cast increasingly deeper shadows. Guessing by the size and shape of the vessel, the man appeared to be administering the same type of potion to Raliel.

Aven staggered toward the two. He experienced the strange sensation of his head suspended in the air; his legs could barely control his floating to where he wished. Yet, on the other hand, he felt if he were just to lift his feet, he could drift away with the breeze.

He arrived in time to see the last of Raliel's cuts sealing shut. Covered in blood, whatever was not steel showed skin through slices. But, unlike him, she remained heavily out of sorts.

"I've nothing for exhaustion, but all her minor wounds have healed," came that muffled voice again, "are you fit to travel?"

"Not sure, but we've no choice," Aven responded, recalling the half-bogran's war horn. The man read Aven's expression.

"Yes, there are more. I did my best to delay them, but for how long?" The shadow shrugged, replacing the bottle on the belt loop.

"How many?" Aven asked vaguely.

"Bandits? Maybe twenty. They were riding up Deragard's road when the horn sounded." He folded his arms. "A small avalanche delayed them. I expect they'll make up for lost time once they recover their animals." He skipped off, searching through the fallen ambushers' belongings. Surveying the carnage, Aven noticed Raliel's pack and cape nearby in the dirt. Feeling more vital and centered, he retrieved the items and returned them to her. She stirred.

"Mum, mmm…" she groaned.

"Rali."

"Yeah?" She stretched her arms.

"Are you OK to stand?"

"I had the most wonderful dream…" Her eyes widened with alarm, and she lurched to her feet, head whipping right to the left. Aven caught her, straining with all his might not to fall himself.

"Take it easy. We're safe…for now," he whispered.

She relaxed slightly but seemed agitated.

"You're hurt!" She attempted to inspect Aven's bloody armor.

"Not anymore." He took both her hands in his. "He healed me."

He nodded in the direction of the shadow, meticulously rummaging through the spearman's pale corpse.

"He healed you too." Aven directed his gaze to her scarlet-painted attire. She withdrew her hands from his to inspect her sliced clothing as if seeing was not believing like she needed the tactile reassurance to soothe her skepticism.

Aven gasped, alarming her, "What?!"

"Your hair," he said, reaching, "it's changed."

"Aven," the muffled male voice called.

"Yes?" Aven turned in time to catch a small leather pouch.

"That's all the valuables I could find."

"Why are you giving them to me?" he asked, confused.

The stranger walked to the half-bogran, whom he first pillaged.

"Aren't you in charge of this venture?"

"Yes, but…"

"Then finances are your responsibility, correct?" The leather-clad figure bent over the half-bogran and continued to search, pawing, "aha!" he rose, carrying the crossbow over his shoulder, cocked and loaded, a handful of bolts in his left hand. Aven and Raliel stood, baffled. She'd retrieved her axe.

"Aven the Adventurer, correct?"

"Yeah, but how do you know that?" Aven asked.

"No time to explain. I'd like to offer my services." He inspected the giant crossbow, nodded, and then replaced it on his shoulder. Raliel took a step forward and stated with uncommon civility,

"We appreciate your timely help. You saved our lives, but do we know you?"

"Introductions can wait." And looking deferentially to Aven, he asked, "On your order, chief."

"Let's head out."

They were on their way as soon as they repaired Raliel's pack straps. Their newest member stopped to retrieve his cloak from a bush just north of their position. Raliel had thought they should drag the bodies behind a boulder amid the grasses. Instead, they kicked gravel and dirt over the telltale combat signs.

They ambled first, then committed to a swift long-striding march. Their mysterious leather-clad companion—with Aven's permission— darted ahead to scout, melting into the deepening dark.

The sky glowed orange-red by the time they reached the trees. The silhouette of Midhaven's massive walls obstructed the sunset, creating a nimbus of glowing red for a backdrop.

"Looks like it's on fire," Aven said to Raliel.

She ignored the observation.

"I thought you died," she said, looking straight ahead.

"So did I. Well…I kinda wasn't sure what happened."

She chewed her bottom lip, still staring straight as they continued to march steadily.

"Aven."

"Yeah?"

"Something happened to me when my belt's magic failed."

"Like what?" he queried.

"Remember the stories our fathers would tell us?" she said.

"Which ones?"

"Of the warriors of Arba," she said.

"'The warrior kingdom of Arba, Keepers of the Flame,'" Aven quoted in his best impression of Fargar.

She smiled and said, "Well, I don't want to sound ridiculous; it's nothing compared to their supernatural powers, but when I had nothing left, no strength to even stand…and I thought you were dead and all was lost…I had failed in our oath…" She looked abashed.

"Raliel,"

"Let me finish," she silenced him. "I thought of those warriors and how they could invoke the powers of their god, and I cried out with all my heart…and, I don't remember anything clearly, not until the end. But, it was how I always imagined the frenzy of the warriors of Arba."

"Doesn't Fargar always say you've got Arban blood? I mean, the race is only legend, right?" Aven didn't know what to say.

"I don't know what to believe, only that it happened, and if you don't believe me, I don't care. I don't even know why I'm telling you," Raliel finished, frustrated.

"NO! I'm listening." He studied her changed hair; new multi-colored streaks gave the illusion of flames. "Even among the Arban people, it was rare, but there may be an explanation. I believe you. I also think you should keep this between us until we learn more."

"You believe me?" she asked.

"I'd believe you, Raliel, even if you weren't my best friend, based on the carnage you caused. You dropped a Bogran one-on-one without enhancement. That's pretty convincing in itself."

"It is." She looked pleased and smiled. "Even if he was just a half-kin."

Yes indeed, he thought. A damn good thing Raliel had been there, or he'd be dead. "Wait till you see your hair." He couldn't resist.

From the shadows, their scout appeared, "We're here."

CHAPTER EIGHT

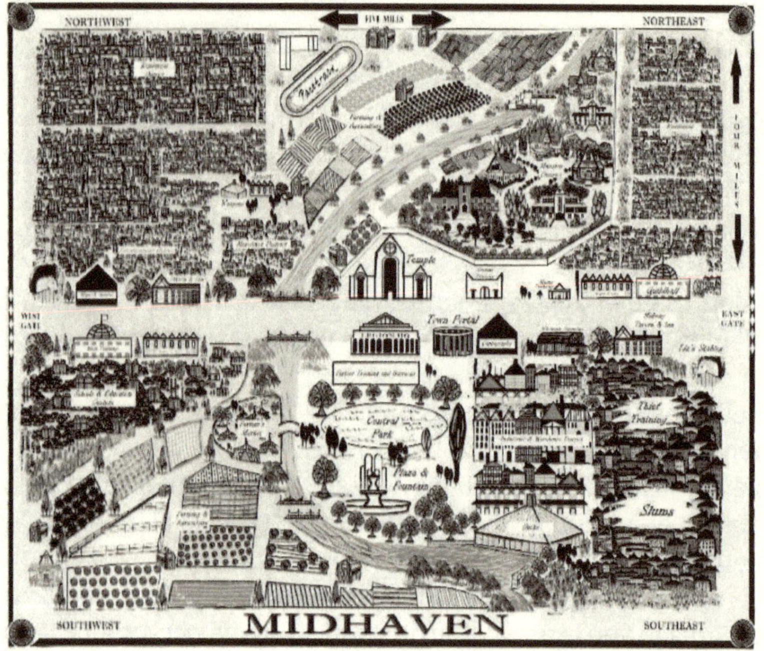

They made it through the East Gate just in time and with no more than a cursory glance from the city guard. Aven imagined they must have seen far worse than bloody clothes in their experience. Unfazed, sure, but ready. All twenty spear men stared rigidly into the coming night, lining each side of the wall around the gate. Aven wondered at the horrors that aroused such vigilance from these green-cloaked, steel-plated, stern-looking men and women.

Immediately through the gate, guards began scrambling to close the immense iron doors. Strange runes caught torchlight as they swung inward, sealing shut with a BOOM. Aven glanced back and saw them slide a massive bar—gliding from a recess in the wall—through fitted rings along the doors and into the other side. Then, with another boom, the doors sealed for the night.

Ahead trailed the city's main boulevard. It was 50 yards wide and ran for five miles straight to Midhaven's West Gate. Hundreds of tiny streets led off to the north, south, and through the various buildings and towers. The 100-foot city wall squarely encompassed the vast refuge.

Midhaven withstood 300 years of wild entrenchment and avoided disaster while providing refuge to fleeing families. Legend said the guards would hold the gate open until the sun disappeared and the last visible traveler reached safety. Just south of the entrance were the city stables. West, and on the northside of the boulevard, stood the Guildhall, the first large building with alabaster walls and domed roof. A light shone through a window next to the closed doors of the entrance, a signal for guild members seeking sanctuary. A large man in a leather apron to the left of the Hall locked up his smithy for the night.

As the three walked down the middle of the cobbled road, their heads swiveled between the sights. Music and activity increased as they neared a building on the south side of the street.

"That's as far as we need to go," their savior informed.

Aven and Raliel were in no condition to argue. Veering south, they sought lodging in a raucous Inn before them. The music came from a type of harpsichord, it appeared. The melody was festive. Even in his fatigue, Aven found himself drawn to the sound. No words joined the keys, yet the song seemed to speak of food, drink, warmth, and fun.

The interior didn't disappoint. The vast taproom of round tables, with a long bar at the back, was filled comfortably with men and women enjoying all the music had promised. High above the back bar extended a balcony with a flight of stairs leading down on the far right of the main floor. More stairs were on the balcony leading up to the third and fourth floors. Again, Raliel and their mystery companion looked to Aven, jarring him back into his role as leader.

"Well, I don't know about you two, but I'm starved, tired, and dirty. Rali?" Aven asked.

"Yes?" she replied.

"What say you go check us in and arrange some baths or whatever's available? Then, meet us here for dinner." As he expected, the mention of 'bath' cast a wistful quality to her weary eyes.

"On it." She walked to the clerk's desk at the base of the stairs.

"Uh…I don't know how to address you?" Aven asked their new companion, who just maintained eye contact but failed to provide a name. So Aven continued, "Okay then, could you find us a table?" Was that an amused twinkle in the man's gray eyes?

"Done," the man replied, and before Aven could study him in the light, he was gone.

Aven went for the bar, spotting several barmaids busing tables and serving drink mugs. The bar was a length of dark polished wood that provided room for dozens of stools and patrons, either scattered or grouped around. Heading straight for four empty chairs, Aven sat just in time to catch one of the rapid-moving barkeeps, drying mugs while taking orders. Upon ordering and paying, the barkeep asked, "Where will you be dining?"

Aven looked back; a leather glove rose from a secluded booth near the stairs. "There," he said, pointing.

"It'll be twenty minutes," the barkeep said.

Before he could leave, Aven added, "I'll have a pitcher of strong ale and three cups, now please," and placed a few coins on the bar.

Pitcher in one hand and the handles of three wooden mugs in the other, he weaved his way to the booth, resisting the urge to steal a few gulps from the pitcher to wash the dust and blood from his mouth and throat. Before he could set them down on the table, Raliel sidled past to the empty side of the booth. Aven slid in next to her, loosened two mugs from his fingers, and poured his to the rim. He drank deep, the strong ale rinsing weariness and dust with a burn. Then, fortified, he set his mug down. "It's time to tell us your name, friend." He directed his eyes toward their companion across from them.

"I'll do better than that," his muffled, but resonating voice replied. He reached behind his head, releasing unseen clasps, and pulled the boiled leather helmet forward to his lap; head bowed. Aven glanced at Raliel, who had lowered her mug, eyes fixed as she absentmindedly licked foam from her lips. Aven looked across at the man, at the black crown of tightly bound hair; a sharp intake of air from Raliel, Aven's heart lurched with recognition.

"Vic!!" Raliel yelled, "of course!"

Still silent, Vic held Aven's gaze with his distinctive gray eyes with his head raised. His aquiline nose and face were barely able to contain his emotions. "How?" Aven asked, stupefied. "I thought you were finishing your training? Gosh, Vic! Tell me you didn't give that up!"

"Relax, Aven, Nazar granted me a leave of absence," he said to their apparent skepticism. But, he added, "More than that, he sent me here to seek some specialized instruction and purchase some rare items."

"When do you leave?" Aven asked, anxiety replacing the gratitude his presence inspired.

"Master didn't say," he explained in his deep yet quiet tone, eyebrows furrowed. He filled his mug. "I can send everything he requested by caravan, and the training should take a while." He paused to drink.

Aven also raised his mug to drink.

Raliel announced, "A toast then! To Nazar's pupils, Okay?" She smiled.

"CHEERS!" all said in unison and clacked mugs. They drank deep. A mouse-haired barmaid came with a fresh pitcher and a heaping platter of grilled meat and steaming vegetables. Then, with ample cleavage bared, a raven-haired barmaid produced plates and spoons, picking up the empty pitcher.

The raven-haired maid looked at Aven with pale blue eyes and whispered, "An' you be needin' anything else, ye ask for Gale, master." He felt Raliel tense with annoyance.

"Thank you, Gale; this should be fine," Aven said, carefully aloof.

"Just be askin'," Gale added and turned, swaying her round hips seductively. Vic strangled a cough in humor at Aven's expense.

"What a hussy," Raliel commented as she shoveled food into her bowl. Without looking up, she added, "Why don't you paint a picture, Aven?"

Had he been staring at Gale's backside this whole time? He had. He reached to fill his bowl as Vic, still smiling, did the same. Raliel blew on a spoonful of hot food. For a moment, they all ate without a word.

The lighthearted melody from the harpsichord had ceased. The player, a slight, balding man with a shiny red nose, took his break, mug in hand, talking with Gale the barmaid. The dull roar of the crowd, clacking wooden dinnerware, and sounds of eating continued unabated through bowl after bowl and mug after mug. After his second bowl, Aven noticed his companions helping themselves to a loaf of brown bread, using it to soak up the remaining juices on platter and plate. He grabbed a slice and was pleased to find walnuts baked into the wheat grain.

"I'm exhausted, guys." Raliel dropped two keys on the table. Each had a numbered square attached. "Our rooms are all close together on the third floor. The registrar assured that hot baths would be ready by the end of the meal." She stretched her arms over her head with a feline growl. "I intend to make good use of said tub and sleep. Move it, Aven."

With Raliel gone, he sat back down across from Vic, who was busily picking clean his white teeth with a very sharp throwing spike. The mouse-haired barmaid approached and swiftly cleared the remains of their meal and just as quickly disappeared. Vic poured them both the last of the ale and sat back, his long arms stretched across the back of the booth seat. His head swept back and forth, following the constant motion of activity around them like a hawk. His actions reminded Aven of Vic's strange leathers and hawkish helmet.

"So, your armament; your design?" Aven asked, point-blank.

"No, mostly Nazar's. I had to fashion a stealth suit for the first phase of my training. The helmet was my idea. It has breathing and auditory ducts hidden by the beak." He inspected his work and added, "You know how I've always been fascinated by birds of prey, their swift and lethal ability to surprise attack." He looked up and smiled. "Master Nazar seemed pleased by my choice." He nodded to the helmet on the bench and continued, "It coincided with his style of advanced training."

Aven thought it was fitting; Vic always looked and moved like the fierce hunter, notwithstanding his own hawk-like 'beak,' a cause of some teasing as a child, the reason his parents sought private tutoring. As though reading his thoughts, Vic turned to him and said, "It seems fitting to honor the reason I was allowed to find my calling." He tapped the tip of his nose.

"Indeed," Aven said and raised his mug. "I didn't think we'd see each other again for a long time, Vic. It's amazing sitting here with you. In Midhaven, of all places!"

"Well, it's a damn good thing I am!" He was angry now. "Listen, Aven, you and Rali almost died. If I hadn't shown up, what would've happened? I almost lost you guys." He struggled to contain his emotion. "You've got to be more careful, Aven. On the road, what you didn't do showed your inexperience as a leader."

"I realize that Vic, seriously, I do. I never planned on having to worry about anybody but myself," Aven defended weakly, "until I got here."

"You see? That's my point, this place," he said, gesturing around them, "and especially beyond, will be extremely unpredictable and dangerous." He leaned forward. "You've got to plan for the unexpected."

"I attended the same lectures as you."

"But," Vic interrupted, "knowing right and applying that knowledge—"

"Are two separate things," Aven finished for him. "Yeah, I know, and mostly I know I let my guard down just like I promised Hori and Raliel I wouldn't."

Then, Aven tried to rub the shame from his face, massaging the muscles of his forehead, temples, eyes, and neck. "Gosh, Vic, having you here is like being lectured by Nazar," he said and opened his eyes, "but you're right to correct me. My error almost cost me my life and that I can accept, but losing Rali because of my stupidity I cannot."

The front door banged open, and a stout massif male entered, the handle of a great hammer stuck over his gray blood-encrusted braids. As he turned to shut the door, Aven saw a battered kite shield strapped to his back. It was almost as tall as his five-foot frame.

"I've never seen a massif before," Aven thought aloud.

"Nor I," Vic replied. "Well, not in the flesh anyway."

The statement reminded Aven of the various practice dummies and artwork depicting great scenes of battle and pre-war life in Nazar's large home.

"Thanks, Vic." Aven watched the gruff-looking massif as the patrons divided, giving him a wide berth.

"You can thank me by doing a better job staying alive."

Again Aven turned his head to study the taproom, avoiding eye contact. The thick massif settled on two barstools at the bar and withdrew his mug—an intricate stein—from a loop on his belt. He set it on the bar. The crowd murmured, some clapping their hands as another figure entered the room from a stage door underneath the balcony.

Crowd approval increased as Aven recognized Gale, no longer in simple attire but wearing a shimmering pale blue gown. She neared where the harpsichord rested on an elevated platform in the center of the room. Clapping and chatter subsided as she reached the stage.

The light source, Aven now noticed, came from an immense chandelier high above. This bright source of light dimmed to multiple embers of orange.

In the darkened taproom, with only the chandelier lighting her, Gale withdrew a miniature silver harp from the folds of her gown.

Aven looked to Vic, pleased to find him as entranced as he was. He returned his focus to Gale. She sat upon the bench with her back to the harpsichord and held out her harp. With a flick of her wrist, the sparkling instrument enlarged. Another tug and the now five-foot harp rested neatly on the floor, frame comfortably secure between her knees. The crowd applauded at the magic show, hooted, hollered, and quieted in anticipation.

Now enlarged, Aven could make out carvings of horned horses and forests decorating the harp's mirror-like frame, which threw back more light than was present. The numerous strings, so fine to almost appear invisible, were made detectable by a golden gleam. One of Gale's delicate hands began to dance, an ivory spider, filling the room with a heartbreakingly beautiful melody. His soul responded to the notes with visceral butterflies tickling his stomach, heart, and limbs. Aven noticed that his eyes were closed as he savored the music. He opened them to study her again, and just when he thought it perfection, her other hand joined the fray to conduct its dance and song. Two distinct melodies blended unfathomably into something inexpressible in any way but this. Elegant and soothing, yet Aven could understand more. It spoke of beauty, longing, love, and an underlying yearning that made a crowd of hearts ache.

Aven wished Raliel had stayed to hear it. The song spoke to all, through an array of feelings no words could express, yet no less a tale, a journey taking all to a particular place within their souls. So enchanting was the sound that it wasn't until Gale stood and placed her harp back in her gown that he and the crowd realized it had ended.

The patrons cheered and stood clapping. Lights brightened, Gale curtsied and disappeared through that same back door. Across the room, the massif reversed position, back against the bar, and wiped his eyes hastily with the back of his hairy forearms. When Aven turned, Vic was gone. Ready for bed, he grabbed the remaining room key and headed upstairs feeling weary yet excited and thrilled to be in the world finally.

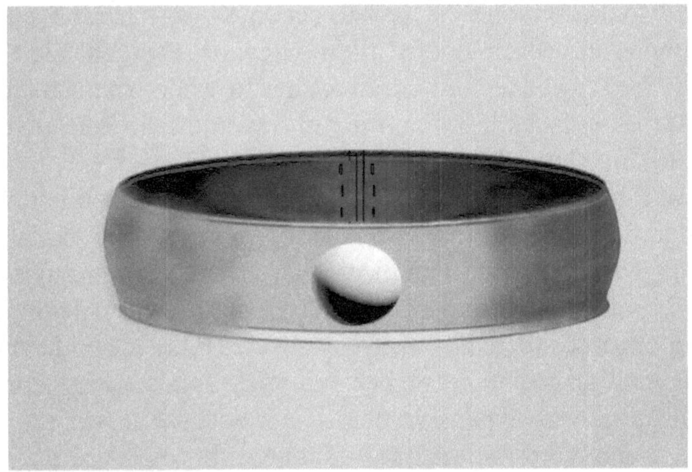

aliel was early to rise. She dressed in comfortable city-wear, lightweight fabric blouse and pants, with comfortable soft leather shoes, and hastily combed and bound her now multi-colored locks into a tail down her back.

Midhaven was civilized, for the most part, she knew, so she decided to leave her chainmail and steel boots. Instead, she buckled on her belt and axe, greatly relieved to find its strength enhancement fully restored. The added strength, sans armor and gear, made her feel she could leap straight out of the third-story window to the street below. After her brush with death, however, she banished the silly notion.

The morning air was fresh and cold on her face. She headed west on the main strip. Even at this hour, people had yet to find their beds, some stumbling from the taverns quite drunk.

Others moved with purpose, couriers, identifiable by universal satchels and colorful hats, zipped to and fro, and workers headed to the warehouse district to the south.

The cobblestone road was broad, allowing various flows of traffic. Raliel had no map but, from talking with Hori, had learned the city's general layout. All significant buildings were on the main strip: the guildhall, temple, legion headquarters, larger inns, taverns, town portal, etc.

Passing the wholesale supplies building, she knew the industrial warehouse district lay directly south. The mansion district could be discerned from the expansive home estates on its hills beyond to the north. Dozens of city blocks segmented the side streets, leading off north and south. It would be easy to become lost in Midhaven.

Staying to the south side of the boulevard, she kept alert for the building Hori explained would direct her to where she wanted to go. She had a few places in mind, only one would take her far from the main road, but she would do that last.

A great ring of marble pillars marked Midhaven's Town Portal on her street side. Specifically, she wanted to see this. The portal was a functioning remnant of ancient magic that made everything possible for surviving civilization. Approaching the front, she ascended marble steps to the upper expanse where city agents conducted daily teleportation travel. She could only spare a moment, but she couldn't resist taking a peek.

Portal travel was expensive. It was not because it was complex or required much from the acolytes in charge, but because of the great demand. With more significant funds and profits, Merchants paid greatly to monopolize the immediate shipment of goods so that travel required reservation. Currently, waiting lines stretched to the steps, consisting of those already scheduled for travel.

A smooth white marble courtyard extended fifty feet across. There were separate circles—of different colored marble—each sectioned off by velvet rope and an attending portal acolyte. There was a ring filled with crates, another with people, and the third remained empty. She guessed this third section to be incoming transport.

Various marble statues, ancient heroes, sorcerers, and clerics of renown, stood between the surrounding pillars, figures that she couldn't identify by sight but likely knew well by a story. The statues represented all races involved in the most remarkable contributions to history, spanning millennia upon millennia. She admired a nine-foot statue of some proud sorceress when blue and green flashes piqued her interest. She spun in time to see the stacked crates engulfed in electrifire, vanishing in a puff of ozone.

In the past, more gateways existed. They'd been deactivated or destroyed centuries ago, during the Great Divide, and would take an expedition to find; hundreds of all sizes throughout the wilds, according to Hori. The passages waited to be rediscovered, lost in time and inactivity, their secrets and treasures revealed. Glad she came, Raliel skipped back down to the street. Her curiosity sated somewhat as she headed west to the Legions' HQ.

***

Vic arrived early enough. An hour before dawn, he headed west dressed in the coarse robes of a student of his craft. Unfortunately, Vic hadn't been completely honest with his friends. He was given a few tasks from Master Nazar, and yes, he wanted to spend time with them, but the latter could only run parallel with the pursuit of his craft. He was here to advance his training, but it was unknown how long that would take and where it could lead.

Nazar had taught him the full of his knowledge, that's true. Some things couldn't be taught and must be learned in time, but through Nazar, he had received all the fundamental building blocks to make mastery possible. All Nazar could offer was a repetition of what he already knew and the skill of that knowledge through repetition.

Vic had come to love Nazar as a father, so it was painful to reject the honor of filling his mentor's humble role. However, he didn't think Aven would understand and would probably be disappointed, so he kept that detail from him. Master Nazar hadn't been surprised at his rejection. Instead, he began treating him like an equal and detailing the brotherhood that Vic's skill set—still essential to some—gave him qualification.

Lounging here near the city Plaza—in the park behind the Legionnaire training grounds—he recalled his last day with Nazar.

"Come with me," Nazar said and led him into his vast study filled with scrolls, maps, and many curiosities. He was shown a position of the network that existed between cells of the craft—told of their place in history, their purpose as an order, for hundreds of generations back. The war of centuries had affected all, but little hindered this ancient Order, which thrived on adaptation and resilience.

"I've prepared everything you'll need for your pilgrimage," he'd said, gesturing to an assortment of supplies. "Of course, you'll need to prepare a few things yourself; I've provided schematics. Your pilgrimage will take as long as is needed; no one can determine this

83

for you. At the end of this journey, know that my offer stands." And with a twinkle in his eyes below white brows, he added, "Though I expect many such offers will accumulate as you progress among our brethren."

And so, here Vic waited, within Midhaven's park plaza, to meet the first of such colleagues. Nazar's instructions did not describe location and name, as this was typical. Much was left to Vic to discover for himself, part of the training and methods he was required to employ on his chosen path.

Nazar had generally revealed the brotherhood's purpose, which hadn't surprised him back home. Nazar had seemed pleased by this as well. Vic had noticed a difference in his training versus his friends. Each received excellent programming, and it seemed to reflect their strengths on the surface. Aven's use of armor and heavier weapons, leadership skills, and tactics suited him. Raliel's ferocity and endurance was tempered into deadly efficiency. His speed, agility, and focus were likewise honed, traits beneficial to any swordsman. However, he was pushed harder and made to learn more than he thought possible.

Each new vista of skill brought him a rush of achievement, shortly before being pressed on to new heights. Stealth, hyper-focus, precision, heightened awareness; he'd spent the last thirteen years training to master these things and knew it to be only the beginning.

It was not power that drew him to the brotherhood, renown, or refuge within his ability to survive in a dangerous world. It was the challenge and quest for perfection, ever-elusive, to pursue the most outstanding mastery possible in one's life; for him, there was joy in the continual practice and meditation. His passion was as Nazar's: mastery of mind, body, and spirit.

The horizon began to lighten with the dawn, dew sparkling on blades of grass and the leaves of his perch high in the trees encircling the plaza.

He could maintain this vigil indefinitely. His focus and discipline silenced the distractions of the body. He was eager for the chance to test himself. He wondered what this new master would be like and what he might teach him. He meditated upon all the possibilities behind ever-vigilant silver eyes.

His breathing deepened, slowing his body, entering a trance state, minimizing the unnecessary expenditure of energy. The world around him seemed to speed up, the leaves flickered oddly, and the sunlight grew markedly. Time was not speeding up, of course, but he was slowing down. People appeared with unnatural jerking movement, darting to and fro.

Eventually, the sun shone steady and a small group formed on marble benches around a fountain. According to Nazar, men came to the plaza fountain to debate and discuss philosophy. Master 'Taberah' could be found here each morning.

The world seemed to slow coming out of his reverie with a quickening pulse. Doing so was always a little disorienting. He allowed himself a few seconds to adapt before descending, branch to branch, trunk to springing turf. Vic headed to the gathering to find Master Taberah.

***

Aven enjoyed one of those moments when consciousness comes to a sleeper gradually and peacefully. When one slowly and lazily becomes mindful of each new detail. First, he became aware that his dream was a dream and of feeling rested. He set the dream aside, a happy dream, and if it's possible to feel the flex of a mental smile, that is what he felt. Then, like a pocket of air, rising from the depths of sleep to the glittering warmth of the sun upon a clear, cerulean sea. Aven drew to the light until the red, orange, then yellow of his eyelids became the only thing between him and the world.

He lay still like that for a bit longer, recalling everything of the past day. Finally, he felt content and could've stayed in bed except for the rising interest in this new day.

His first day in Midhaven, with so much he wanted to see versus what he needed to do. That notion roused him more than the warm sunlight. A ray shone on his face through the open window. He'd left it cracked for fresh air, and now he noted the twitter of small birds in a tree outside, the footfalls of people echoing on the small backstreet below.

He sat up, stretched, and walked to the dresser, leaving the bed unmade; a luxury of travel he appreciated. Pouring fresh water from porcelain jug to basin, he splashed and rinsed the sleep from his eyes, thoroughly wetting his shoulder-length hair. He spied a terry cloth towel, pressed it to his face, and swept his hair back before looking at his image in the dresser mirror. He ran a comb through and tied around

85

his hair with a leather thong, bundled his padded leather armor, folded it where possible, and tied it with a strap as a handle.

He donned a short-sleeve shirt, sparse leather breeches, leather shoes, and belted-on sword and items pouch.

A knock rapped on his door. He found Gale, cloth bundle in hand in her plain apron, all raven hair and blue eyes above a pink-lipped smile.

"Mornin' master Aven," she said.

"Good morning," he replied.

"Care for some breakfast? Prepared it myself."

"Yes, thank you," he said, gratefully receiving the bundle.

"You can leave the cloth in your room." She was off for the stairs with quick turns, displaying her shapely figure. Aven smiled, appreciating the woman's refined looks and kindness. He stepped out, locked the door, and left for the desk registry to make arrangements for the week. That done, he was out the door amid the hustle and bustle of the city's main thoroughfare.

Breakfast consisted of three big portable meals of egg, pepper, and sausage wrapped in thin flatbread. Aven devoured one and rinsed it down with a delicious apple cider in one of two stone bottles. The rest he tied to his belt for later.

His first two stops were directly across the street, to the north. So he cut through the flowing foot, carriage, and horse traffic for the giant alabaster dome. Inside he found a clerk's window next to a broad wall filled with bulletins, pictures, and scraps of paper tacked in cork. Then, through an arched walkway to the far right, he saw a landing of wood stairs. A grand hall was ahead through an enormous archway, for meetings and activities he assumed.

"May I help you?" a male voice called from the window.

"Yes," Aven said, as he reached the clerk's station in five strides, "I'd like to register as a guild contractor."

The man's eyebrows rose slightly. Likely on account of Aven's age.

"That'll be twenty-five silver marks, registration fee, upfront." The balding clerk paused, eyebrows raised over gold spectacles, mouth a hard line amid a sharply trimmed silver goatee. Then, his cue unread, he added, "You have the fee payment ready, correct?"

"Oh! Of course." Aven reached for his leather pouch, counted twenty-five silver, and handed them over with a clink to the clerk, who nodded approval.

"I'll get the forms, one moment." He left the window to run the errand. Aven inspected the desk and cabinets through the window. Before he could begin to peruse the bulletin wall, the clerk returned shuffling papers.

"Okay, I'll need some general information," he said, then asked for Aven's name, home region, and other basics.

"Company name?"

Aven admitted that he didn't have one ready.

The clerk replied, "I'll need a company name. Most are simple word-names like color or weapon."

Aven thought of Raliel, his home, dreams, future, hopes and exclaimed, "Bright."

"Bright Company it is then." He nodded and scribbled in his records. "Your numbers then?"

"Numbers?" Aven asked, confused.

"How many do you employ," the clerk enunciated slowly.

"Uh…sorry, two others beside myself."

"To qualify for most contracts, you'll have to hire at least one more unless you select freelance jobs on the wall," he informed Aven. Then, with a point of his quill to the miscellaneous papers tacked to the left. "There's an annual membership rate of one silver royal, due in a year, once paid, you'll receive your guild crest, which will afford you a ten percent discount at most shops. In addition, you'll receive a twenty percent discount from any guild certified blacksmith, inns, or other services. You and your party will be required to obey all laws of any city containing your guild halls." He then fixed Aven with a stern look and added, "But don't think that allows any kind of lawlessness in between. A royal warrant will suspend or revoke your membership."

"I understand." Aven nodded solemnly, placing a silver royal on the counter. "I'll pay my dues now, if I may."

"Excellent," he said with genuine respect, "sign here."

After Aven signed, he stamped the documents with the guild seal. "I'll be right back with your identification crest."

This time, Aven glanced at the bulletin notices: mostly missing person's posters with written descriptions, details, and rewards. These were the freelance jobs posted by people who couldn't afford or didn't require a guild registry. He wondered if there was a fee to post a flier in here. Probably.

"Sir?"

Aven unclasped his hands from behind his back and returned to the clerk. He noted the crest, a small patch of leather with the guild crest: a sword and quill crossed over a shining star. It rested on the counter.

"The crest is imbued with a charm that will keep it attached to whatever you affix it to, unremarkable and unable to reproduce. We don't advertise this, but you receive a travel package with your initial crest, including a scroll of town portal, a fire-wand, compass, and a city map. You must have your crest visible to receive any discounts. Listed behind the desk are Guild quests, available upon request. Any questions?"

"No." Aven shook his head, feeling anxious to get going.

"Well then, welcome guild-member and good fortune."

The clerk stood, suddenly cheerful, and thrust out his hand, which Aven shook firmly. He then sat down, resuming his paperwork.

Finished, Aven pressed the crest to his sword-belt; it sank, fusing into the leather. "Neat." He whispered and rifled through his new travel case, a quality leather items pouch with ties to fasten to his leg. That done, with a wistful glance at the bulletin wall and mental note to request the quest list when he finished his errands, Aven exited the guildhall.

He stepped outside, a bona fide guild contractor. He wondered where he could solicit team members in the future but put it out of his mind for now.

The next stop was the guild's blacksmith armory, next door, to see about replacing his armor, or at the very least, repairing the puncture.

***

"Not much can prevent damage from a bolt like that, but chainmail or plate may reduce or deflect it," informed the armorer.

Steel was expensive. Aven didn't have nearly enough for a suit of plate, and a chain ensemble would leave him without much left to live on, minus unforeseen expenses, so he settled on repair work. With the twenty percent discount, he reinforced the chest piece, shoulders, greaves, and boots with layers of scrap mail available for a low cost. It wouldn't be fancy, but it would work.

He stared in awe of the items displayed, weapons of differing shapes and designs from rough iron and bronze pieces to polished steel. He couldn't resist picking up a beautiful two-handed claymore of burnished steel. It had a good balance and long reach. The blade hummed through the air. He pictured the damage he could do with such a weapon—something to consider once he could afford better armor.

In light of his near-death, he decided to supplement his defense further, selecting a heavy bronze kite shield that looked like it could stop anything with its inch-thick chassis. It fit well, overlapping his left fist to the elbow by two inches, raising half a foot to a horizontal line, good combination of visibility and coverage. Its base came a foot and a half below his arm, tapering to a point, as compact as it was heavy—the cost of near impenetrable bronze.

He'd manage the weight. If anything could stop a bolt, it would be a bronze shield. He thought it best he start getting used to its weight now as he strapped it over his back. The top corners were just short of his shoulders, covering well; the heaviness was reassuring.

Aven stretched and tested his mobility. Finally, he paid, scheduled the retrieval of his armor, and thanked the guild's blacksmith before heading out.

Midhaven was twenty square miles, completely encased within a rectangular wall, according to his map, that ran four miles north to south and five miles east to west. A wide boulevard and the 'Icepeak' river divided the city. The Icepeak flowed a mile from the northeast corner of the wall. It ran in a great arch, crossing the boulevard south, then southeast to exit nearly a mile from the southeast corner.

Crops were irrigated from the west side of the river, while some fields existed north of the boulevard. However, the most extensive farmed land was in the southwest corner, a district nearly a quarter of the city. The farm culture explained how the community had survived over the centuries.

Other districts marked on the map represented upper, middle, and lower-class housing; an industrial district, central park, entertainment, and merchant district.

Midhaven was a world within itself. Civilization separated from the wilds by only fifty feet of stone, more than just an outpost, as many people viewed it; it was a testament to the possibility of taming the wild world west of the gorge. But Aven guessed one had to see it to comprehend.

By all accounts, Midhaven was isolated, pressed on all sides by dangerous wilds, but to walk its boulevard was to understand that life here conveyed anything but seclusion. Instead, it was full of opportunity, action, and promise.

Aven still had enough money to live comfortably for months but knew the sooner he began to work, the better chance of managing costs, primarily if he intended to take on more help.

He walked west for some time, enjoying the thrum of city activity. Then, he wondered about Raliel's day and what she was doing, bringing on a curious sensation, a tug. Not physical, but from the glyph around his neck, a knowing. With it, he knew, without a doubt, that Raliel was west-southwest of him, about a mile away. He could feel the distance viscerally. It felt as pleasant and natural as relying on any other sense.

Smiling, Aven decided to see if he could catch up. He was just plotting to cross the busy street when the movements of a small group caught his eye. Something about the scene seemed sinister, and another tug, this one moral, urged him to investigate. The group bustled out of view into an alley between a magic shop and a clothing store. When Aven came around, he could see teenage ruffians jostling a younger red-robed boy, tossing a large jeweled ring back and forth. Probably intent on robbing and beating the youngster. Aven remained hidden around the corner, looking into the alley, ready to intercede if things got out of hand. However, something about the boy made him curious to see.

"Give back my ring, fool," the robed boy commanded.

"Come n' get it," said a pock-faced teen, one of six and at least two feet taller than the boy. No longer willing to play, the boy stopped chasing after the ring, stern-faced and looking much more mature than expected from one his age.

"Tell us where you stole it from, and we'll give it back, eh?" another teen prodded, bouncing the ring in his hand.

"I didn't steal it; it's mine." The young boy lunged again. The ring flew to the next thug, forcing him to reverse direction. The new bearer inquired, "What else ya got on ya, to trade for this ring then?"

The boy's back was to Aven now, and he looked ready to comply, raising a hand. Just about ready to step in, Aven noticed strange light reflecting off of the faces of the tormentors. The sparkling within the huddle cast shadow outside the group.

"I have this," the boy offered. His audience leaned forward to better look at whatever sparkled in his hand.

The whole world disappeared in a blinding flash. Completely sightless and surprised, Aven barely registered the scamper of light feet as a small body dodged past his groping hands. Blinking and rubbing his eyes, Aven's vision returned peripherally but with a purple blob seared into his eyes. He could barely make out the forms of the teenagers, similarly reaching out or rubbing their eyes, worse off, due to their closer proximity. He tried to look up and down the street for the kid, but he had disappeared.

Aven laughed, stumbling off, rubbing his eyes, and probably viewed as a loon.

Then again, probably not. Seemingly unnoticed by those around him, Aven imagined that such a sight would affect someone from his upbringing. The residents of Midhaven likely had become dulled by so much activity. Finally, it occurred to him that a person could be hustled into an alley and murdered without straying more than twenty feet from hundreds of preoccupied citizens. Among thousands of eyes, it would be too easy to disappear.

He shook away the dark thought, though with a lot more respect for his surroundings. It comforted him to rest a hand on his sword, as he closed on Raliel's location.

When he reached the indicated building, he had to step back, amazed by the immensity and magnificence of the marble sculpture and pillars. His curiosity was piqued. What would bring Raliel to this place? Shaking his head, he bounded up the steps.

***

"It's a disaster in the making; we can't hope to push back the hordes without the aid of our ancient allies, and their numbers haven't replenished nearly as much as we hoped during the last 300 years. We're just not ready yet, and won't be until the requisite signs—I've listed—are evident."

"And so, Demarcus, you expect us to do nothing? Even as the hordes become further entrenched, spoiling the world with their filth, erasing the advances of the past."

"I didn't say 'do nothing.' We can work to encourage the completion of the requisite signs of readiness, such as assisting our allies in replenishing their numbers."

"And if they cannot? If their power is unable to be revived, leaving

91

us to deal with the ever-growing scourge? Why should we wait? The best we can do for all allies and humans alike is follow good King Gershon's decree and secure new land. We should be supporting this now, strengthening our territories while we can."

"Stern, my boy, even if possible—and perhaps it could be secure for a while—are you sure it's a good idea to claim our ancient allies' homes for ourselves?" In his seventies, Demarcus, a balding man, raised his great white eyebrows and smoothed his toga.

"This is a matter to be left for the day it becomes relevant," said Stern, another toga-wearing man, broad of shoulders and draped in dark red with black sandals.

The men continued debating current events. The conversation shifted here and there, with three main discussions spread around the fountain. Smaller groups of men and women, similarly dressed, discussed various topics ranging from astrology, philosophy, history, and anything of interest.

The plaza was a place of political and social activity. Among those who could afford the leisure, Vic thought pointedly.

There was still no mention of or a way of identifying Taberah. Of the near sixty citizens gathered, none looked anything like he expected a master of the brotherhood to look. Though he'd only seen one master, none looked like Master Nazar.

He'd never imagined such styles and colors of what was, in his view, a fancy bed sheet. Clasps bound the togas, an obvious nod to wealth and status to make up for general drabness. These ranged from simple to intricate knots, metal badges, and precious jeweled ornaments. The ladies' hairstyles became extravagant. Sandals, too, served to express one's fashion sense. However, many plain-dressed individuals equally engaged their peers in vigorous debate.

Vic saw how this could be a civilized bridge between the classes of Midhaven. As he drifted from circle to circle, in search, many showed open disdain for his attire, to which he politely explained his foreign status. Then, naturally, he was directed to this or that merchant of formal wear. He had been discreet in his meandering and was just about to start asking of Taberah by name when someone spoke to him near his right shoulder.

"And what's your position regarding the King's new decree, young man?"

Vic turned to this new speaker, an ordinary-looking man of average height and size, brown eyes and hair, in a tan toga held by an intricate knot upon his left shoulder.

"Is it wisdom or folly, Mr. …?"

"Vic."

"Ah, a fine name indeed. Short for winner, champion, conqueror, vanquisher. Excellent. Well, champion, we'd like to know whether you believe it worthy of action in the first place, of course, hmmm."

Hardly a new topic, Vic had discussed it a dozen times since its proclamation, so he didn't hesitate:

"I believe the hordes and evil can't be allowed to encroach forever upon the lands of goodly races; the King's decree has wisdom to it if only to spur us to action."

"Action that will cost the blood of innocent lives."

"Their life; their choice." Vic held out a palm to buy him time to explain, "Humanity is versatile and resilient; by setting off a chain of events, we'll begin to learn from our experiences and become better at challenging the scourge."

"So the lives lost are, to you, nothing but the necessary cost of learning?"

"There's danger, for sure, yet a choice as well. We can't expect it to be easy, but action trumps stagnation. The residents of the wilds will only become stronger with time while we remain limited to our fallen back position." Vic countered.

"Well spoken!" stated a gray-bearded man in encouragement.

The ordinary man smiled, and Vic continued, "It's possible to limit the loss by a cautiously and well-planned undertaking. I don't think it wise for families to begin settling recklessly, but it's encouraging to think of increased expeditions to learn what we can. By increasing reward, claiming ownership of land, the King knows people will find a way."

Nodding, the plain-looking man tried, "And what of the families, the ones with ancestral rights to some of this land, preceding their forced departure, should they sit back and let anyone who would lay claim take their property?"

"I think they lost their land when they left it. If anybody has more reason and motivation to reclaim it, it should be them," Vic said.

"Splendid, my boy," a man in the crowd called out.

"Yes," a woman cried out.

The man in the tan toga adjusted his garment. He continued, "I assume that goes for our ancient allies who unfortunately cannot carelessly throw their remaining numbers away. Should we not expect them to become bitter and feel betrayed by our ambitious seizure?" he finished with a dramatic rise of his eyebrows.

"With all due respect to our esteemed allies...." He gestured around him. "This whole calamity began with their warring against each other. But, for the sake of honor, when it comes time to seize foreign land, we should offer the Massifae and Elden the option to settle with us until their numbers are sufficient to join the fray in earnest."

Sighing, Vic became weary of the topic, "This may take many years. The real obstacle is discovering if there's a way to eradicate and restore tainted areas. Until that happens, true settling would be unrealistic."

Applause startled him. Vic was unaware that a crowd had gathered during his debate with the ordinary man. Several hands reached to pat his back, and the plain man beamed, taking a bow amid chuckles and hoots. Then, people began to disperse, finding other discussions.

Vic's tan-clad opponent took a step forward and confided, "Many people were wondering whether you had bumbled here, lost," he said, grinning, "my apologies for the barrage of questions. It's just our way of getting to know a new attendee. Walk with me." He didn't wait for a response, forcing Vic to catch up, before continuing, "If it's any consolation, I agree with most of what you said, as do many here," he clasped his hands behind his back, surprising Vic with a display of well-developed shoulder and arms.

"I'm flattered, truly, but I've not come to debate," Vic said, mirroring the shorter man's posture, "I must be going."

"Hmmm, no, I don't think so." The man's voice underlined this statement with a quiet authority that unnerved Vic.

"I'm looking for someone...."

"Aren't we all," the man interrupted.

"I'm in no mood to argue the point, sir, but...."

"I meant no offense, vanquisher. You see that clearing up ahead?"

Vic nodded and looked to an opening in the path. The park had trails weaving in and out of the foliage, offering marble benches and tables for respite.

"Be kind enough to accompany me there, and I'll see if I can't help with your dilemma, young man."

They continued in silence, the fecund scent of nature, the cool breeze rustling the leaves, the colder shadows dispersed by warm rays of the sun. That cheered Vic, lightening his mood. He would have all day to locate Master Taberah.

They reached the small clearing, secluded from all the rest. His instincts prickled; something was wrong. The simple man of average age, height, weight, and build had veered to the far right of the space. The light seemed to dim with menace as he studied the man's back. Vic braced himself and asked, "Who are you?"

"Oh, I think you suspect." The man chuckled.

"Master."

Turning, Master Taberah faced Vic. "The beginning of every battle is fought and won here," he pointed to his temple. "It's the mind that tells the body what it can and cannot do. If you expect to learn anything from me, you must be ready to cast all aspersions aside. Brother Nazar taught you most of everything you need to perform your duty. Each master, in our order, possesses a unique ability or technique. You've proved your worth to our elder brother and no longer required. However, skills do come at a cost; you'll work for me if you choose until you've learned what you must, or decide to journey on, understood?"

"Yes, master."

So far, none of this was unexpected, not the speech and especially not the casting aside of doubts. Vic was ready and knew what was coming next, or thought he knew. Taberah covered the twenty feet between them with incredible speed in two violent pumps of his legs. Fists struck at Vic as he dodged, blocked, blocked, and struck out again. Taberah continued bearing down on him with a vicious series of punches and kicks, driving him back. Vic found himself blocking and dodging more than striking, each block catching fist to forearm or wrist as he turned the blow away. Only to avoid another fist while blocking the ensuing kick.

"Good, Conqueror, you keep up well," Taberah commented without the slightest slowing of random strikes or a catch in tone. Vic was not near tiring himself; he had not even broken a sweat. Instead, his breathing remained deep and steady.

Taberah said, "Try and keep up," and unbelievably, Taberah's movements sped up, forcing Vic to add rolls and great sidesteps to his purely defensive position.

"You must strike me, Champion; you cannot hope to tire every opponent."

Vic gritted his teeth, abandoning all thought of preserving stamina, and committed to a ferocious endgame. He called upon all the speed he could muster. He scored a glancing blow to Taberah's shoulder, which cost two solid punches to the chest from the superior warrior.

"Good," Taberah encouraged.

Vic struggled to keep up, blocking a snapping kick with a sweep of his left wrist and a punch with his right.

"Faster," Taberah's fists and feet shot out rapidly, battering away Vic's feeble attacks and striking him in the thigh and stomach. On came the master with ridiculous speed. His strikes began to make the very air 'pop.' Another strike sent Vic reeling, yet when he regained his footing, the master did not pursue.

"Observe," Taberah said. He proceeded to strike with an increasing fury, which caused the air around him to quiver and crack with the thrust of fists and feet. His movements began to blur, disrupting the atmosphere with explosions of air.

Vic could feel the impacts even at a distance. He stared in wonder and respectfully bowed his head. Taberah was beet red when he looked up, glowing with heat, steam rising from his head like smoke. Vic understood the principle behind what Taberah had done but never before thought it possible.

"You're familiar with the concept then?" Taberah asked.

"Yes. Master Nazar taught me how to do the reverse," Vic replied.

"Excellent. We'll see if you can learn both while you're here." Taberah cooled down just as swiftly, displaying his ability to do just that.

"Do you require somewhere to stay? Food?"

"Neither, thank you."

"No matter, come, brother, let me acquaint you with our sanctuary here in Midhaven."

***

Adam studied Edmund—a preceptor of magical arts—across the counter while awaiting his response. The sign out front read, 'Magus Pedagogy, Artifacts, and Enchantment.' Adam hoped to find enough work to survive, perhaps even apprentice for the precept. At the very least, get off the street for a while.

"Sorry young fella, but I can't afford to hire you."

Adam sighed with open disappointment. He had expected as much. None of the finer shops even gave him the slightest consideration, sometimes ushering him immediately back to the street, he thought to try the more humble shops; Edmund's being the last in a long line of refusals.

With the grace to express concern, Edmund added, "If its money you need, perhaps I can offer a price for your enchanted ring and robe, but I must admit I can't meet their worth."

Adam met the preceptor's eyes, this not being the first offer, "Sorry, can't part with them, been in my family for some time," his voice softened, "it isn't money I need, but food, shelter, and training. I've come from very far and possess some instruction already."

Edmund raised his brows, for the boy could hardly be older than twelve. Then, with his sigh, he gestured around the store. "I empathize, lad, but as you can see, honest business and charity haven't gotten me much; any more than that would be taking bread from my wife and child," he paused, brow furrowed, "though you say you've had training, you might check with the guild companies for hire."

"I've tried," Adam replied while fighting back the hopelessness in his voice, "none would take me." It'd been two days since his travel rations had expired, and the effects of hunger were quickly acquainting him with a desperation he'd never known.

"Well, that could change. See a relative of mine at the east stable, ask for Liz, and make sure you tell her Eddie sent you. Then, if you're lucky, she'll put you up for a bit in exchange for work."

After a moment of thought, Edmund added sternly, "I don't do this lightly, lad, don't risk my reputation. But, if she can help, you had better make her glad she did. Understand?"

"Yes, thank you!"

With several hasty bows, the slim boy was off in a swirl of red robes. Edmund smiled and shook his head at his kind, foolish heart. The boy had been his only visitor that day. He was unsure if he'd be able to stay off the street himself if he didn't do something soon. It wasn't that he lacked skill, only reputation. He'd opened the shop only a year ago, spending all he had, hoping he could secure a clientele base quick to support his family. Unfortunately, it was proving more difficult than expected.

He banished the negative thoughts and took heart in what little reprieve he could offer the boy. Perhaps he'd receive the same from the world. Hopefully soon.

***

The Legion Hall training grounds consisted of a moderate arena-like bowl filled with sand and gravel. There were several training sessions at the moment; group formations, battle simulations, relays, and sparring, to name a few. Amid the clack and clatter of equipment and practice weapons, Raliel stood across from an instructor mirroring his movements as she memorized the sequence.

"Pause right there," his deep voice instructed, "ensure your feet, hips, and shoulders pivot together behind each swing—Okay, better."

She'd come to the Legion Hall to peruse its renowned library. Then, having done so, for much of the morning, she'd come to see what these grounds could offer.

A twenty-year veteran, Marcus was a revered quasi-retired master axeman doing what many aging warriors do to survive and, as an instructor, highly desired. The sequence she was learning was basic, but from watching his previous session, she knew it could become challenging. The first thing he asked was for her to remove any enchantments. She was able to retain her axe. It wasn't exactly heavy, it had a graceful balance to it, but without her belt, it was not long before her shoulders, thighs, and forearms burned with strain. She focused on holding each position and waited for the next. Just when she was beginning to worry if she could go on any longer, Marcus finished with an agonizingly slow double upper-swipe and thrust, which he held steady until Raliel followed.

"Okay. At ease." Meaning for her to return to the neutral stance: feet and shoulders square, axe held across her chest. "Not many have completed that on their first try; I believe you'll receive training well. Most students need about a year to grasp the more intricate patterns. However, four months of that is spent on fundamentals. So beginning a little ahead shouldn't be a problem for you."

"Probably not. I've been training with weapons for over a decade," she said.

"Excellent." Marcus enjoyed what he did. However, teaching didn't scratch the surface of what he knew. Raliel intended on learning all she could from him and as quickly as possible. She had no doubt she could; she knew she was proficient but understood that prowess must be a work in progress, a lifelong journey filled with intense training.

98

Especially if she wanted the edge to survive and keep Aven alive, his path would be incredibly dangerous by nature; the more profitable the contracts, the more risk of death. She didn't doubt that she could; she knew.

"Realize," Marcus continued, "I don't offer this option lightly, it'll save you a considerable sum, but I must admit I see potential in you, which would be a shame to ignore." He held her attention as he considered, "I'll do it for two silver royals, which is a third of my usual fee; will this be possible for you?"

That was double what she had to her name. Her heart dropped initially, but she recalled something Nazar always said, necessity determines a person's ability. She hoped that included finances because she would need all her knowledge to produce another silver royal.

"Will you accept half now?" she asked as she fumbled with her purse.

"No need," came a familiar voice, "greetings instructor, my name is Aven, of Bright Company," he glanced at Raliel, standing straight and looking entirely professional.

"Ah, guild members, as well." Marcus nodded with approval. "Training guild members is highly encouraged by the legion. The royal treasury covers twenty-five percent of my fee."

"Really?" Raliel was shocked.

"Really," replied Marcus. He looked to Aven and continued, "You'd be the company contractor then?"

Aven nodded.

"Well then, please excuse me, Miss Raliel, while I arrange for training with your contractor."

She felt relieved and grateful as she picked up her belongings and restored them to their proper places.

Aven and Marcus walked off toward the grass, rimming the training grounds to talk business. Raliel took the opportunity to roam.

There was quite a bit of noise coming from a sizeable well-equipped force, about a hundred men. They were currently broken up into five groups of twenty, displaying five separate domes of a shield. Curiously tipped spears protruded between as they maneuvered and shifted, careful to maintain formation while instructors scrutinized and barked commands. On order, the armored domes braced, hunched, and tightened shields. Then, the groups would attack on specific sides and in various sequences per command. First, spears appeared and thrust patterns with swift and lethal accuracy. Raliel could empathize with the workout these fighters were receiving. Then, just as swiftly, the groups merged into a line. Some shield men maintained a solid wall, but the rest supported their line as they fanned out, filling the gaps seamlessly as the wall stretched. Every so often, an instructor would bellow, and the line would launch a series of deadly thrusts, boots continuing to crunch in sequence, each strike punctuated with a collective roar "Hoo-Hah!"

"That'd be the new excursion corps, the legion contribution to the King's decree," Aven said, approaching her unexpectedly.

"Mmm…hmmm," she mumbled, distracted and mesmerized by the spectacle.

Aven continued unperturbed, "Those must be the new spears, bone-splitters, they're callin' 'em."

"Sent to explore the Witherwood then?" she asked.

Aven shrugged. "It sure looks like it, but probably not for some time yet. Be a helluva sight, though, won't it?"

"Mmm...hmmm."

They studied the corps for a few moments more. Then, after silence, Aven asked, "See on the reverse end of the spears?"

She did: foot-long steel blades to meet a broader range of threats. Considering their other swords, axes, hammers—and even crossbows—it seemed they could do that and more.

"The legion expects to have the new corps, much like the hereditary positions of the Wall, ready to clear the near wilds soon," Aven said.

Only time would tell how effective they'd be. It made sense, too; not only would these men be paid well, their families cared for, but they would be securing the new ground for the Kingdom. One day, their own families could have land rights, not an insufficient incentive. Plus, excellent training, equipment, and support. If only venturing out in the wilds was not such dangerous business—a mystery. Nobody had traveled far from the outposts in hundreds of years.

Raliel and Aven headed west, across the river, then south down a wide street to the farmer's district.

After perusing a wide selection of fresh produce, they assembled an eclectic lunch of fruits and nuts. On a sloping grass bank, stone tables and benches were looking west over the southern flowing Icepeak. Across the river, the trees of the plaza park provided a magnificent view. The distant waters of the park's artificial lake glittered majestically through an emerald canopy.

They sampled strawberries and cantaloupe before lethargically munching on a mixture of hardy nuts and dried fruit.

"This would make great travel rations," Aven thought aloud, "and it's inexpensive."

Everything sold at the farmer's market came directly from the bountiful acreage of crops along the Icepeak River. Aven remembered the stone bottle of cider on his belt and handed it to Raliel. She popped the cork, took a sip, and set it between them.

He'd given her an account of his day, showing her the guild crest and including the brave kid's story, which amused her. She loved stories of an underdog coming out on top. It felt good sitting here with her. He was content.

A cool breeze could be felt and seen over the waving trees, grass, and river, but the bright sun's heat kept the chill away, just so, under a pristine blue sky. Raliel relayed her morning, detailing her experience at the town portal. Aven showed her the scrolls of the town portal he had. Her eyes sparkled jade with the anticipation of using one.

He finished the cider and asked, "What were you looking for?"

"I intended only on seeing the legion library, which was as big as expected," she said. "I wanted to research my possible ancestry, you know, that could explain…what happened." She touched her hair and widened her eyes.

"Maybe you can learn more about this ability's potential," he offered.

"Yeah, there's that and, I dunno, I just need to know as much as I can. It's all I've been able to think about," she finished with a pleading look in her eyes.

"Well, you couldn't be in a better place to find out," he encouraged, "you'll be coming to the training grounds regularly, which means you could study regularly as well." Seeing her perk up, he continued, "I guess; as your team leader I find both time properly spent." He smiled, delighted to see she appreciated the support.

"Thanks for funding my training from Marcus. I'll pay you back."

He shook his head. "Rali, that money is well spent; training is necessary. It's part of my responsibility as a leader." He placed a hand on hers. "And my gift as your friend."

They both returned their attention to the view.

After a moment, he said, "Besides, with those skills, you'll have plenty of opportunities to justify the investment—OW! You didn't have to punch me!"

They both laughed.

***

The small passenger carriage turned north off the main boulevard. Horse hooves clip-clopped as the carriage creaked and clattered behind. Vic split his attention between master Taberah—who stared placidly out of a small window—and his own, with a view of unfamiliar people and residences.

They'd entered the vehicle as soon as they reached the boulevard and sped east back the way he'd come that morning. The ride so far was made without conversation, even as they passed his inn, and turned into unfamiliar territory.

Without slowing, the carriage was allowed through a hastily opened gate, entering a community sealed off from the rest of the city. He studied the streets and structures, all residential, probably upper-middle-class working families. Each home had room for grassy yards or gardens. What struck him most was the number of children of all sizes and ages playing. The occasional adult raked, swept, either coming or going. Compared to the city's chaos, filth, and general dangerousness, it was almost tranquil.

"There are other enclaves like this throughout the city," Taberah explained, "some much wealthier. But, for the most part, Midhaven is civilized."

Vic noticed a gold wristlet behind Taberah's right hand, which he absentmindedly twisted with this left while staring out the window.

"Seems so normal," Vic remarked.

"Oh, I suppose it is for some, and perhaps not so much for many others; we do enjoy a portion of peace here, but not without a price."

They rumbled along and turned seemingly at random before reaching their destination.

"Come, brother."

Upon their exit, the carriage and driver wasted no time departing. Its racket receded to nothing in moments. The plot before them was more prominent than those in the vicinity. On it stood an abbey, surrounded by an imposing wrought-iron fence with foot-long spikes topping each rod. The gate was open and warm light glowed from large stained glass windows decorating the face of the building.

Gravel crunched underfoot as they walked to the front steps. Taberah paused before the stout iron door, then knocked in a distinct sequence. Immediately, the lock mechanisms began to release, and soon the door swung in on well-oiled hinges.

"Come along," Taberah said, stepping inside, Vic close behind.

The abbey was candle-lit. Candlesticks were visible throughout, in various wall mounts and standing candelabra. As the door thudded shut and Vic's eyes adjusted, he noticed others moving about, nearly invisible in the shadows because of the dark hooded robes. Two were helping Taberah into a similar robe, distinguished from the rest by its vibrant red color and a large glyph upon its back, marking him a master.

Soon, they were walking side by side down a wide spiraling corridor with a steep decline. The air took on a subterranean chill. The floor leveled as Taberah led the way through a stone arch and into a dormitory filled with beds. Each possessed its footlocker and nightstand with a single drawer and candle. Sleeping mounds inhabited some beds. The atmosphere was serene, and neither made a sound as they glided through.

Beyond, a door led to a shared room. A fireplace burned low, and a robed man leaned over a desk writing.

"Now, brother, I deliver you into the capable hands of brother Azure. You'll receive a summons when the time comes to further your training." And with that, Master Taberah made his exit.

Azure continued writing, oblivious to Vic and the recent introduction. This lack of acknowledgment continued for a while, and —though he maintained discipline and patience—Vic wondered if he should use his ability to speed things up. Azure looked to be mid-forties with black short-cropped hair peppered with silver. Vic was just about to speed through the wait when the brother put down his quill, rolled up the parchment, poured wax from a candle, sealed it, and set it aside. Azure looked up and met Vic with ebony orbs.

"Welcome, brother." He began in a deep baritone. "From this time on, you will be addressed, within this sanctuary and by fellow brothers of the order, as brother 'Agate.' Do not share your former name or past with any other member."

So, 'Azure' was not his name, Vic thought. The man reached into a drawer, retrieved a few items, and placed them upon his desk before looking up again and continuing.

"You're able to stay here for free. Here's the key to your designated bed and chest, which contains a robe, clothes, and other items for your use."

Azure lifted a small scroll and continued, "Here's a map of the complex. Before you scoff, study it and carry it with you. This place is much more vast than you may understand. We can't have you lost or late for appointments.

"We offer training, services, and products particular to our work and not commonly found outside.

"When you're ready, come to me for assignment." With that, brother Azure began working on another parchment.

Vic gathered the key and map, nodded, and went to locate his bed and chest.

***

The following day, Azure instructed Vic to report to general training. He learned that when he wasn't on assignment or allotted free time, this was where he should be.

The compound's gymnasium was a massive cube of a room. Brothers engaged in various types of exercise independently, but mostly in pairs or groups. Cream-colored muslin suits wrapped their bodies; nothing but their eyes were visible.

Instructors—distinguished by thick, brightly colored belts tied around their waists—faced their groups.

Various scaffolding lined the walls high up to the ceiling. Many giant lanterns lit the expanse, spaced and hung from frame and canopy with bright yellow light leaving almost no shadow. Above was filled with ropes and bars from which students adeptly skittered across.

They appeared to be competing to reach a single yellow belt hanging precariously from a center bar twenty feet above. As they neared, the competition grew aggressive. It seemed that knocking opponents from their holds was allowed and encouraged. Nimble bodies fell amid whoops from their peers. The soft earth padded their landings but not their egos as they skulked off in failure to join other groups.

"And where are you supposed to be?!" the strong demand shocked Vic and brought him to attention.

"I'm not sure. Azure sent me here. I'm new," Vic explained.

"Brother Azure, initiate, and you'll address me as Coach Jin; report directly to me for your training. Got it?"

"Yes, Coach Jin."

"Good. You'll start by mastering the brack." Jin flung a silver ring to Vic, who quickly plucked it from the air. The 'brack' was a little bigger than his head.

"You'll be expected to wear it at all times." Jin motioned for him to slip it over his head.

Vic complied. He immediately felt heavier. The brack itself was weightless, but his arm felt nearly too heavy to lift when he reached up to adjust it.

"It'll take some getting used to. See, it's not your body that's inhibited, but your willpower. So expect it to hinder you in many unexpected ways."

To Vic's surprise, the brack shrunk, snug around his neck. Though it wasn't tight, panic fluttered a moment.

Jin smiled. "Before you leave today, pick up your initiate uniform. You'll also be required to contribute to daily duties and responsibilities— while not here. These I will assign to you as you progress."

"When will I begin training with the Master?" Vic asked.

Jin scoffed, "I'm the only teacher you need to be concerned with. If you do well and are lucky...." He raised his eyebrows. "He'll request you after your training."

Vic wanted to pursue the topic, to point out that he meant to train directly under Taberah, but he sensed that he wouldn't get far with Jin. He'd likely only embarrass himself. Indeed Taberah was aware of the expectations of an initiate. So he resolved to be patient and humble. The last thing he wanted was to give the impression that he felt entitled, especially on his first day.

A good reputation would do more to speed his advancement.

He followed Jin farther into the gym, noting other students struggling under bracks. Their faces shone, uniforms soaked with sweat, as they performed basic movements.

Hours later, Vic stood at his designated post. Jin had instructed him to keep watch through a small viewing port until nightfall. He was to memorize all activity observed from this vantage: a small street abutting the abbey property. If he found anything out of the ordinary, he was to pull a plain braided rope hanging from a recess in the wall to alert a scout to investigate. There was a red rope to be drawn in an emergency.

The duty grew tedious because he couldn't entirely rely on his slowing skill without the risk of missing something vital. Not that there seemed much risk of that, he thought glumly.

He tried to avoid imagining what kinds of fun Aven and Raliel were having. But, unlike him, they elected to pay for training directly from an expert.

Vic was required to sleep on the compound should his presence be needed for anything, striking a dismal chord in his heart. Something about the collar, for that's what it was, no matter what they called it, and the control of every aspect of his time outside the gym. It felt like captivity. It wasn't what he'd expected. Nothing like his time with Nazar, but what did he expect?

He silently chastised himself. He wasn't usually this gloomy. These feelings never occurred until he'd put on the brack. What had Jin said? To expect it to inhibit his willpower?

Vic shook his head, then grinned. Jin hadn't had to offer that clue. Perhaps Vic was receiving more consideration than he'd thought. Everyone had their approach. This chapter—of the brotherhood—was militaristic. Perhaps all were. He'd just have to follow through with an open mind. First, though, he resolved to test these new limits. He didn't like limitations. But, on the other hand, he was perfectly capable of maintaining his discipline.

Tonight, as soon as his relief arrived, he intended on having dinner with his friends—like every other night—he'd take off before Jin could assign him anywhere else.

He refocused on watching the occasional pedestrian stroll by or the random child chase ball or pet, nothing unusual for a residential street, with the concentration on memorizing each activity. Why? He was sure it was to train him in observation, and he could easily recite its virtues, but it felt far beneath his level of training.

Most of the recruits he bunked and trained with were within their first year of martial training. Vic had been at this his whole life, under a master, no less!

The sun seemed frozen in place with no intention of lowering. With a sigh, he concentrated on memorizing each activity. Vic cleared his mind and took control of his breathing.

CHAPTER TEN

Adam woke an hour before dawn, as he had since he could remember. For him, this was the perfect time for introspection. The stable's loft was pitch black, the presence of animals marked by scent and the occasional sleepy huff. Adam went through this mental checklist and exercise he'd learned in mage training. He felt for the sources of power, renewed after a night's rest. Adam breathed deep and steady through his nose. Scanning from the toes and lesser sources, all the way to the top of his head, he stopped at each bundle of nerves holding the secret of a mage's wellspring of power. Not everyone could tap into that power, but it was essential to ritually remain acquainted and comfortable with each one for those who could. Only this way could all of them be broached, some more than others, and only through repeated use--or enhancing artifacts--could the strength and endurance of each one's power increase. Like physical training, except this power had the potential to exceed measurable limits. No one knew their true potential, so it was important for the gifted to regularly stretch and exercise their power connections.

With inherited advantage and mental acuity, some began their lives with a more significant edge. Adam was such a one, though he didn't feel so. His family had started his training as soon as he showed ability at three years young, a prodigy. His forehead wrinkled at the memory. That label had been the cause of all discomfort since. He was never allowed to do what other kids could but expected to 'know better' and live up to a standard he didn't choose. He'd wanted nothing more than to be a normal kid for a long time. Toward the end, he gave his family a good share of trouble. Though he wasn't a bad kid or evil in disposition, he did at times suffer from severe boredom, which had led him on several misadventures. This, in turn, led to his parents doing what they did. His lip trembled for a moment, and in his inner darkness, he tried to cry, even forced a gasp and shudder. No tears came, only the burn of bleary eyes.

He focused on his weakest power-ganglion, as taught. He sought the tiny spark of energy at the base of his tail bone, disposed to specific flows of magic. All ganglion produced power, each best used for particular types of casting. However, the energy could be transferred to a particular one if a person was adept, so it was important to exercise all, even those not within a mage's forte. He cast a fortifying spell of endurance that depleted the ganglion. A wave of vitality washed over his legs, receding in power as it reached his upper limbs. The enhancement was weak and would last only a few hours, but there had been a time when he could only get a few minutes out of it. Others, he knew, hadn't achieved such progress for decades, if ever. That made him smile a little, and his mood lifted as he exhausted his weak sources. He flexed his stronger one—which he would be sure to drain through the day—and diverted sparks of power from more vital points to weaker, to expand and deplete again. By the end of this practice, he detected the rising sun's first light right on time. Animals began to stir, anticipating the feeding, brushing, and mucking he provided.

Adam conjured, from his most potent source, a spark of light. He moved in among the rafters, quickly adjusting its brightness to acclimate his sensitive eyes. Trying to get the dimness right was challenging, to fine-tune when dealing with a powerful source. He thought of the teen gang from yesterday, wondering if they had any clue how easily he could have seared their eyes blind forever. In his heightened perturbation, it was tough to control the intensity of the flash.

Adam observed the corner of his small loft and the nest he'd made of hay and blankets. Then, stretching, he stood and summoned a globe of water before him. Sticking the hand in with the ruby ring first,

Adam used it to heat the blob in a steaming mass. He shoved both hands within the rippling globe, then face and hair, conducting his morning ablutions. The sphere flattened and frosted over into a suspended pane, buffed with a sleeve, creating a decent reflection even as Adam cast darkness behind. As he combed damp hair with his fingers, he thought about how loneliness wasn't so bad. He couldn't grieve too much when he had his abilities to comfort and protect him. Undoubtedly many were much worse off.

To the sound of chirping birds and hungry animals—careful to dispel the mirror—he descended the ladder to begin his chores.

***

The watcher stalked his prey through bustling crowds. His responsibility was to shadow and monitor the objective until a replacement arrived, reporting any vitals to base upon his return. He wanted to cheat by using his ability to speed time but couldn't risk losing his target. Earlier, during the subject's long and leisurely midday meal, the desire was extreme—challenging Vic's belief by the enormity to which even an obese man could punish his digestive system.

Vic stared beyond his target—though keeping him locked in view—as they swam through tides of pedestrians, merchants, officials, and city guards, ebbing and flowing. He heard in stories that city navigation could be like acquiring 'sea legs.' Walking among the press of people took some adjustment. On a visceral level, one could intuitively feel when to press and when to let the flow carry them. Sometimes, he'd need to aim for C to get to point B from point A the quickest. His target took to it effortlessly, displaying a lifetime of experience.

Vic had been surprised to learn that other brothers didn't share his ability to speed time. Many were openly envious of the advantage during long waits. Not to mention when injury demanded the stanching of blood flow or playing dead, as some pointed out. He'd never thought of those applications. There were others with unique talents; Sister Onyx's ability to stick to any surface; Brother White's, to regenerate tissue. Both enviable, beyond staunching a wound or 'playing possum.'

Taberah's branch offered great training opportunities and requisites that he looked forward to with anticipation and earned through a task. Learned skills determined future work and thus more opportunities to learn. Never before had he felt more driven with purpose. He could easily stay put, learning from this single chapter for a lifetime. He wanted to.

His target took a turn down an alley. Vic, getting a visual once at the entryway, pursued. He was to monitor without being seen, but losing the subject was not an option. He rounded each corner and obstacle just in time to catch the hem of the fat man's robe swiping around the next bend. Evasive tactics? It could be nothing more than a precaution.

Stone buildings pressed high on each side connected by lines of hanging clothes. Discarded crates and trash littered the ground. A gutter of slow-moving sludge ran down the center of each twist and turn of these back alleys.

Vic peered around another stone corner to see his subject greeting a silver-robed and cowled figure at the end. Then, from a break in the roofing above came a beam of sunshine lighting upon the duo, causing the silver robe to sparkle; Vic tapped an earring on his left ear, then twice, focusing on the pair until he succeeded in tuning into the conversation.

"...Followed?" asked a woman.

"No mistress," the target replied.

"Do you have it with you?" she asked, stepping forward with impatience.

"I may."

"You dare to play games with me?" she snapped, commanding respect.

"No mistress, I only mean to assure that I place it in the right hands," he replied, cowing and dabbing his forehead with a sleeve.

The woman—much taller than the man—pushed back her silver hood, revealing full and beautiful silver and white streaked hair. It reflected bright and pale in the sunlight. She tilted her finely sculpted youthful face proudly back, chin out. Then, with a few fingers, she displayed her heritage by the point and structure of her ear.

"Is that confirmation enough?" she asked in a voice almost musical in its natural eloquence.

"Ye—yes, mistress." The man reached in his robe, retrieved a small package, and handed it to the Elden beauty. He remained, head bowed, his hand held out expectedly.

"Oh, yes, of course, this should do," she said, already losing interest in the man. She tossed him a coin purse, attention diverted to the article in her hand. The man peeked inside the silver bag as she inspected the package.

"Most excellent, mistress, will you require anything else?" he added, greed in his eyes.

"No, not at this time. You've done well, very well; I will call on you again."

Vic spotted movement in the shadows above. Onyx had arrived to relieve him. As the target disappeared beyond, so did Onyx, smoothly negotiating the building walls—quick as a lizard. He reached up to disengage the earring's magic but paused as the Elden woman began mumbling. He quickly increased its strength.

"…If this doesn't work, he'll surely kill me, foolish girl." Then she took off at a jog.

Vic wanted to follow her, was intrigued, but only had so much time to report upon being relieved so he could get dismissed for the day. Duty first, he thought and began his trek back to the abbey.

***

"We've got a job!" Aven declared, barging into Raliel's room to find her engaged, rather embarrassingly, with her chamber pot device.

"Get out!" she screamed.

"OH! Sorry!" he stepped out, shielding himself from view, without closing the door. "As soon as you're ready, and we can find Vic, I've managed to contract a good-paying quest in the slums."

"What, no more escorting tourists?" she mocked.

They'd been accompanying visitors for a week now, with no foreseeable change in sight. While the work was sustaining them, barely, her legs and feet—endurance enhanced or not—were killing her. "Because if I have to deal with one more snotty brat or a snobby tourist, I'll start cleaving heads!"

"No, no, not today or this week, though the faster we finish this job, the more money we'll have to live on."

Through a week of personal guarding, traveling back and forth, up and down the city limits, they had become well acquainted with the better parts of Midhaven. But, namely, the novelty had long worn away. They conducted most jobs themselves because Vic was usually busy with his continual training. It was frustrating how secret he was about it, even if that was his way, and they'd been too busy or too tired to complain. Besides, he always made an effort to meet up for dinner, though he didn't stay, claiming his lodging was provided.

"So, you gonna tell me the details?" she asked.

"At dinner, when Vic gets here. I think we're gonna need a hire-on, if not now then soon."

"Wow, a hire-on, aye," she commented, thinking that this job must be profitable indeed, as tight as Aven could be. "Lotta money involved?"

"Well, if we manage just us three sure, but we may need help, there's the possibility of treasure."

"Ah, treasure," she said, rolling her eyes. "I will at least get to cleave a head or two?"

Aven's tone turned grim, "Yeah, Rali, this one could be serious."

She'd been making that comment with each job, but now her blood ran cold. So, their first dangerous job. Butterflies welled up in her stomach. "Okay, Aven, now get out!"

The door slammed, tinkled, and clicked as he engaged the lock. Whose idea was it to share room keys anyway, she asked herself, then got back to what she was doing.

***

The taproom was pretty empty, as it was most weekday nights. Real crowds only showed up for the special weekend performances. However, one could expect festive tunes from the resident harpsichordist every evening.

Aven was early but was too excited to do anything else. After a week, he had grown accustomed to the usual residents and patrons. Occasionally, the sturdy massif would appear, looking worse for wear. He'd always go straight to the bar, same stools, same drink from his mug. Aven hoped he would show tonight to offer him work though he was clearly out of their league. If the massif wanted, he could probably do the job himself. Single-handed, with his monstrous war hammer. To say the massif was quiet or terse was an understatement. In passing, Aven had made attempts at conversation, to which he'd been summarily ignored and nearly trampled. However, the night before last, when Aven shouted a greeting forcefully, he received, to his surprise, a grunt in reply. Fortified by this, Aven was set on cornering the massif until he could persuade him to help on this job. Yet, to his dismay, the massif man was nowhere in sight. It *was* a bit early.

Aven's leg bounced under the table, causing a jingling and catching his attention; the scrap mail on his greaves rattled. Aven thought of the guildsmith's ingenuity and felt pride in the dark scrap mail sown over his leather armor with twine and covered the chest, shoulders, forearms, legs, and boots. He thought it looked pretty tough. Raliel said it looked ridiculous as she strutted around in gleaming mail and plate boots. She said he looked like something for scrubbing pots, more than a company leader. But that was Raliel. It was next to impossible for him to get an outright compliment out of her. Though it was hard at times, he loved her all the same. Of course, it didn't hurt that she was beautiful—more than any other—in his eyes.

It dawned on him that through all the years growing up together, nothing compared to the closeness they were achieving here, on their own. Their journey here, working together, things were changing. Sometimes, as Raliel stood before him, he was overwhelmed with a desire to have her, kiss her, and hold her tight. He pulled out his rune chain and inspected the artifact suspiciously. He sensed Raliel's exact direction and distance: forty-five degrees to his right, angling upstairs. The accuracy this close was uncanny and reassuring.

"Am I interrupting something?"

Aven found Vic standing to his left, leather stealth suit on, gray cloak folded over one arm, sheathed long slim sword in the other.

"Sit. I've got great news." He began to summarize, careful not to expose too much until Raliel arrived.

"When exactly will I be needed? My mornings—to noon or a little later—are usually required for training." Vic's 'training' was seven days a week, while Raliel's was four, sometimes five. It hadn't been too much of a problem, but Vic would eventually have to choose as the jobs became more demanding.

"No problem. I was thinking the later, the better, like tonight." The thought sparked a gleam in Vic's silver eyes. Hunger? For what? Adventure? Carnage? Did it matter? Aven wasn't sure. Even he fought to check an animalistic urge to rush into danger. "We might finish it in one night, hopefully, but I'll explain in more detail when Raliel gets here." Vic nodded, glanced to the stairs, and looked about to say something, but Aven beat him to it, "Should be down in a moment; let's order." Aven gave a signal to a server and looked back to Vic, who lounged, both arms resting on the back of the booth. "When did you start wearing an earring?" Aven asked.

Vic smiled. "When it became part of the job." He must have noticed Aven's confusion, so he added, "It's enchanted to increase hearing. I can focus it precisely too." He looked across the taproom tapping his earring. "See that woman and man leaning close?" Aven did and nodded. "Let's see." He paused, eavesdropping, "ah, he's professing his undying love," he chuckled, "she's expressing her desire to eat." He tapped the earring again, disengaging the device.

"Useful," Aven said, grinning.

"Yeah," he agreed, "I can also broaden its range to detect movement." He waved a leather glove, dismissing the thought. "It's not mine though, only on loan. Tried to return it today…" he seemed to restrain himself a bit, "…but was told I'd need it. For training tomorrow."

With the straightforward honesty of lifelong friends, Aven asked, "What's up with all the hush-hush business anyway?"

Vic shrugged, "I dunno, comes with it, I guess." His brows furrowed. "Hasn't been anything worth hiding," the chuckle again, "but I had to promise, at least while I'm here training." Vic smiled.

Aven smiled, satisfied that one day his friend could explain what it was like to excel as he had. He spied Raliel jogging down the stairs, mail jingling as she neared.

"You did say the job's within the city, right?" she asked, looking at Vic's cloak.

"Yup, and underground." Aven looked around and still didn't find the massif anywhere. But, he thought, if they couldn't find a hire-on, they'd work it out.

****

Mendelonius No Name was tireless but weary. So weary of it all. Life hadn't panned out how he'd expected, no reflection of the hard work he'd put in, indeed. Nor as sensible as his upbringing, himself being more realistic than most Massifae this generation.

His generation. Was he the last? He couldn't know, hadn't seen any of his kin, and very few Massifae of another lineage, since he'd left his home. Not that he hadn't looked; he'd searched high and low. For how long? He wasn't sure anymore. Finally, the grief of his loss, the tragedy of it, had driven him to abandon all he'd known; there was nothing left from those days, just an empty shell of what once was. Initially, his clan and home had been more fortunate since the Great War. After all, he was alive. No matter how he lived, he continued to live.

All his closest friends had been gone for a long time; he'd lost so many dear ones that he didn't try anymore. He couldn't afford to lose anyone in this world; they'd certainly die. He was a massif, after all, one of the last of his kind. The new majority race: humans, would come and go, leaving him and a few other long-living ilk to walk alone. And so he had. He was doing the odd job here and there to fund necessities and travel on a never-ending circuit—the futility of which he pondered now.

In the beginning, he and his friends had a purpose that cost their lives. His chest burned at the thought, and he shook his head. He'd been a fool, right along with them, thinking they could make a difference, and how they had! But alas, they were gone, and he never expected to find love and camaraderie as he'd known then until he'd seen the boy and girl.

At first, he thought he'd seen ghosts or suffered a stroke, so stunned was he at the resemblance. It was uncanny, eerily so. Not precisely in look—for his friends had been well into adulthood when they'd met— but something visceral. He reached under his breastplate, retrieving his glyph. Could it be? Each time patrons came or went through the front doors, he could see the three friends talking seriously among themselves.

Time for him to leave. He didn't want to go through this again. It was painful enough to live with cursed longevity, with his already significant loss, without adding more fragile friends. He huffed a sigh, which to passing humans was a startling blast of air. Mendelonius turned to leave this place. He'd be back in twenty years or so, and if they still lived? Well, he'd worry about that then.

***

"So, what's the big job?" Looking at Vic, Raliel added, "While you've been on your butt, probably meditating, Aven's had me babysitting all over town."

Vic smiled, batting a glove her way. She glared.

Aven cleared his throat and began, "There have been reports of a possible infestation of river boglins between the warehouse district and the slums."

"River boglins?" Raliel asked.

"They're like regular boglins, but smaller with an elemental affinity to water." Vic explained, "Common near rivers and lakes."

Aven continues, "Yeah, so a possible lair has been discovered. The warehouse district is offering 200 silver to eradicate them."

"Plus a legion bounty of 10 silver for each boglin nose," Raliel interjected.

Aven looked impressed, "Exactly. This job could turn out very profitable." He paused, looking his friends over, "we need this, guys, and I need this chance. We'll not get many like it and need the funds, not just to live, but to get ahead. To hire help and better equip ourselves for bigger jobs." Then to Raliel, "I don't know about you, but I'm not trying to live in an inn babysitting tourists forever."

"Well, the inn isn't bad, but I'm in if it means avoiding another tourist job," Raliel assured.

"What about you, Vic?"

"I'm in, of course, considering I'm available."

"I think we should go tonight before losing the shot," Aven continued.

"Let's do it," Raliel encouraged.

"No time like the present," Vic added.

"Good. Let's get going; it's about a half an hour walk from here."

"What about our order?" Vic reminded.

"Already took care of it." Aven stood first, grabbing his shield and sword and leading out.

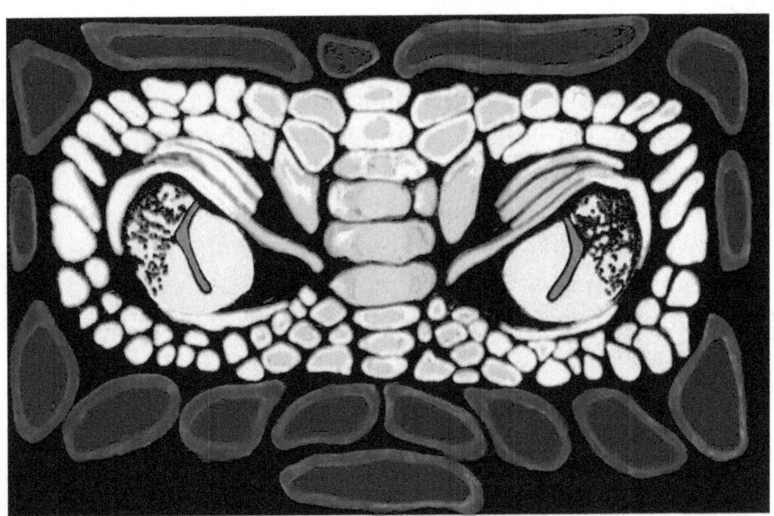

CHAPTER ELEVEN

"How much farther?" Raliel asked, anxious for action. They'd been skulking for a quarter of an hour in the slum's upper sewer system.

"Just up ahead." Aven droned as he consulted the crudely drawn map that'd come with the job. The sewer-works was a successful attempt to use much older ancient tunnels carved into a network of natural caves under the city. Unfortunately, the map only showed a rough sketch of the entrance of the slum and the estimated source of boglin activity. So they headed in that general direction, making turns when needed, among many intersections of alternate passageways. The tunnel they now traveled was wide enough to afford a narrow canal running down its center filled with slow-moving black liquid, its depth unknown. Here and there, a small bridge appeared for crossing.

An occasional stout door emerged between each intersection of corridors, always locked. Vic provided the scouting for their party, skittering out into the dark, where he spent most of the time. Aven had brought a bundle of small torches slung over one of his shoulders. He hoped they'd be enough. He eyed the half spent example in his left hand, sword out in his right, and bronze shield guarding his back.

"Hold on," he whispered.

"What is it?" Raliel hissed back.

"I think this is it," Aven explained.

Vic seemed to materialize from the darkness ahead, on cue. His long slender blade leading, knife handles glittered from all over his stealth suit. "There's a broken door ahead to the west." His voice sounded ghostly and hollow from behind his hawkish helm. "There are prints, and boglin, er…looks like droppings."

Aven looked to Raliel, pleased to find her braced for combat. "Alright, we secure that room before we move on."

The scene was just as Vic described: the thick wooden panels of the former door looked hacked up from the inside out. Splinters of wood and twisted iron lay before them. Motioning everyone back, Aven lit a new torch and threw it through the entrance, to the right. His older torch went to the left as he donned his kite shield—no sounds of response within. From the surrounding tunnels, a faint drip echoed in the distance.

Aven shield-rammed the busted door with a nod to his team, sending its remaining frame tumbling before him. He veered left, placing his back just inside. Next came Raliel, taking a right. Vic blurred straight into the shadows on silent feet. Retrieving his almost spent torch, Aven held it high, revealing a flat stone ceiling. He threw the torch farther to the back, showing more signs of mindless destruction.

"Looks like the remains of some type of storage room," Vic remarked, holding the new torch over shattered shelving and various rusted bits of metal. Rotted wooden splinters covered the area.

"Over there." Raliel indicated with her axe. The darkness seemed incredibly dense to the far right corner, despite the light, and strangely rounded.

Aven lit a fresh torch just as the first began to gutter out in a small point of blue flame. He stepped forward, already feeling the strain of the torch and shield extended on his left arm. He found a crude tunnel, barely the height of a man with no room to stand side by side.

"Aven," Vic warned.

They observed the grim remnant of a horrid meal: the small bones of a human child. As Aven leaned to inspect the poor soul's remains, the light disturbed thick black maggots feasting on putrid flesh. They wriggled and burrowed beneath soiled rags. It was amazing they hadn't smelled it before.

"You can still see the teeth marks on the arms and ribs," Vic observed.

Raliel edged forward to see. "Do river boglins eat humans?"

Aven looked to Vic, who shrugged and admitted, "Those teeth marks look too big for a boglin."

"Aren't their teeth pig-like?" Aven asked.

"No, that's bogran, the bigger kind." In Nazar's collection in his study, many curiosities included the bones and skulls of various creatures from bogran and boglin to half-kin and even the massive claw of a grawl.

An authority on the subject, Vic added, "Bog-kind can vary according to their elemental affinities."

That was sufficient for Aven. "Well, it looks like we found what we're here to do. Shall we?"

***

The cramped tunnel went on for almost an hour, primarily due to the tight space forcing them to walk in a low crouch for long stretches at a time, broken by steep declines. Eventually, the burrow-work reached a natural crack that broadened into a vast cavern.

"Looks like a fresh break," Aven whispered.

"What could have done that?" Raliel hissed.

"Probably an earthquake," Vic answered.

"Whatever it was, it opens into a much larger previously sealed cave," Aven thought aloud, "sealed on this side anyway."

They entered the chamber, sticking to the right wall, keeping lit only one torch, held low to hide the light as much as possible. Probably pointless, Aven thought, but no sense in trying to be careless. As far as they could see, there extended, into the dark, a veritable forest of stalagmites, hinting at lofty twins far above. The 'forest' served to conceal their passing, but Aven couldn't help but wonder what else they covered. He had the increasing fear that they'd delved into something beyond their ability. The growing dread was palpable and evident in Raliel's eyes. Vic seemed ready but equally wary.

Their torch was a pin-point in the greater darkness. An abyss felt, if not seen. Nevertheless, there were signs that they were on the right track. There were obvious indications the same route had been used many times recently. These boglins were filthy creatures. Running water could be heard now, roaring somewhere distant, and the visible cavern wall became moist with condensation. In some places, among the stalagmites, small showers drizzled from above. Aven, having long returned his heavy shield to his back, decided there it would stay unless under immediate attack.

"Ahhh! Ewww!" Raliel called out.

"What?" Aven hissed, glaring at her.

"Another one! I'm gonna have to have these boots boiled when we finish this damn trip."

"Keep it down!" he ordered.

She huffed, glaring back, cleaning her boot on a rock to rid it of black boglin feces.

"Quit that scraping, Rali," Aven said over a shoulder, studying the darkness.

"I'm not scraping," she whispered, likewise studying the dark.

"It's coming from ahead." Vic pointed with his sword, his other hand he held to his left ear.

"Should we put the torch out?" Raliel asked. It was a good question.

"How would we see to fight?" Aven whispered. Thinking quickly, he wedged it into the wall above and motioned for everyone to take cover behind the stalagmites. The scraping continued to near as they watched their solo torch flicker. From just outside its penumbra, two puny gray-skinned bipeds tugged on a large iron cage with wooden wheels. It was too big to turn around, so the two creatures pulled it backward. Its heavy steering handle scraped behind with each lurch. Silent, by comparison, came double lines of river boglins, armed crudely with sharpened bones, rocks, driftwood hammers, even an occasional rusty knife or small sword. They paid little attention to the torch above.

Aven counted 16, including the wagon bearers. When he looked at his friends, he saw them jolt with surprise: a garbled growl sounded, stopping the march. From the shadows strutted a nightmare incarnate: a bogrock.

Just like boglins, the larger bograns had their affinities too. A bogrock was a dangerous example. This specimen's eyes glowed yellow in apparent pain from the torch's light. The bogrock roared--gesticulating orders—like tortured gravel. Standing eight feet tall and powerfully built, Aven knew that it wasn't its enormous maul in hand or its tremendous strength that sent chills cascading down their spines. Instead, it was a fact that a bogrock's hide was notorious for being impenetrable. Their only hope was that it would pass without noticing them.

Just when Aven thought things couldn't worsen, while the boglins hurried to extinguish their torch by hurling projectiles, the probable source of the gnawed bones appeared, scampering up to the semi-blinded bogrock. His pet, a wicked reptilian creature, was more horrendous than anything imaginable east of the gorge. A hundred pounds of black scales. Darker spines bristled around its neck and ran down its back to the tip of its tail. The latter, whipped back and forth sporadically as it locked eyes with Aven, making a lunge their way. The bogrock seized its spiked neck holding it at bay and focused on their light source.

Their torch exploded in a shower of sparks. Their last image: the group scraping on; the bogrock's lizard writhing and hissing in their direction.

After a long, intense wait in darkness, Aven dared ignite his fire stick. Then a new torch.

"What now, Aven? That monster blocks our retreat!" Raliel whispered.

"Don't worry, our retreat is covered. The real question is, should we move on or bail out now?"

"We move on," Vic said, "makes no sense to go back empty-handed. If we're lucky, that group was the majority of the nest; worst case, we find a nest of bogrocks and bail."

Aven nodded grimly. "Any ideas on dropping one of those if it comes to it?"

"I might be able to slow it down with my axe."

"Or piss it off," Vic said, jabbing her in the shoulder.

"What about stabbing it through the eyes?" Aven asked Vic, clearly thinking of his throwing knives.

"Difficult, but not impossible." Vic considered the challenge.

"If Aven and I distract it, you could land a throw."

"Sure, I could blind it at least."

"Yeah," Raliel said, "if twenty river boglins don't stop us."

With a sigh of resignation, Aven led, "Okay, it's settled then. Do whatever we can and bail."

They set off at a jog. A ledge appeared in the wall in no time, leading to a flat summit. Vic returned from a quick scouting trip below.

"How many," Aven asked.

"Eight, all boglin, but I can't see in their shacks to know for sure." Vic stood straighter. "There were ten," he added, displaying two slender gray noses dangling from a twine loop on his belt. "Sentries."

Aven beamed, motioning for them to gather close, "Okay, here's the plan...."

***

Igal was hungry. Ever since the crusty no-wet grocks came to their home, they'd known hunger. He closed his bulbous eyes, sniffing the irresistible scent of tenderflesh. His distended gray belly grumbled from beneath prominent ribs. Grock would know and squish him like he had others of Igal's clan if caught stealing a bite or two.

Again, drawn to the remains of the last meal at the camp center, he found two of his brethren gnawing on the bones and gristle of grock's leftovers.

"Igal hungry." He clicked, popped, and whistled in the language of river-kind, one better suited for underwater. Then, busy eating, each reluctantly indicated, with grease spattered chins, toward a garbage heap a few feet away. Only grock was allowed to eat the 'tenders.' He would feast upon the more significant part of their meal and then, once sated, pass it to his boglin warriors. Soon after taking up a fresh, wriggling, and screeching 'savory,' squishing it for consumption.

The lowest enslaved individuals in the pecking order: camp attendants, servants, and wagon pullers—like Igal—were only allowed to feed on what remained. Igal poked and prodded the pile of sticky bones, prying a piece of slobbery meat. He missed eating fish and frogs, his favorite. The memory caused him to drool copiously from his lip-less serrated mouth. His extended black tongue sampled the piece before he munched it ravenously. He could get used to these tasty meaty 'tenders.' Even if he missed the way things were, it would be impossible to go back after acquiring a taste for these. So engrossed

122

in his meal, dark bulbous eyes squeezed shut that he hardly noticed a squishy crunch from each of his fellow diners. So it was to his great wonder to find himself tumbling forward from a bone-jarring knock between his shoulder blades. So dizzy, he hardly registered the abrasive cave floor as he crashed and rolled. Paralyzed with shock, Igal struggled to breathe. *He couldn't feel his lungs*. He couldn't feel his lungs. All he could do was blink his big eyes and stare at a boglin corpse above, convulsing with wisps of smoke rising from its headless neck. Feeling very tired, too tired to watch anymore, Igal slipped into oblivion with the pleasant aroma of seared flesh fresh in his long nose.

***

Aven made for a cave to the right of the camp upon another ledge; it glowed with strange lichen that hung from the ceiling and walls like blue cobwebs. The shelf was outlined in the same lichen, making navigation without torch smooth and swift. Sword and shield ready, he crept into the cave. It was empty, but for a wall of bars at the end. There was a movement within. The lichen had been removed within the jail, leaving its confines in complete darkness. He edged closer, conscious of the increasing sound of shifting inside. The bars looked secure, so he lit a torch.

The bright light revealed five small children huddling in the farthest corner of their prison. The sight wrenched at his soul. He set the torch in the wall and inspected the lock on the cell. It was crude but strong, requiring a heavy key. One he didn't have. "Does anyone know where the key to this lock is?" Although he spoke slow and gentle, his voice sounded too loud and harsh in his ears. No response, just a trembling mass of quivering limbs. They were terrified. He tried again, "I'm here to help. Does anyone know where the key is?"

"Uh-huh…heee…he, the bogrock, has it." A slight little girl in a soiled dress—that seemed to be of fair quality—separated from the group, coming his way. She looked unsure, then set her chin, hands fisted and rigid at her sides. She exhibited strength beyond her youth. Was she six? Seven at most.

"That filthy bogrock keeps it around his neck." She voiced bravely enough but began to quake and shiver, collapsing into wracking sobs.

"I'll be back." He left the children, though he didn't want to, setting off a chorus of pitiful cries of despair. Almost immediately, he ran into his companions.

"Camp's clear," Raliel reported as he registered the stench of burned hair and flesh. Then, he looked to the head of her axe, glowing on her shoulder. "It's self-cleaning," she explained.

"Anything in the cave?" Vic asked.

Aven quickly explained the situation. There was no sure way to expect they could kill the bogrock, get the key, and free the children. They considered the fact that other raiding parties were due to return.

"I won't leave them," Aven was adamant, "but I can't force you to do the same." He'd come up with a plan, but it was dire at best. "I have an idea," he sighed. "I brought a scroll of town portal, which was our escape. I could pass it through the bars, instruct a brave little girl to use it, and facilitate their escape." He met their eyes as the implication settled.

"Which would trap us here," Vic began.

"Leaving us to find a way back," Raliel finished.

"I won't pressure either of you. We could always use the scroll to alert the city guard."

"That would take too long," Raliel dismissed the idea.

"I'd be here with them," Aven reminded her.

"Don't be ridiculous. Aven, they're eating them," Raliel emphasized.

"I'll stay," Vic volunteered.

"Vic that could be suicide, and you're supposed to be the Voice of reason. No, we all stay, send the children, and either make it back or die trying." Raliel decided for all, "Are we in agreement then?"

Everyone nodded.

Aven sent Vic to scout and serve as an advanced warning should the enemy return. He asked Raliel to raid the camp for valuables and search for anything that could break the lock. He returned to the children.

He found the brave girl, face pressed against the bars. "Mister! Please don't leave us, please!"

He could see clean streaks—from tears—stark on her tiny face. "Hush now, and don't be silly. I'd never do that." He soothed and set down his shield and sword to focus on digging through his pouch. "Do you know what a scroll of town portal is?"

"Uh-huh," she affirmed.

"If I told you how, you think you could use one?"

"I-I can try, mister."

He sighed; if Raliel had found anything to break the lock, she would've returned by now. "I'm here with friends, but we need to hurry, Okay?"

"Uh—Okay."

"My name's Aven; what's yours?"

"Drina."

He slid the scroll through the bars, "All you need to do is...wait, do you know how to read, Drina?" she shook her head. He took the scroll and quickly memorized the small incantation before handing it back. "Okay, when I tell you what to say, you've gotta say it just like I do." His heart was ready to break at the sight of her solemn nod. Then, her tiny hands manipulated the coarse parchment into the ready position per his instruction.

"Now repeat after me." The words were foreign and nonsensical to him, but she did remarkably well imitating his words, tone, and inflection, as best as could be hoped. She threw the scroll down and hopped back perfectly.

Nothing happened. Aven's worry and disappointment must've been evident because she stared at him, eyes threatening to overflow with tears.

The four other children, who'd relaxed enough to watch the proceedings, emitted whimpers of freshly lost hope. Brave little Drina hiccupped and wiped her eyes, determined again. Aven vowed that if he lived through this, especially if these children suffered, he would take his vengeance upon the maker of this scroll. Drina stepped forward. "Should we try it ag—"

"Back!" yelled Aven. The scroll began to smoke, sparking into blue flames. The children backed away as much as possible. It sputtered, flashed then—accompanied by a strange otherworldly humming—a portal appeared, wavering like the surface of a puddle. Waiting.

"In you go, all of you!"

The four small children inched forward, it cleared, showing the town portal station beyond, and they darted through screaming. Drina hesitated, "Mr. Aben?"

"You need to hurry, child." He handed her a folded note he'd prepared. "Give this to the portal acolytes, as soon as you're through."

She looked torn, glancing at the portal then him, "Kay." She ran to the bars and whispered, "Thank you." And she was gone in the blink of an eye.

Aven felt relieved, even resigned to their fate but didn't leave until the portal vanished in a puff of smoke. He took one look at the remaining pile of ash and turned heel, scooping up his gear without missing a step. He had the comfort of knowing they'd done the noble thing but hoped it didn't cost the lives of his friends. Maybe they'd get lucky.

***

Aven trotted down just as Raliel began showing Vic the spoils of her search. It wasn't much, just items looted from previous victims, primarily children. However, the trip had funded some living expenses for a while, including the boglin noses collected already. In addition, there was a small collection of coins from the bogrock's shack—judging from the size and smell.

Also, the mangled body of a man, a fighter, judging by the destruction surrounding his corpse, was discovered. His battle recently ended with a crushing blow that shattered his chest and torso, stuck to a wall in a frozen image of gore. Stuck and hardened like a squished bug. His face contorted in a fierce determination as if he never gave up, not even in death. Had he, too, been captured? Or attempted a rescue? They could only speculate. If only he'd waited, he would've had unexpected allies. Oddly, his body wasn't looted. Vic retrieved the fighter's sword, of outstanding quality, the blade shattered. The jeweled hilt looked too valuable to leave, so they took it with great respect.

"He has no supplies, not even a torch. Not a planned expedition," Vic observed.

"He must've traveled and fought in little to no light." But, Raliel said with admiration, "Can you imagine it? All alone? He must've known a captive to display such courage." She decided.

"Let's hope he finds peace now that the children are safe." Aven's tone was solemn, and all understood the underlying message: that they too should find peace in that knowledge. "We should get going before the bogrock and his party return."

Raliel and Vic hesitated, looking anxious.

"What is it?" Aven asked.

"Vic found something that you need to see first."

The ground had risen to the right, over the camp and the prisoner's cave. Its summit ended in an abrupt drop. From this height, they could

126

see the entrance to a tunnel beyond the center. A large pot of ancient design was on each side, capped by tiny tongues of ghostly green flame.

"Massif, most likely," Vic surmised, "the flames burn without fuel and don't create smoke." Just like the stories. Vic pointed beyond, over the entrance. "What does that light out there look like to you?"

The tunnel backlit by green light itself appeared to cut through a colossal mound. The distant source was magnified and refracted all about by unseen waters. There were more fire pots and more to discover beyond the tunnel.

"We've gotta come back to explore these ruins," Aven thought aloud.

"It's for the best; without knowing how far they go, we'll have to resupply to do it properly," Vic agreed.

With one last glance, the team turned to go. There was some talk of taking the right wall back to explore and possibly avoid running into the bogrock, but this idea was rejected. Instead, it was agreed to take the same direct path and rely upon Vic's scouting—and heightened hearing—to buy them time to hide. If necessary.

As far as they could estimate, the necessity came—at the halfway point. The companions settled behind dark stalagmites to wait for the procession to pass. Aven held ready his firestick, prepared to light a torch at the first sign of trouble. They were nearly out of torches.

Almost out of the cave, too. They'd be free to move as soon as the caravan of horror passed. After waiting an appropriate amount of time, Aven lit a torch.

They made progress along the cavern wall as quickly as they could. The bogrock's party would've reached their camp, possibly even hunting them now. No sooner had the thought occurred to Aven, Vic said, "We're being followed."

Pointed out, the group could easily spot a pair of yellow eyes to their right, flickering in and out of view. The skitter of scaly talons and familiar hissing betrayed the bogrocks pet. Finally, Aven spoke, "We should run, NOW!"

Thinking quick, Aven lit two more torches, passing them out with instructions to place them strategically should it come to a fight. He almost believed they'd make it to the exit fissure when the first boglins came rushing from the stalagmites. Instead, they'd taken a shorter route—not good.

Vic and Raliel tossed their torches in front of them, long sword and axe ideal for long sweeps, slowing the advance. Aven stabbed his torch above their heads and took his place, back against the wall, covering their right toward the camp. The boglin's initial wariness, for fire and weapons, was abandoned when a fierce roar reverberated from far beyond.

The river boglins became quick and desperate in their fighting. From the shadows rushed five simultaneously. A crude trident of bone shattered on Aven's bronze shield, answered by an overhead chop from his broad blade, exploding right through boglin skull. Its lifeless form collapsed, forgotten. He shield-rammed a stone hammer strike. The stone head cracked and hung limply from its rag-wrapped handle. To its credit, the boglin wasted no time in swinging the instant flail. It came close to landing a strike but was met by bronze even as its gray thigh was bit by iron. Aven's blade hewed straight through, embedding in the calf of its other leg. Three more boglins came to take their place. One leaped over the fallen with a shriek and overhead swinging rock. Aven met it with an extended blade, skewering it and using his shield to remove the body.

Seeing the carnage, the other two became wary enough for Aven to risk a glance at his companions: smoking limbs and corpses lay before their blades. The circle of boglins grew increasingly dense.

"Tighten up! Let's keep moving!" Aven ordered.

They snatched torches and marched warily, careful to keep their backs to the wall, as Aven covered their flank with shield and blade. Five boglin weapons rained blows upon his shield, emboldened by their retreat, searching for a hit. His counter-attacks were reduced to wild swings under the tumult, scoring only glancing blows. The river boglins soon realized their advantage in numbers and pressed in harder. The friends were unable to continue, trapped. Spears, hammers, and small blades beating down.

Aven knew his friends must be receiving the worst of it. The sound of it tortured his conscience. But, because of his more excellent defense, he remained relatively unscathed. So he had to turn the tide, even if it meant taking some damage. With good timing, he shield rushed the next volley, cracking weapons hard and leaving the safety of the wall. In three monster strides, he managed to topple four boglins, stomping his heavy boots hard on their tangled bodies. The pleasing feel of cracking bones was surpassed only by the music of their howls of pain. Still fending off blows with his shield, Aven thrust his blade down into each fiend, methodically backing to his original position. Then he dropped his shield, took his broadsword in both hands, and rushed headlong, swinging wildly into the press of bodies. Aven charged, striking and slicing, moving in an arc; now, Aven was behind the enemies engaging his friends. Once through the press, he turned full force on the backs of the six boglins trading blows with Raliel and Vic. Each unexpected chop and cleave felled a boglin in a heap. Spinning around to meet the next wave, Aven found only fleeing shadows. Not missing a beat, he quick-stepped to his shield, returning it to his arm. They stood catching their breath.

Raliel wasn't exhausted but had several purpling lumps covering her arms and head. Vic seemed unharmed, at odds with the many scuffs and nicks in his leather suit. Before Aven could retrieve his torch, Vic warned, "Aven."

Another group of boglins approached, squinting at the light and carrying a small cage on poles; crude weapons came to hand, their burden abandoned as they absorbed the scene. For a moment, the groups faced off in silence. The crackle of the torch flame. The creak of leather. Then the boglins fled into the dark, abandoning their load. Aven signaled for them to grab their fires and move on.

***

Drina scowled at the acolytes. They'd sent for the city guard—at the children's unexpected arrival— mainly because they weren't sure what to do. Several of the children had broken down bawling for their parents or out of relief when reality dawned on them—causing quite a scene. But not Drina. Not when her rescuers remained in danger. She'd heard enough to understand that they'd given up their way back by saving her.

Nevertheless, she was determined to do all she could. The portal acolytes refused to do anything but—to her frustration—implore that she wait patiently for the authorities. They wouldn't let her leave. She glared at them then turned, on the pretense of checking on the other kids, to hide the tremble of her lip and tearing eyes.

She mustn't cry. Not yet. She shuddered at what could be happening to their saviors, which brought memories of the horrors she'd seen. Things no young person should endure. She held onto the face of her hero 'Aben' and whispered, "Bright Company," with a distant look. If only they could make it to safety.

Boots pounded up the marble steps as the city guard arrived.

It felt counter-productive to scout by torchlight in the dark. Vic's enhanced hearing couldn't alleviate the fact that he was blind without light, his blindness reducing him to scout a mere measure of terrain and nearness of their goal. He tried to move swiftly, careful to not extinguish the weakening flame of his fluttering half spent torch. Left behind, Vic could no longer see the light from the others but would only have to follow the wall a short run to meet them. The exit seemed much farther than he remembered.

He was just beginning to wonder if he should head back when the pitch-dark fissure appeared on his left. Just big enough for a person to fit. He stuck the nearly spend torch between a narrow split in the crack on instinct. His right glove glided over the cavern wall, his sword extended in his left.

The darkness played tricks on his eyes. He imagined colors and flashes as his brain processed the complete lack of stimuli; he resisted the urge to shut his eyes, knowing he must spot the others and gauge his approach to avoid an accident. Instead, he concentrated on steady movement, mentally envisioning the terrain he passed. The wall continued smooth, with only a slight curving. He stepped as light-footed as speed would allow.

His stealth and heightened auditory senses allowed him to detect the skitter of claws, among other inexplicable indications of life. He sped up, and so did the clawed pursuit. As he slowed to negotiate a curve, the chase accelerated. He squeezed his eyes shut, focusing on the nearness of the sound. He had to time it just right. Then, the noise vanished at the last possible moment—a leap! Vic swung his blade in a broad upward sweep, a swift backhand that seemed almost a miss until he felt the slight catch, rasping ring of a clean sever—followed by a furious thrashing and scrambling on two fronts.

He quickly moved on, eyes wide but sightless, ears ringing from the dead calm. He seized control of his breathing, relaxing his body. He wouldn't be able to hear over the beating of his heart otherwise. Then, far behind, he was startled by a roar that chilled his blood— gravelly rage.

Aven's torch appeared around the next bend, and Vic whistled before approaching them. Raliel's torch was near guttered, while a fresh one blazed in Aven's shield hand. Both had their weapons drawn and ready.

"The exit's near. I marked it with my torch; it will guide us if we hurry."

Aven perked up visibly and pressed on, lighting the way. "We've got this."

The need to vocalize—quite possibly their last word—was outweighed by the hope that silence and speed might bring escape and life. Shortly, they discovered the remains of the bogrock's pet, split neatly in half.

As calm and collected as Vic attuned his body, as much as he relied on his martial skill, nothing could diminish the plunge of his heart as they rounded the next bend. They arrived just in time to see—two spans ahead—the bogrock smash Vic's torch with its colossal stone club.

A shower of sparks. The fierce glare of glowing yellow eyes turned on them. Two bursts of sparks lit from well-aimed throwing knives. Both ineffective. Aven paused, only to place his torch and don his shield. There was no need to say a word; they all knew the best strategy. Aven would draw the attack to his greater defense, Raliel would harry, and Vic would seek a sure kill.

Aven shield-rushed, drawing back just in time to escape a wind-buffeting swing of the monstrous club. The bogrock positioned himself between them and the fissure in a few more sweeps. From the dark came glowing axe, Raliel connecting blow after blow to its left flank. Sparks showered the ground with each hit, leaving red welts on the rugged hide, but they didn't penetrate. They did enrage it. Aven launched a series of thrusts and feints to regain the massive bogrock's attention.

Vic lurked unseen, calculating and biding his time, envisioning the perfect maneuver. The 'grock's eyes flared as he swatted club and fist at his foes in frustration. Now. Vic took his shot, coming low from the shadow, into a vertical corkscrew. His sword point hit its target, but the angle wasn't perfect. The tip pierced under the lid and through the left eyebrow with a loud pop of toughened hide. It was all he could do to hold onto his sword as the 'grock stood its full eight feet and swatted at the wound, whipping to and fro. Finally, Vic's sword broke free, sending him tumbling out of sight.

With a two-handed flurry of enormous blows from its club, the grock unleashed its rage upon Aven. It ignored the welts from Raliel, its backside thick with muscle and rock. Each hit made a 'bong' sound on Aven's shield, finishing with a crunch of breached bronze.

Raliel attacked with increasing panic as Aven abandoned the sword to brace his smashed shield with both hands. The bogrock's blows intensified, beating Aven down into a crouch, clearly holding on for his very life.

Before Vic could circle the 'grock, two things happened: the bogrock's club glanced off of Aven's shield, knocking him unconscious, and with a wild back fisted swing, it caught Raliel by her hair. The bogrock shook her like a doll, slamming her with finality between it and Vic. The bogrock absorbed a shower of throwing knives and spikes.

It was over unless Vic could end it now, so he led with a series of vicious strikes, doing his best to dodge that whirring club. Finally, the torchlight winked out, leaving only glowing yellow eyes visible. Holding back, Vic was out of range of the invisible stone club. The bogrock took pleasure in the anticipated kill and uttered a gravelly gurgle. With complete darkness, the 'grock's vision cleared, eyes widening to the size of yellow saucers.

Strangely, its silhouette sharpened, as white light, engulfed it from behind. From the fissure a blinding flash seared the image in Vic's eyes. The bogrock was sent to its hands and knees, with a now visible look of utter disbelief, mirroring Vic's.

The bright light source stepped away from the fissure, bathing the cave in true light for twenty spans, enveloping the bogrock. A dozen boglin spectators fled. Something big screeched angrily above and departed in leathery flapping.

An earth-toned massif brought his hammer down, hammerhead shining so bright it couldn't be seen, slamming into the top of the bogrock's skull. The head didn't split; instead, its contents exploded through sightless eye sockets, painting the ground with bone shards and mush, transforming the head into a rock-studded bag of refuse.

Though the river boglins were no longer near, their distant shouts echoed gleefully.

Aven lay still as death, while Raliel groaned softly. Vic rushed to Aven, skidding on his knees, and checked for breathing. Aven snored, a fist-sized bulge covered the left side of his head.

The massif was muttering over Raliel's body. Vic tensed as that devastating hammer rose over her. Wisps of light poured down upon

Raliel as she sat upright, her groans subsiding. The hammer's light diminished significantly.

"Is he fit to travel?" the massif barked at Vic as he rifled through the bogrock's scant belongings. Then, finally, he seemed to find what he was looking for: a small bulging leather pouch. He prodded gruffly, "Well?"

"I don't know," Vic answered.

Irritated by the response, the burly massif conducted his inspection, "We'll have to carry him." Then, the massif negotiated Aven onto his left shoulder with one strong arm, "Get the girl."

Vic sheathed his sword to retrieve Aven's fallen broadsword.

It seemed the hammer's light waned further. The surrounding dark pressed in, and so did whispers of movement beyond. The glint of strange colored eyes flickered in and out of view.

Raliel and Vic were herded into the exit and left in its dark shade as their savior's light ventured back into the cavern. The massif returned with Aven's ruined shield, setting it just inside the fissure. His hammer dimmed orange. The shield began to radiate a molten glow, throwing heat back as if fresh from the forge.

The massif veteran began pounding and welding the metal with his hammer, sealing off the cave. They watched in fascination as the massif blew a veritable gust of wind, cooling the metal quick enough to make the bronze and rock buckle and creak.

With Aven draped over a shoulder, the enigmatic massif warrior eyed them like an exasperated parent. "Move it. No sense in hangin' around."

CHAPTER TWELVE

A ven first noticed the pleasant drone of conversation as he slowly surfaced from a deep and restful sleep. He was in no hurry, enjoying the warm comfort, not yet trying to recognize or make sense of the talking around him. Probably mom and dad preparing the morning meal. *Now that piqued his interest.*

"He's smiling."

Strange, what was Raliel doing over this early?

"Maybe he's in worse shape than we thought." Vic too? Heightened consciousness brought on the unwelcome awareness of several deep aches all over his body and head. "Oh…my head." The muscles of his temple were bunched in a knot. "What's the matter with my head?" Aven tried to sit up but was forced down. Voices protested his movement.

"Take it easy, there's nothing broken, but rushing will only make you dizzy."

The strange voice spurred him to open his eyes, but only the right one responded. He blinked his right eye repeatedly until its bleary vision cleared. The fight with the bogrock came back to him; he was relieved to find the others were fine. He relaxed involuntarily, and restraining hands withdrew. He tried again to open his left eye but only managed a painful peek. They were all in the abandoned storeroom. Still under the city. "Bogrock?"

"Destroyed," Vic said, "Our friend Mendel here showed up—"

"And a good thing I did, or there'd be nothing but bloody smears to mark your existences." By the light of a small fire, Mendel was fashioning a torch with what looked to be a thigh bone and filthy rags.

Mendel lit it and approached Aven. He raised a thick hand over Aven's head. From the calloused palm sparked small beams of light. They grew into white tendrils, descending to bathe Aven's face and head. There was a flicker, the tiniest moment, when the pain felt excruciating, but it was gone fast—followed immediately by comfort and warmth, like waking from a nap in your favorite chair. Aven's eye, though no longer in pain, remained swollen shut. He reached to feel it.

"That'll have to do for now. Can you walk?" Mendel growled.

Aven sat up and got to his feet without a hitch. "I feel fine."

Raliel smiled, then scowled in thought. Something was bothering her; Vic looked more severe than usual, offering a nod before heading to the broken door to wait. Mendel held his torch high, giving Aven a chance to study his features. As the only massif he'd seen, possibly the only one left, the urge to stare was hard to resist. Mendel was part of an elemental species, as much part of the world as the hills and mountains deep.

"Well, don't just stand there—here," Mendel said, giving him the torch, followed by a nudge no less imposing than a leaning boulder.

Aven found Raliel, axe in hand, a stern look on her face. Did he do something? He reached for his sword, finding an empty scabbard.

"Looking for this?" Vic tossed the broadsword hilt first. It slapped Aven's palm with an iron thrum. "Afraid you're shield had a higher calling," he smirked.

"Higher calling?" Aven asked Raliel.

She just shrugged, marching off with her axe lighting the way.

When they finally exited the sewer, the sky lightened with the early dawn. The air was crisp and welcoming. Aven took a deep breath through his nose. Never believing he'd see the day when the slums smelled so sweet. He heard the others doing the same.

They dutifully checked their equipment and each other once more. Finally, a shuffling of boots gave them pause as they exited the service alley.

"Halt!" From cover, and outside the alley, rushed several pikemen in gray conical helmets, mail suits, and forest green tunics—city guard.

"Aven of Bright Company," he said, careful to keep both hands visible as he displayed his guild crest. The pike points were uncomfortably close, hemming them in a tight crescent. The guards noticeably relaxed at the sight of the emblem crest but kept their pikes trained.

"We got a report of boglins in the city. Kidnappings."

"At ease, men." Weapons lowered, and men divided, making way for a tall man. He matched the guard's uniforms except for the addition of a slate-colored cuirass encasing his torso, and a mail-gripped, two-handed greatsword sticking at an angle over his right shoulder. He displayed a patch of his own. "What brings your company to the slums at this hour…Aben, is it?"

"Aven. We have accepted a contract to investigate boglin reports too. 'Sergeant'?"

"Sergeant," he affirmed, looking over Aven's shoulder to the sewer entrance and the party members, "good morning Mendel."

"Sergeant Land," he answered with a nod.

Land focused on Aven's swollen eye. "What's the status of your contract?"

"Complete." Aven hadn't had the time to acknowledge the fact until now. But, with it said, he felt pride.

"What inn are you staying in?" Land inquired; his men were already drifting off to inspect the sewer entrance or speaking quietly.

"Midways," Aven said.

"I'll walk you as you fill me in."

They walked and talked as the sky brightened. Aven described their adventure, leaving out the possible massif ruins. When he described the fallen fighter near the camp, Land muttered, 'Scion's Shield', and nodded for Aven to continue. Vic took over, telling of the battle with the bogrock and Mendel's improvisation with Aven's shield. Aven was surprised when Land chuckled. Mendel just nodded. At this point, the sergeant paused to order his two remaining guards to rouse the city mason so that they could reinforce the barricade.

Soon they were standing in front of Midways. "I bid you all good morning, Bright Company." Land smiled, then added with all seriousness, "You've done a service for the people of Midhaven; we thank you." He clapped a fist over his heart. "A report of your actions will be made as per policy. You should check in with your guild master." With that, he marched off.

Aven addressed his team, "I guess I'll meet you all at dinner unless anyone wants to share breakfast in an hour or so."

"I'm going to sleep…after a hot bath," Raliel said.

"I've gotta check-in and get rest too," Vic said, looking to the north.

Aven turned to Mendel, but before he could say a word, the massif rumbled, "Don't you know how to do anything right? First, we split the treasure!" He reached his belt and produced a small leather pouch, filled to bursting.

"From the bogrock," Vic recalled aloud.

Mendel made a pouring motion with it, Aven cupped his hands, looking conspicuously around the abnormally empty street. Mendel upended the sack. Four stones tumbled free. One large uncut gem, and three fine jewels of green, red, and blue. All but Mendel drew breath and neared. "Beautiful," Raliel subconsciously touched the red gem, which glowed like an ember. Even the customarily subdued Vic grinned, eyes sparkling.

"There's one for each," Mendel asserted, "that's the way it works, the adventurer's code, but it's your call." He looked at Aven, waiting.

"Sounds fine to me, one for each. Thank you, Mendel." But the massif continued to look expectant. His eyes looked pointedly from the gems to the others, then back at Aven, brows reaching record height.

"Oh! Uh, let's see here; Vic, the green is yours. Rali, the ruby calls you." She nodded vigorously and retrieved it. "And it would only be fair to give you the largest since you not only found it but saved us."

"Agreed." Mendel snatched the uncut gemstone. Aven stared at the remaining blue sapphire and closed his fist.

Raliel wasted no time entering the inn. Without further ado, Vic struck off as well. The sound of sweeping and door latch disengaging increased as the day began.

"Mendel?"

"Yeah?"

"Thanks for your help." Aven wasn't sure, but Mendel winced a little at the acknowledgment.

"Don't mention it. You were just lucky I happened to be passing through." He, too, turned, stalking off before Aven could continue the conversation. He stood alone and looked again at the sapphire. It looked valuable. Tucking it away, he entered the inn. Not to sleep, there was no time but to clean up, eat, and head back out. Though duty called, as a leader, it was more than the excitement of success that made it impossible to sleep.

He was sobered by how close they came to being destroyed. The remains of the bogrock's victims flashed in his mind, curdling his stomach. Especially the scene of 'Scion's Shield.' A skilled fighter. His life ended when he'd been overwhelmed. Aven had to do everything he could to ensure their safety. With that firmly set in mind, he headed inside.

***

Raliel stared in the mirror, brushing the tangles from her hair with a scowl. Her skin was still flush from the hot bath. Her small clothes hung to dry over the tub's rim. She continued taking a good long look at herself: brown towel wrapped around her ample bosom, strong arms—well within female beauty—muscles rippled as she combed. Her changed hair—now blond, red, and white locks—gave the impression of flames. Hair she had never been allowed to cut growing up, 'you might have the Fireheart mane,' her father always said, 'something to be prized and shown,' he'd expressed as if she was one of his horses.

Her eyes flicked over to her ancestral axe, its crescent blade etched in red designs, balanced by a spike. It rested within reach against the wall.

But back to the full head of hair that had nearly cost her life and almost broke her head from her shoulders, she recalled the sensation of her neck joints popping back into place and feeling flooding her hands and feet as she regained consciousness. Vic had confirmed the rest. If not for Mendel, she'd have died. When she'd decided to join Aven, she never imagined things would get this hard. It frustrated her. She'd trained in the axe; she had enhanced strength and endurance—

a flaming axe—yet instantly, all negated because of the hair. Prized or not, she couldn't allow it to hinder her again.

It humiliated her. Tears stung her eyes, and homesickness overwhelmed her. She yearned for the simple, carefree life across the gorge. I am not a little girl, she thought. Raliel's anger reinforced her resolve to refuse self-pity. Failure was not an option.

She turned her attention to the rune talisman around her neck and instantly knew Aven's presence in the next room. Renewing her resolve, she looked at her hair, then her axe, and sighed.

***

Adam seldom had downtime. Liz kept him busy seven days a week. But things would slow enough occasionally, and she would send him on errands. Like right now.

Stable work and hearty eating had served his body well. In addition, his meditations, and practice with enhancement magic, helped him build up and adapt much quicker than expected.

Everyone knew each other in their area, and since his affiliation, with Eddie and Liz, he'd never been bothered by hoodlums again. However, he didn't push his luck. Twice he'd seen the gang of teens who'd harassed him when he'd been lost and hungry. They'd acted like he didn't exist each time, actively looking past him. Fine by him.

It was early, and Liz sent him to her brother's with a list of items and a steaming pie stuffed with eggs, cheese, green peppers, and sausage. Adam just finished cleaning his hands of grease—noticing only slight smudging on the list—as he approached Ed's shop.

Ed was always open early. In the hopes of securing as much business as possible. Liz always sent for as many of the stable's needs as he could provide. For this reason, Ed dealt in other than magical items—out of necessity—like animal care products. Since the city funded Liz's stable, its patronage helped keep him afloat.

Adam enjoyed running errands. He could browse a little and talk with Ed about new items, lore, and what new abilities he'd taught. Liz didn't pay Adam, besides food, clothes, and shelter, but Adam was content. Not only was he alive, thriving, and learning skills that would serve him all his life, but he was allowed a quiet place—in the loft—to meditate and practice his sources. Not to mention how much the siblings helped fill the void of family in his life.

The familiar jingle of bells sounded as he entered Ed's shop. He found a rare surprise this early: a customer engaged Ed over the counter. Ed's eyes flicked to Adam, then to the shelves, instructing him with a tilt of his head to browse or otherwise occupy himself for a while.

Adam ensured he was far enough to give privacy, reached a source in his neck, focused on the desired application, and then surged some energy to this aim. Instantly he could hear their quiet conversation.

"I can't afford to ever pay for something like this—it must be worth a fortune!" Ed hissed, then asked suspiciously. "Where'd you get it?"

In response, a deep growl rumbled, "Found it on a legitimate quest, Ed."

"Since when did you take quests, Mendel?"

"Not important. Do you want my business, or should I take it somewhere else?"

"It's not that. It's just that I could never pay you the way things are, not even in a year," he said, gesturing around the empty store, forcing Adam to hunch and feign interest in some bottle in his hand.

"Ed, I know things are slow, but you're a friend. Consider it partial payment to what I owe your uncle."

"You can't always use that excuse. It's just not right. I feel I'm taking advantage."

"You're not. How about this then: half is yours, and for my half, simply account it to my tab, and I will only shop here for supplies."

Ed huffed, knowing Mendel shopped nowhere else, but also knowing when to concede to the stubborn massif, "Do you need more potions?"

"Yes, please."

"Okay, I've prepared the usual, but I'm doubling it! I don't like owing."

"Thank you, my friend."

Ed went off mumbling, "He thanks me? Massifae!"

Massifae? Adam sneaked a peek at the customer: unusual stoutness, a massive hand—containing double the bone and sinew of a large man's—tapped the counter with resonating thumping.

"That's bad manners, you know." Adam winced from the still-amplified rebuke. He hastily dispelled the enhancement, then subconsciously cooled his eardrums with a healing rush.

"Spell-caster, ay?" the massif turned, "I sense some real talent in one so young."

Adam's face flushed, put on the spot.

"What's your name, human?"

"Adam, um, sir massif." Mendel smiled benevolently and subtly waved a hand in Adam's direction. Then, his eyes widened. "Light have mercy, boy, you possess strength not commonly found in humans so young."

"Um, yeah, I practice every day."

Still grinning, Mendel mouthed the word 'practicing' with a roll of his eyes. "Light and healing are strong." Mendel's eyes were hooded now, his hand held out, swaying. "Clothing enhancement," he muttered to himself, "and what is that now?" Then, finally, Mendel's eyes popped open, and he roared, "HO!" His eyes shot straight to the ruby ring, or instead to where it hid—on Adam's hand—beneath the folds of his red robe. Mendel grinned at Adam and winked.

"Here you go, old friend." Ed's eyes flicked, reading the scene, "Everything okay?"

"I've just been talking to this wonderful young man." Mendel winked at Adam again. "But I've gotta run; you both have a nice day." Mendel hefted the sack of potions, then paused to rummage through it, "Ed, this is triple the usual." He sighed a blast of breath, and before Ed could respond, said, "Tryin' to keep me away eh? Well, it won't work! Ha!" He left, patting Adam's shoulder with surprising gentleness, and was gone in a tinkling of brass bells.

"Who was that?" Adam looked star-struck.

"Just an old friend." Ed wore a dreamy, lopsided grin, staring at the door. Then, he shook his head and focused on Adam. "It's a good day, Adam. If you brought a list, go ahead and put it together, you know where everything is, but I have an errand for you before you leave. So check in with me when you're ready."

Ed had already started preparing parchment and ink and set down a rough gray rock. It had a deep pink sparkle shining through. "Well, go on now." Ed motioned absently with his quill.

Adam leaped into action, heading to the back with his smudged list and a mind filled with questions.

***

Vic stood outside Taberah's sanctum, turning the emerald gemstone in the torchlight. Pricey. More valuable than what he sought, but not more important than preventing failure. The cavern's utter darkness had been as close to vulnerable as he'd ever felt. Fighting blind was not something he wanted to repeat, especially with creatures of the dark.

Moreover, he knew the brotherhood possessed magical items not found in shops. So before going on any more excursions—guild or brotherhood related—he wanted to make a better effort at properly equipping himself. He raised his fist to knock, but the door swung inward.

"Master," Vic greeted. "Sorry to intrude."

Taberah was stripped to the waist, covered in a sheen of sweat. He was going through a series of martial forms unfamiliar to Vic.

"It's no interruption."

It didn't seem to be. Taberah continued to stretch and balance, strike and hold, all with supreme control and calm. Finally, he asked, "What's bothering you, son? I thought you'd be exultant after you and your friends' recent success."

Vic started, then relaxed; this was a master of the brotherhood. If anyone knew, it would be him. "That's what bothers me, master...I felt unprepared and was unable to do anything." Taberah's eyebrows raised at the shrill tone. Vic quickly calmed himself before continuing, "There was a point where we almost failed because of my inability. I could hardly use stealth or scout because of my blindness. I couldn't puncture the hide of the bogrock or execute a proper kill-strike. But, if it weren't for a random stroke of luck, we'd be done."

"You mean the massif. Hardly random." An odd remark. "What is it you seek?"

"Training, master, and access to specialized items." Vic wanted to be as direct as possible about it. Rejection was preferable to lack of assertiveness.

"You are indeed ready for training. Enhancements, access to enchanted items is something earned. Never bought," Taberah said with a look at Vic's clenched fist. "Visit our armorer to replenish your items. Once completed, return to me for your next lesson." He continued his routine, dismissing Vic.

"Yes, master, thank you."

As the heavy door boomed shut, master Taberah smiled with approval, then struck and held.

***

Aven bathed, dressed in civilian clothes, and buckled his sword around his waist. He crossed the street, following the chimes of the guild smith's hammer. His battered leather-mail armor was bundled up, boots and all, for exchange against the cost of what Aven sought. With Mendel's find, he hoped to afford a significant equipment upgrade.

Weaving through light foot traffic, he was greeted by the sun, barely cresting the city's massive east wall. The air still nipped with morning's chill as the wall's shadow began to retreat. He shivered but from excitement.

He entered the shop; a slight pause in hammering suggested the smith had noticed. Aven walked straight to the armor section and looked upon a newly completed suit of plate armor configured on a sturdy stand for display. The steel wasn't shiny but slate-gray like the city guard's armor. It was a well-engineered piece, built not for flash or beauty but for durability. His heart soared at the thought of trying on—or walking out with—something he'd dreamed of owning since he was a boy. Beyond that, though, Aven was haunted by the memory of being battered with only a shield to block. He was blocking with no ability to strike back. With a suit like this, he could've done more. The plates were attached at the joints by ring-mail and well-hidden straps for adjustment. The plates overlapped, just so, for maximum coverage. Steel plate covered the entire body, like an insect's carapace, giving the appearance of musculature in the torso and limbs, complete with steel boots jointed for movement. The helmet looked intimidating. The single thick piece of solid steel was rounded for fit and broken by a slit from base to the nose bridge and two scowling eye-ports. Aven leaned close to inspect lumps of steel made to look like a bunch of brow muscles. Not all functionality then, and skillfully worked in a purposefully crude manner that only enhanced the menacing appearance.

After investigation, he figured he could afford the suit using the sapphire and have some change left over for living expenses. Or he could seriously upgrade his weapon. But he couldn't do both. After a moment, he decided that defense with a broader range of movement was more important. Attack strength could be balanced by sheer ferocity. He would make it so.

Still, he couldn't resist looking at the weapons wall—a familiar gleam brought on a longing sigh.

He still needed to exchange the jewel for cash at the guildhall and pick up the contract funds. But not without taking care of this first. The smith had just quenched his current project in a barrel of liquid, hanging his heavy tongs before approaching Aven. 'Onin' patted his gloves on his leather apron, freeing himself of invisible filings of ore. "What can I do for you guildsman?"

"I'd like to discuss selling my leather-mail armor and purchase that one."

Onin's eyebrows raised with the corners of his mouth. "A durable long-term piece, truth be told, I had a mind of keeping it as I made it. I can have it ready now if you like. You'll, of course, need an instructor and training?"

"Uh, training? How much is that?" Aven began to worry.

"Not much, only a small fee, for a guildsman, but it'll take a week or two. Go see guildsman Malek for that." Noticing Aven's look, he added, "You can find him or any info on guild member instructors at the guildhall."

"Okay, thank you, I'll be right back to pick up the plate." Aven took the last look at the silver prize he so coveted on the weapons wall. Sighing, he thought, it'll have to wait.

Onin smiled, a knowing twinkle in his eyes. "You should have Cassandra look at that eye while you're there." Then, he set about preparing the suit of plate.

A dozen strides from the smith, Aven's stomach fluttered with anticipation at the guildhall entrance when it dawned on him: they'd completed their first major contract as an honest company. He donned his best professional look and approached the front desk.

The front room was empty, and the padding of his leather shoes seemed loud. The bulletin board continued to show various posters and promises of reward, but he noticed some blank spots; someone had been busy, or perhaps people had just given up.

The clerk acknowledged his approach with quick eye contact before returning to his paperwork. Again, he paused to open a ledger, inking in notations and returning to the stack. Aven noticed a rectangular placard with 'Erek' stenciled in gold.

Patiently waiting, Aven watched as Erek scribbled on, maintaining professionalism and calm, though he didn't feel either. His mind wandered back to the plate armor and the many other things involved that he hadn't thought about. He pondered whether he should go find Malek and Cassandra when Erek interrupted his thinking with an "ahem." Aven didn't hesitate, "Good morning, I've come to report Bright Company's success in finding and eliminating the boglin threat…including one bogrock." Aven finished with pride.

"Any evidence of the bogrock?" Erek asked.

"No." Aven struggled to keep a stoic face.

"Well, I wouldn't mention it; the guild can lawfully acknowledge only verifiable acts. Claims without proof can require serious sanctions," Erek said this without a hint of smugness and genuinely wanted to help. Aven just nodded, humbly accepting the correction. Erek shuffled his papers and continued, "The city guard has confirmed that your company is responsible for ending the boglin threat and completing your contract. Congratulations and thanks, from the guild; here's your payment," and pushed forward previously counted coins. It was much less than anticipated and would cover little expenses. He might have to review his spending plans. Without complaint, he dutifully scooped up the payment and poured it into his money pouch.

As he turned, Erek spoke, "Not so fast, guildsman."

Aven turned back to find quite a few more silver and even gold stacks on the counter.

"For the rescue of the missing boy, Zan: 100 silver; quest complete. For the rescue of missing sisters, Ginnie and Lia: 200 silver; quest complete." Eyes bulging, Aven began carefully filling his coin pouch. He was going to need a bigger one before long. "And for the rescue and safe return of Alicia Lumin: one gold royal, and this invitation to Lumin Manor."

"Lumin Manor?" Aven asked, feeling overwhelmed and giddy by the implications.

Erek raised a brow and slid a sealed envelope with the invitation printed in bold black ink. "Guildsman, Aven, you've brought us honor among the citizens of Midhaven. Perhaps even more than you realize yet. Either way, the guild wishes to reward you with 72 hours of free training from an instructor." He slid a parchment voucher to Aven. "Also, a scroll of town portal and these assorted potions." Over the counter came a small sack.

"Thank you." Aven didn't know what else to say.

"Keep up the good work, guildsman; new quests are also available.

In addition, your company's stature will continue to qualify you for more demanding jobs."

"I'll return when we're ready, Erek."

The clerk nodded and got back to work. Aven tried as hard as he could to depart without too much jingling of the coin; it was almost comical how loud it seemed. A huge grin split his face. They were rich. At this rate, he seriously considered shopping for a strongbox. The sapphire!

He turned back, producing the gem just in time for Erek to notice, "I almost forgot; I need to have this appraised."

Erek's eyes sparkled with genuine interest. Taking the gem, he murmured, "No proof of a bogrock, eh?" shaking his head; he retrieved a curious eyeglass, which he held by squinting an eye, examining the stone in the light. Then, nodding with approval, he told Aven an amount very close to what he'd expected. It was worth just enough to buy his suit, with a good amount of loose silver. With his cut of the contract pay, he could even afford a new weapon to complete it. He didn't try to hide his joy, as he thanked Erek and headed out to finish his errands.

***

"A practical look for you, Raliel." Marcus approved, "Much more battle-worthy."

Raliel ignored the compliment while holding out a soiled linen sack.

"What's this now?"

"Payment for more training."

"In boglin marks?" he noted her seriousness and shrugged, "money's money." Then, after peering in the sack, estimating the severed noses, he said, "This is more than necessary."

Vic had given over all the boglin marks to her to take to legion HQ for compensation. "I need to learn."

"You're good already. You can't rush mastery; it'll come with time and experience." Marcus stood outside his living quarters, on the southernmost edge of the training grounds. He wasn't used to his students prodding him so early in the morning. But he already figured that this warrior wasn't the average student.

"I need to do better, now." She allowed barely restrained fury to pour from her eyes and was almost distracted by the twinge of surprise in Marcus's own.

He broke eye contact with a shake of his head. "Come on then; it's time you began to learn."

Her forehead bunched. "What have I been paying for then?"

"What people pay to be taught. Nobody wants to learn anymore, and they're certainly not going to pay for giving up too much time and effort."

"Well, I don't have much time," Raliel added, clearly impatient.

"Of course not; they never do; It'll be up to you to compensate with effort or waste what time you have. You're more than welcome to waste all the money you want. I'll do my best to make you dread coming here to train for the next several days. One complaint or failure to give your best will terminate the program."

She noted they were angling toward the sparring ground and instinctively unhooked her axe.

"No more practice blades, and NO MERCY!" She barely blocked his battle-axe in a jarring ring of steel and sparks. Recovering her footing, she fell into the familiar routine—or tried to. Marcus pressed on mercilessly, keeping her unbalanced, reeling back on her heels. Even with her enhanced strength, she was hard-pressed to prevent a fatal blow from landing. He couldn't mean to kill her, could he?

She couldn't spare the focus to ponder. Everything became a blur of motion—a daze of nearly concurrent impacts. Her numbing hands held onto her weapon with all her might. Something inside her seemed to scream, a rage that clarified her vision and movement—a heightened combat awareness of her body position with her opponent's. She yearned to release a bellow of fire. Instead, she restrained it with a growl, meeting strike for strike, no longer blocking, and just knocking blows aside in smooth arcs of perfect anticipation, grace, and focus. She was in her element, in the zone now, but so was Marcus.

He unleashed a flurry with a growl of his own scoring a slice across her mid-section. She'd left her armor at the inn, so it burned and felt wet; a cut that would've scraped chainmail now seared her every movement. Another gash across her forearm caused her to hesitate in shock—he's really trying to cut her! The realization sent a spike of fear through her system. A crushing boot to the chest and she was on her back, blinded by bright blue sky. Marcus towered into her vision, raising his axe to finish her off, "NO MERCY!" rolling to a crouch, she barely escaped the killing blow. Sand exploded where her chest had been. She had no time to worry over a fresh burning sensation on her side, she blocked and parried to stay alive. Raliel didn't have time to think, only to react. She began to believe that the veteran had lost his mind. Something she'd said or done had triggered him. Survival focused her mental energy leaving pain and strain forgotten.

Marcus lowered his axe, and tossed her a small vial. "Now we're getting somewhere. Drink that—and take off that damn belt—so we can begin."

Begin? The vial's contents sealed her scratches in a warm wave. She unclipped her belt, letting it fall, and immediately felt the weight of her axe. Shoulders burning—where any average person would slump in exhaustion—she took a deep breath and launched herself at Marcus—infuriated by his self-approving grin.

CHAPTER THIRTEEN

Mendel had made up his mind. What was the point of living if there was no feeling? If there was anything he'd learned in his long life, it was that nobody was exempt from pain or loss. Trying to escape it was a fool's errand. By doing so, one risked missing everything worthy on the way.

There was something special about the young adventurers. It drew him powerfully, and if they'd have him, he intended on seeing things through. Oh, the thrill of adventuring with companions. There was so much he could show them, so many ways he could enhance their short lives.

He scowled at that, but only for a moment before shaking off the gloom for good. He wouldn't allow himself to become rigid or damaged by life anymore than some fiend for that was a sure path to insanity.

He'd had everything to live for long ago, a reason to fight and live fully. Yet, even now, so long after, his heart suffered a pang of loss at the mere thought. For he knew love lost and missed his companions of old. How long had he moped through life in a fog? 40 years? A century? Helping only here and there, stalking his companion's descendants. How many times had he walked the boulevard of this city? Alone. And other cities? Mendel continued to haunt their old routes, maintaining as much as possible of what they'd achieved, and inevitably losing ground. The world continued, *and so could he, so should he.*

There was something else too. Mendel was sure now that the amulet was responding to the friends. He hadn't felt the tug in so long that he hadn't been sure. Perhaps unwilling to believe. Like the presence of a loved one's ghost. Both frightening and thrilling. Surety had come once he'd decided to follow their trail, like a spirit calling him. Into— of all places—the sewer works, and just in time too. It felt good to fight to protect. It felt better to use his healing skills again. There was much he wanted to learn from these exceptional youth, and to do that, he would need to keep them alive. He chuckled at their naiveté in entering a cavern containing man-eaters. He smiled proudly at their perseverance and self-sacrifice as well.

For all their boldness, they still couldn't last long in the business without proper instruction. Who better than he? Mendel's heart warmed at the prospect for the first time in ages.

Midways appeared through the crowds. The sun hung low in the west, ready to disappear behind Midhaven's wall for the day. Here and there, the glint of dun steel belied the occasional patrolling guard. He walked through the entrance, surveying the patrons. By rote, his body gravitated to his regular seats at the bar. He spied Aven sipping from a wooden mug just as the leather-clad youth joined him. Both turned to regard him, but he kept walking past, suppressing a smile as he reached his seats. Mendel unhooked the goblet from his belt, set it on the bar, and waited for it to be filled. The goblet was a relic from his distant past.

***

"I thought Raliel would've shown by now," Vic said, sitting across from Aven.

"You're a little earlier than usual, but you're right. Raliel hasn't been to her room all day."

"Maybe she's shopping," Vic offered, smiling, not believing the statement.

"Yeah," Aven joined, "soon she'll appear with shopping bags in full dress, all lace and ribbons."

He laughed sarcastically.

"So, what's in the cloth?" Vic nodded to a bundle leaning against the table. Aven reverently retrieved it and unwrapped it. Vic whistled, "Wow, now that's a sword."

The two-handed claymore was quite literally a 'great sword.'

"Give it here." Vic held the iron scabbard, examining the gleaming cross guard—steel polished to a silver shine—stylized as the jaws of some mythical beast, silver fangs each side pointing parallel with the sheath. A polished mail handle and pommel sported a helmed human head, its face frozen in a bellow of defiance. "That's unique," Vic said, smiling.

With all the intricate detail, Vic worried that Aven got duped into buying a purely decorative piece. Something for tourists. He unhitched the clasp, unsheathing the blade a bit. Another whistle as he stared into his reflection, noting the well-honed edge, which reflected iridescent, hinting at an intense fusion of ore.

"Silver-steel alloy," Aven explained. "The blade itself was found by a guildsman some years ago and sold to our smith. This crosspiece," Aven said, taking the sword back. "He said he possessed it for longer."

The eyes of the raging head glinted as the light caught in tiny chips of polished gemstones—the white shine of living orbs. The illusion was impressive.

"Only recently did he have the inspiration to join the two. I guess there is a certain risk involved."

"A great weapon. Silver-steel alloy?"

"Well, on that, he can't be completely sure. But, he said it's very likely because he had to heat his forge five times as hot to work it, and even then, it was difficult because it hardened so quickly. He said he'd heard of the exact problem with the older high-end alloys." Aven shrugged.

"You lucked out." Vic smiled.

"Wait till you see the rest." Aven mirrored the smile.

"The rest?"

Aven laughed as he looked around. "You'll see. So, what did you buy with your share?"

"I'm still working on that," he said. "Now, it looks like I'll need to work hard to compete with that!"

They laughed.

"Compete with what?" They looked up to see Raliel standing over their table, a stern look on her face.

"Aven's bought himself a new sword," Vic explained.

"What'd you buy with your share?" Aven asked, scanning her for new items and noticing her head. "Hey, where's your hair!"

She turned to show tightly braided tresses corded straight down her back.

"It looks good," Aven said unconvincingly.

Her eyes flashed angrily. "Some of us aren't concerned with looks, more than staying alive."

Aven noticed bags under her eyes, which looked like bruises. Overall she looked rumpled and worn.

She took a seat next to him, nearest the edge. He waved for the closest barmaid, then asked, "Are you okay?"

"I'm fine," she said, "just exhausted. I spend all day training. Most of my share on it too." Her eyes flicked nervously to Vic, who didn't seem to notice.

"Money well spent then," said Aven, "though, in the future, I can do that for you. Training is essential. So I'll be training this week too, to handle some new equipment."

Aven began to outline his interaction at the guildhall, noting the positive effect on his friends. Their food arrived. Aven looked over his shoulder as the server placed their meal platters down to see an identical platter forced on Mendel at the bar. The massif seemed equally frustrated to find his attempts to pay for drinks repeatedly refused. Aven went back to detailing his day, finishing during a lull in taproom chatter.

There was one thing left to do before he could focus on his food. His stomach grumbled. Aven produced two hefty coin pouches. "For your service to Bright Company. Our company."

"This isn't necessary, Aven," Vic said.

Raliel was shaking her head 'no.'

"Don't tell me how to run this company," Aven said in a severe tone. He'd anticipated this. "I'll have nobody say that I don't pay a fair wage or take advantage of friends." He paused, daring them to protest, "I've covered our living costs for the next two weeks, Rali. I added the difference to your pouch, Vic, and you both may eat and drink freely here during that time."

Vic nodded and retrieved his money without a word, followed by a shrugging Raliel.

"Okay, boss," Vic said, smiling at her. All three burst into laughter, drawing a few stares. Scraping stools silenced their mirth. All attention turned to Mendel as he gathered his mug and headed toward their booth on his way out.

"Have you talked to him yet?" Raliel whispered.

Mendel veered directly toward them and, without preamble, said, "What's all this nonsense about my money being 'no good'?"

They were all stunned to silence. Aven remembered it was for him to answer, "It…was…it's the least I could do for your help, sir massif!" he exclaimed, looking to his companions for help—receiving none.

Finally, Mendel relaxed, "I'm looking for work. You wouldn't happen to know of any companies interested in an old veteran with a few skills, would you?"

Their shock doubled. Mendel was over-qualified. A veritable one-person company. Aven smiled, eyebrows raised in disbelief, joy, or both before composing himself, "We'd be honored to have you, Mendel."

"Good!" He pulled up a chair, the seat dangerously creaking as he settled in. "We can discuss pay another time; what I wanna know is what's next?"

"Okay, I trust everyone has restocked and re-equipped? I've taken on a few escort jobs," Raliel groaned, "but only to stay earning for one week. A week we need to train."

Everyone nodded at that, even Mendel, who offered, "I can take point on those, to keep the money flowing, anyone with free time can provide relief."

Of course—Aven thought—Mendel was a seasoned warrior probably accustomed to command, a qualified leader. "That'll be helpful, Mendel; I'll be training with the guild—"

"And I at the legion," Raliel voiced.

Everyone looked to Vic, who shrugged. "A week dedicated to training sounds good to me, but I fear I may not have time to relieve escort jobs."

Everyone knew this, that the brotherhood—though they knew not the reason—demanded almost all his time. He said it more out of consideration, with the grace to look contrite.

"If Vic can escape to training, so can I." Raliel thrust her chin out in defiance.

"That's fine, Rali; training's a priority." But, for some reason, this didn't appease Raliel as much as he'd hoped. "Looks like I'll be with you, Mendel, every chance."

"Just as well." Mendel agreed.

A barmaid showed, clearing the meal and supplying each with a mug of honey mead. It was something Aven had recently discovered and made him feel sophisticated to order. He suddenly worried that it would make him look foolish in front of Mendel, but the massif—after pouring it into his mug—took a whiff, grunted approval, then drank deep. They all talked about work and their recent job. It was strange how something so dangerous that'd nearly been their death could become something they could laugh off.

As the strong mead warmed them, they loosened up, talking more easily—even Raliel, who had seemed plenty uptight, visibly relaxed. Mendel avoided questions about himself, deflecting inquiry with a curt 'just an old traveler tryin' to get by.'

"You've acquired training as a cleric," Vic prodded.

"I've picked up a few tricks, such as that, but it's limited." They eyed each other for a moment.

Mendel had repaired a broken neck and likely a fractured skull, among everything else. If that was the limit of his healing capabilities, it was welcome indeed.

"So, Aven, what're you gonna name your sword?" Mendel nodded to the new blade.

"Name it?"

"Every weapon deserves a name, Aven. This," Mendel paused as he reached behind his head, "is 'Attiel-garga,' in the Massifae home language."

Over his shoulder came the big hammer, the head of it looked over 20 pounds—yet he handled it with ease—spinning it to an abrupt stop for display. The entire hammerhead was engraved with runes, scenes of battles, and other indescribable art. The handle was as long as his forearm, made from the same piece of ore, grooved for grip, thick and sturdy. Though it was undoubtedly ancient, it shone with a smooth luster.

"Mythrallum?" Raliel asked.

"Yes, an ancestral weapon."

"What's it mean, Attiel-garga?" Aven inquired.

Mendel had all their attention. "There's no natural way to say it in human…the closest translation is Bright-Smacker." Just then, the hammer flickered. A silver flash traveled along the runes' outline, gone as quickly as it had come. He replaced the weapon.

"Fireheart," Raliel showed her axe, "named after some ancestor." Its long thin handle—wrapped in red leather—led up to a crescent blade, joined to a wicked spike for balance. The blade glowed red, orange, then yellow until flames threatened to ignite.

"Show off." Vic shook his head. "I've gotta long piece of sharpened metal myself," he said, largely ignored.

"Fireheart," Mendel repeated, "not only a name but an attribute. Raliel, does your ancestry reach back to Arba?"

"Just a family legend," she said, but Mendel looked thoughtful.

"Well, there is a history behind my new blade, but shouldn't I get acquainted with it first?" Aven wondered aloud, "Before I name it of course."

"Your weapon should become your best friend. Let me see this new sword of yours." In Mendel's hands, the great sword seemed almost proportionate. It was a lot lighter than it looked. Crafted large and menacing. Mendel studied the helmed visage on the pommel, "This is older, from one of the greater human forges. Post-war, while humans fought to hold back the wilds. Did you know it's enchanted?"

"You sure?" Aven's eyes were wide, face serious.

"Oh, yes, but dormant. It's not the original blade either. A finely wrought one: Elden silver-steel." The last bit, Mendel growled out without seeming to notice. At the mention of silver-steel, Aven nodded at Vic.

Mendel continued, "The enchantment possibly disrupted in the separation from the original blade, but silver-steel is highly compatible for enchantment. Will you permit me to try and discover its purpose?"

"You can fix it?" Aven was eager, Raliel yawned, and Vic seemed more entertained by Aven's reaction.

"Oh, it doesn't require fixin'; it's more like the separation diverted the flow." Mendel saw that this topic was becoming too advanced for his audience.

With a gust of a sigh, he said, "The enchantment lies here in the helmed figure and should flow through the blade, but the circuit's broken, and so the enchantment remains dormant. If I could somehow reconnect the flow, there's a chance it could," he paused, "heal."

Mendel used the term to encourage comprehension.

Vic chimed in, "One of the tricks you've learned?" sounding almost snide. Aven wondered what was going on with him; he'd never known him to act like this.

Mendel smiled. "One of my *oldest* tricks, you could say."

"What other tricks do you have, old warrior?" Vic's gray eyes bore like lasers.

This time Mendel chuckled, "Usually, the interview comes before the hiring. I'm good with maps, weapons, armor, and such—nothing unusual for Massifae adventurers." That said, his eyes returned to Aven's sword. He slid it back in its sheath. "Whatever you paid for it; you got a bargain; the silver-steel alone is worth a small fortune."

Aven smiled broadly. "I hope we can do half as well as we have this far. Now, I do have plans for next week. But, first, I'd like to know how you all feel about returning to the cavern."

That cast a shadow upon all but Mendel, who seemed indifferent. What must've been a likely death sentence for them, rated pretty low in difficulty to him.

"The Massifae ruins." Vic leaned forward. "You want to explore them." It wasn't a question.

"I do."

Mendel also leaned in, radiating a chilling new intensity. "What's this now, what ruins, boy? And how do you know they are massif?"

Boy? Aven decided to ignore the term; for now, Mendel indeed had cause to be fervent. But, first, Aven explained to Mendel the ruin entrance they'd discovered.

"What else could it be but Massifae?" Raliel asked Mendel, who'd grown contemplative.

"Hmmm, it may be, but I don't recall any of our cities or havens near here. However, it stands to reason that there could be from before the war. I'll need to inspect these myself. But how? The city masons sealed the entrance in mudstone. If we had a work crew, it would take over a month to clear it all. You can bet it's guarded, too, until fully set. How?"

"With this." Aven produced half of a scroll of town portal.

Mendel looked confused. "With a half-spent scroll?"

"It's the return half of the town portal used in the cavern, the one the children used."

"Children?" Mendel asked, "There were children?"

Aven ignored the question, "It'll take us directly there."

"Directly to a cage, you mean." Vic added, "A cage with a likely repopulated camp."

"Exactly. Which is why we need to prepare," Aven agreed grimly.

"I'll tell you what we need to do something about," Raliel scowled as she spoke, "the lack of light. I'm not going back down there, or any cavern, with just torches."

"What about your hammer, Mendel? It provided great light when we needed it." Vic looked hopeful.

"Yeah, but too wasteful over long periods, and more so if I need to heal or…make use of other tricks. But it's true; we need something or someone to render that irrelevant. A powerful weapon of light hinders creatures of the dark, as much as the dark does you."

Aven recalled the bogrock's fury at the light of their torches, "Let's make it a priority; everyone keeps their eyes peeled for a solution."

Mendel shifted the topic. "I'd like to take your sword to a friend of mine, someone I'd like you to meet. He'll know what to do about this."

"Okay, how about tomorrow morning? I can go before training, and you and I have an evening job too." Aven sorted it out with Mendel. "Then it's settled," Aven stifled a yawn, "I'd better get some rest; gotta full day tomorrow." Finally, it dawned on him that Mendel might appreciate some night-time accommodation, "Mendel, if you want a room, just check in with the desk; I'll take care of it."

"Ya know what, Aven, I think I will, thank you."

Aven bid everyone goodnight and tromped up the stairs. Floorboards creaked behind. Raliel also took the stairs to her room. She'd looked tired all evening. Though a dozen feet apart, they reached their doors simultaneously. Aven had just about unlocked his when she called, "Aven?" he looked to his left. She had her door opened, one hand leaning on the door frame.

"Yeah, Rali?" She looked on the verge of saying something, struggling with it, "…Um, goodnight."

"Goodnight, hey, if you—" Her door shut. He was too tired to try and figure out what he may have done wrong. He'd deal with everything tomorrow. In his room, nothing looked more inviting than the bed. After undressing, he climbed into bed and positioned his sword hilt up against the headboard. The helmed figure on the pommel snarled vigilantly. Aven fell asleep immediately upon extinguishing the bedside candle.

CHAPTER FOURTEEN

Aven had forgotten to mention the jeweled sword hilt they'd found on the fallen warrior. He suspected that the man was related somehow to the captives, so he was sure to snatch it up on his way out.

He left early and could hear Raliel—in the next room—rising as well. He arrived on the street in his newest leather street clothes, boots, pants, and vest over a clean white linen shirt. His new sword was much too large to hang from his hip. With careful adjustments, he arranged a back harness—suitable for today's needs. Its gleaming hilt rested just over his right shoulder.

He'd also forgotten to mention the invitation. In all the excitement, it had simply slipped his mind, which was just as well until he could figure out what would come of it. So he used his city map and followed the instructions on the invitation, heading west.

The bustle of Midhaven's inhabitants already ebbed and flowed. Activity increased as the sun rose. A woman staked out a space of cobblestone to intercept traffic, with a small girl by her side. Both wore drab gray dresses and heavy shawls, baskets in hand, offering small pastries for sale to the crowds. Aven's stomach grumbled at the scent of cinnamon and fresh-baked dough. Finally, after a quick transaction, he was on his way with a fritter half crammed in his mouth and another in hand.

Best he could tell, the quickest route would be to aim for the temple, somewhere around there should be the turn north into the mansion district. Unfortunately, he'd had no opportunity to enter the prestigious neighborhood on his growing excursions throughout the city. It was gated and well-guarded, containing the homes of the most wealthy and influential residents.

It was impossible to miss when the entrance appeared, just short of the temple property. With invitation in hand, Aven made for the security post through the warning glares of four heavily armed and armored private guards. He approached the gate and waited. Their gaudy plate armor and snowy-white capes took nothing away from the steel in their eyes; these were well paid pros.

A guard approached to check the invitation's authenticity with puckered scar visible from beneath his gleaming skull cap. At the sight of its seal, his eyebrows furrowed, and he grumbled, "You're expected," and gave Aven directions to the proper structure, including instructions not to dawdle or wander.

A tar-paved road wound ahead. As Aven followed it, he felt transported to a fairyland of manicured woodland. The ground rose and fell with small manufactured hills of green turf and trees. Groves peppered green grassy knolls, reducing his ability to see more than the next mound. Nevertheless, the clever landscaping gave the illusion of rolling moors, and the thickets of wood provided a feel of open country, though on a masterfully rendered miniature scale.

He walked for a quarter of an hour before passing two other paved trails with a gilded iron signpost on either side of his own. Neither matched the symbol of the Lumin seal in his hand. The small knolls and trees gave the impression of distance, while in actuality, the trees were no taller than himself. The 'hills' could be crested in three to four strides. However, the illusion was powerful, so he almost felt vulnerable out in the wild as he walked. He resisted the urge to check the release on his sword.

After some time--and his other fritter--he reached a single paved trail. The signpost was decorative ironwork gilded in brass, depicting the flame of the Lumin family. The path curved out of sight amid full-sized pine trees, thick for privacy.

Aven enjoyed this surprising break from outside the city, within the city, and marveled at the chirping of small birds darting through the air. The sun's golden rays reached through gaps in green to warm his face, reflecting off the waters of the occasional pond and fountains. Marble benches were placed to take in the carefully created views, suggesting strolls and the ease of wealth.

The path opened up to an expansive meadow, cut through by a more comprehensive cobblestone drive, leading to a great stone fountain and beyond the manor house itself. The place was more significant than any he'd seen, though it gave that same impression of a miniature copy. Three floors of windows faced forward. A broad rectangular stone and wood compound raised just over the tallest pines. The iron double doors were each twice his height and wide. Affixed to each door were heavy door knocks of burnished brass. They depicted heavy rings dangling from the beaks of fierce feathered creatures.

"You two don't seem to like the taste of metal." Aven joked aloud at the grimacing fowl. Straightening, he reached for a brass ring—at least as thick as his wrist—and knocked with a startling resonant boom that echoed like an enormous drum. After a few quickened heartbeats, he tried again. The knock was still booming when the great door shuddered and swung inward, revealing a beautiful expansive foyer—glassed skylight ceilings, and white marble floors with delicate dark brown veins. A slight man dressed immaculately in a gray and white tailored suit stood just to the side. His suit complemented his silver hair, swept back tidily from intelligent gray eyes, eyes that crinkled in a friendly smile as he studied Aven. In a deep voice—almost as resonant as the knock—he said, "You must be master Avenderan Amoniel of Bright Company," his hand extended, and though he meant to shake hands, Aven gave him the invitation instead—cringing inside at his ineptitude. The handwritten card disappeared smoothly before he clasped his hands behind his back.

"Please follow me, sir."

***

Raliel found Marcus in his workshop, abutting his living quarters. He was rummaging through a vast chest, one of many, on the far wall. A large worktable divided the room, presently cluttered with haphazard pieces of mail and plate, which he tinkered with when not instructing. Two high windows opposed each other—one cast rays of morning light upon the large table.

"Ahem!" she announced herself.

He cast a dark look over his shoulder. "Well, there you are! So you think I've nothing else to do than wait for you to get here?"

She opened her mouth to point out that this was the earliest she'd ever shown, then closed it to match his grin. Marcus had a strange sense of humor. Most people took him to be grumpier than he actually was, but she understood and enjoyed his temperament. She'd grown fond of him. He was like the uncle she always wished she'd had.

"So, what's in store for me today?" She was eager to begin, to learn as much as possible before next week.

"I've got some new forms to focus on and a few changes to implement." He rummaged, throwing back the odd scrap of armor or weapon in his search.

She'd told him everything about her recent fight—omitting quest details, of course—even her feelings after her failure. She could do that with Marcus. He reminded her so much of her father; it just came naturally. Since she'd confided this, he determined to train her to master those situations, and he was succeeding in at least building back her confidence.

"Ah-hah!" He stood up, holding a plain axe. The long handle resembled an overlarge woodsman axe, but its head bore a lumbering blunted crescent blade, weighted by an opposing block of ore.

"Here we go, this here's an excellent practice weapon. The head and handle are made of lead and iron; I made it myself. Here, try it." He lobbed it her way, and she felt its weight even with her strength-enhancing belt.

"Off with your belt and axe," he urged.

She complied, voicing, "This must be thirty pounds or more!"

Marcus pondered a moment, "Can't be that much, maybe close, no matter, it'll serve."

'Serve?!' she thought. She could hardly gauge the balance without losing control of the weight. The ponderous block showed a recently marked numeral that looked suspiciously like a 4 and 0. Raliel cocked an eyebrow at Marcus as he walked around the table, leaving the mess.

"Let's get started on forms, get you acquainted with your new weapon."

'Forms' meant she would mimic his movements, often repeating one until she met his standard while he stood barking critique from behind a cork pipe. It was strenuous enough with her much lighter axe. During their last session, she'd severely notched Marcus's personal weapon. She'd also seared the hair from his forearms, enough to anticipate this replacement. With a heave, she rested the lead practice axe on one shoulder, her belt and personal weapon dangling from the other. She limped after Marcus, back arched to avoid unnecessary strain.

She knew that she would exhaust every muscle by the time they reached their noonday, and that was *without* having to contend with a lead weight. This adversity would discourage or crush the spirit of most others, but it only fueled her resolve. Now wizened and with Marcus's instruction, she truly believed she could improve enough to prevent herself from being a liability in an increasingly dangerous lifestyle. As they approached their usual spot on the sand, she noticed others—a group of six. One man was massive, near seven feet tall, and built like an ox. His company only exaggerated his size by way of their shorter stature—none over five and a half feet. So why were they stretching and warming up here? An odd place to choose.

The lummox rolled his massive shoulders, looking directly at her! As they arrived, she noticed the uniforms, marking them of imperial ranks.

"These fellas are your new sparring partner. We'll start with forms then measured combat. I expect you'll be able to perform fairly in multiple scenarios when we are finished." Her opponents chuckled, making her heart rate spike in anger. 'Mattu,' the behemoth, commented in a voice like mashing gravel, "take it easy on her, Marc."

"I'm sure you will," Raliel grumbled. She took a deep breath and let her belt fall before stepping into the sand. It was going to be a productive day indeed.

***

The room could be called a den. Aven's dad had one at home where he conducted business stored ledgers, books, and trinkets. This room was much the same, just magnified. An entire wall was devoted to volumes of all sizes and colors, with the topmost tomes accessible by a tall rolling ladder of light varnished wood, the whole room accented in the same wood. Mounted heads of exotic creatures filled the remaining wall space, some recognizable, most not. It was a comprehensive collection, and where the physical specimen was not, hung expertly wrought painted sculptures and paintings. Across from the books loomed three vast windows overlooking the back of the estate where the man in the gray suit stood looking out, hands still clasped behind his back.

Aven neared, looking out as well. He viewed green manicured grass leading down to the banks of the large flowing "Icepeak" river. Beyond, he spied extending farmland speckled by regular size trees.

"My name is Arman," the man said as he turned from the river view then sat in a high-backed chair behind a dark mahogany desk. It was a 'desk' as much as this room was a simple 'office.' Its surface was polished to a reddish-brown gloss and was large enough to serve as a small stage.

Arman gestured for Aven to take the seat across the sea of glass.

"I'll stand, thank you," Aven said. His great sword made difficult to sit, so he continued studying the room. "Sure, that's fine," Arman assured.

In a brown and white uniform, a woman entered bearing a tray. Arman remained silent and shuffled papers away as the woman arranged fresh fruit and drinks on the desk.

Aven studied a massive skull of what appeared to be a horned gorilla with giant teeth displayed in a ferocious snarl. The head was as big as his entire torso, even without flesh. Next to the specimen was a glass-encased portrait and written description depicting a frightening demonic creature. It carried an armful of unlucky children away into the night, with bat-like wings too small for flight. "Minor Balor," Arman supplied, along with a tall glass of red liquid. "They're said to populate the wilds, but none have lived to relate the experience. The skull was recovered from Northgate during my master's travels." Aven sipped his drink absently. It was a delicious concoction of melons and fruits with the telltale warmth of solid spirits—intense and delicious enough to warrant caution. "Your master?"

"Yes. Master Mikael is away on business. Leaving me, in his stead, to care for things."

Did Aven detect a wince in that? It was gone too quick to be sure. "I must be honest with you, master Arman—"

"—just Arman, Sir."

"Okay, Arman, my company was on a contract that led to the children's discovery. We hadn't planned or known—"

"I'm quite aware of the circumstances and your actions. If we could sit, please?"

Well—Aven thought—if there was no avoiding it, he labored to disengage his weapon. Then, with a final click of steel clasps, he removed his scabbard from the harness and set it beside his overly stuffed chair.

Seated, Arman looked across the massive desk. "Alicia has told me of your bravery—"

"—Alicia?"

Arman looked puzzled for only a moment, "Drina is a pet name of her mothers. Anyway, her proper name is Alicia," he added sternly. Then, he sat straighter, "it was brave to give up your only escape for the children."

Aven looked incredulous as if to say, 'who wouldn't?'

Arman continued, "It isn't lost on me that you, a newcomer, were unaware of Alicia's…status. So your actions are all the more worthy of reward."

Aven took a big drink at that and sat straighter.

"To be quite frank, Alicia, though heart of ours she is, can be difficult to look after." Arman took a drink, straightened his jacket, and sighed. His glass sat with what seemed a loud report in the serene den. "We've been frantic here for the few days she's been missing." Then, another deep breath, "You've saved her life and the Lumin legacy. But, unfortunately, her Shield has gone missing too."

Aven lay the bejeweled sword hilt before Arman and, without preamble, said, "I'm sorry."

Arman's eyes bulged, looking horrified.

Aven relayed as much as seemed proper about the man they'd found, emphasizing heavily upon his bravery.

Arman had taken on a faraway look. Eyes bloodshot, unblinking.

"Was he close to you?" Aven asked to draw the man back.

"He was my only son…employed here only a few years...thank you for returning his sword. I'd intended on hiring you to rescue him." Arman swallowed hard, clearly distressed. A flurry of emotions seemed to be fighting to the surface, but he changed subjects.

They spoke of Bright Company, though hollowly, as the news

dampened the occasion. Still, Arman asked many specific questions regarding Aven's intent and goals. Aven shared freely, over a few more drinks. He learned that master Mikael was a wealthy collector of antiquities who always traveled and was held in very high esteem by the ruling council. One of the most powerful men in the city.

"The sword," Aven nodded to the jeweled hilt, "was it valuable?"

"Very. A Lumin heirloom that Mikael bestows only upon the Scion's Shield."

Aven realized just how much his company had saved the Lumin family. He felt overwhelming relief, surely only a fragment of what Arman must be feeling despite his significant personal loss.

"The creature is dead?"

Aven gave a firm nod. "The bogrock is dead."

"Do you plan on returning?" A glimmer of hope twinkled in Arman's eyes.

"The passage has been sealed."

"You must be impatient to get back." Arman reached into a drawer, withdrew a small chest, unlocked it, and placed the sword hilt inside. The lock clicked with finality." The reward. "The reward was sufficient?"

"Yes, sir, very generous."

"Excellent. It's getting late, and I don't want to keep you. I've arranged for our coach to take you to your rooms." He produced a velvet coin purse, "take this as well, for returning the sword." It was his pouch, with a golden flame embroidered in the velvet over the initials 'A.A.' Aven tucked it away dutifully, returning Arman's smile.

"If you ever need work, remember you're a friend of the Lumin's."

They both stood, and Aven replaced his sword on his back.

"I'll be informing master Mikael of your service—"

"—Aben!" a tiny voice shrieked from the doorway. Before Aven could entirely turn, four feet of satin and lace collided painfully under his left arm. Alicia squeezed incredibly tight before letting go.

"Mistress! You should be in bed recovering!"

"I feel fine, Arman." She gave Aven a dramatic roll of her eyes, then perked up. "Aben! You came to see me; I knew you would, my hero!" she added a dramatic swoon before finally releasing her vise-like hold. "I told everyone how you came to save me. I knew someone would come, nobody believed, but I knew...."

Aven wondered if she truly understood how close she'd come. A thought too grim to voice. Arman gave a helpless shrug as she continued to tick off everything she believed and 'just knew' would happen while in captivity. It struck Aven how resilient a child could be. She indeed experienced terror and grotesqueness that he'd never imagined at her age.

"Mistress Alicia," Aven attempted to interrupt her verbal onslaught.

"Drina." She shot Arman a scowl.

'Whatever,' Aven thought. "It was an honor and a privilege to be the first to arrive and rescue you." He played along, adding a sweeping bow.

"You must be hungry; we'll set you a place for supper." Her eyes widened. "You could stay over!"

Aven looked to Arman for help, but the man only smiled, as if to say, 'I told you so.' He then came to his rescue. "And what of the other little girls and boys, hmmm?"

"Others?"

"Well, yes, master Aven must have other little boys and girls who need his services."

She was wringing her hands, clearly torn. "You're so great Aben! You have to come back, as soon as you destroy all the meanies and creepies, or they'll be sorry they messed with Bright Company…" she continued to rant, as they walked to the front door.

As Aven settled into the waiting coach, Arman reminded him, "If you ever need a favor, don't hesitate to ask."

Alicia rushed into the carriage for one more hug, simultaneously commenting, "Nice sword!"

He was still dazed from the intensity of it all by the time the manor was out of sight.

***

Mendel stood in front of Midway's, trying to maintain his dwindling patience. Aven was late.

***

Vic rushed through his ablutions, drying himself with a thick towel. His new schedule hardly left a minute to spare. His assigned regimen was rigid: every morning consisted of rigorous strength and endurance training, focusing on the ability to climb, jump, swing, and rappel from various equipment in the massive underground networks of courses and gyms.

These sessions were immediately followed by a meal. Then it was off to the sparring chamber, where initiates practiced using various weapons. By noon, it was time for the hot spring in the complex's lowest known level, which accounted for the unnatural warmth this far underground.

It was difficult for him to tell how deep the complex went. Its main corridor spiraled down for what seemed a mile, with endless tunnels offshooting the entire way. Getting from one activity to the next in good time required constant movement. Initiates and disciples alike constantly jogged up and down the wide corridor throughout program hours.

Thoroughly dried, Vic donned muslin smock, tied the drawstrings to his cloth trousers, and slid on canvas slippers.

He was due for meditation training with master Taberah. They were working on proficiency in what Taberah called 'fluttering.' He'd been right in his instinct not to complain. He would've been ashamed by the speed he was called upon had he done so, a close call that peeved him. Frustrated by his impatience, he reminded himself that it took a decade of training with Nazar to get where he was. What was it Nazar would say? 'Impatience only dulled the learning of the moment.' Something like that. Also, 'To do your best, you must enjoy what you do.' So Vic would work harder to enjoy everything he did. Including the most difficult.

Vic arrived at his barracks, smoothly negotiating the corridors by rote. His plain cot, nightstand, and chest looked like any other in the chamber.

He was rarely called for watch-post duty, another indication of his quick ascent. And when Jin had tried to force it, Vic had been immediately relieved by another initiate. Jin no longer tried, and Vic suspected that the overzealous coach had been corrected. After his session with the master, his assignment would be to survey the usual assortment of civilian targets. He wouldn't know the precise task until he reported to 'Azure.' He often repeated the same objectives, but he never again saw the beautiful Elden female.

He'd cleaned and oiled his leather suit. The brown, so dark it seemed black, had needed repair after their duty in the cave. He retrieved it from his chest in exchange for his more straightforward attire. Donning the stealth suit felt good. The steel handles of his throwing knives crisscrossed from shoulders to hips. He slid his long slender sword into a built-in quarter sheath on his back which left most of the blade bare.

For a moment, Vic admired the boiled leather helm he'd created to capture the aquiline features of a hawk. Two slits made sight possible, but no openings were visible other than that. Folds and ridges hid the air and ear ducts—jaw and nose tapered in a viciously pointed chin. The ear ducts reversed the hearing range: one ear backward, the other forward, creating an uncanny heightened sense that amazed him for thinking up the design.

He felt for the green jeweled earring still in his possession. He'd offered to buy it, but Taberah said that it was a tool he could use as long as he needed. It had been invaluable in the dark cavern. It enhanced both ears, and in conjunction with his helmet, he enjoyed quite the advantage, in typical situations, barely surviving the last one.

Their recent close call still weighed heavily on his mind. He felt like a failure for not being able to bring the bogrock down. He'd felt useless, a memory that made his pulse quicken. He needed to master Taberah's fluttering technique. With that, the bogrock would've never stood a chance. This thought heartened Vic. Imagining himself from his friends' perspective blurring into a kill strike made him smile.

Another thing he'd been too busy to investigate: the strange golden hilt he'd found in the Witherwood. He retrieved it from his chest; its fire opal sparkled even in the dark. He removed one of his throwing knives and stuffed it—handle first—into the vacant spot. He'd ask Mendel to take a look at it when he got the chance. Perhaps the old massif could shed some light on the strange grave too.

Equipped and ready for his next meet, he tucked his helm under one arm and sprinted off to the master.

***

The carriage deposited Aven in front of Midways in time to discover Mendel leaning against a wall with a scowl. Aven raised a hand in apology, but the racket of the departing carriage drowned out his explanation. All he could do was catch up with Mendel, who'd already

168

turned to go.

"Morning Mendel, sorry for being late; I was held up." Aven relayed the morning events, pleased to see Mendel visibly relax. The massif even arched a bushy eyebrow at the mention of Arman's offer. Finally, he nodded approval; you've made a strong ally saving the young heiress."

"You know of her?"

"Of course, everyone does; her family—the Lumins—sat on the council for The Triple Alliance. They are powerful still."

"Great luck then," Aven said.

"No such thing as luck," Mendel grumbled as he marched. Then in a softer tone, "Why have you chosen this line of work?"

Aven responded without hesitation, "I wanna contribute. Make the world a better place, I guess."

"And how do you expect to do that?"

"Uh, I'm not sure..." Mendel began to scowl. Aven continued, "But I aim to do something. I'll figure the rest out on the way."

Mendel's scowl deepened, but he nodded, "Fair enough. The heiress was saved because you wanted to do 'something.'"

"I'm sure anyone would've done the same."

"Would they? Why haven't they? Most wouldn't have sacrificed their only way out to save anyone. Even more, wouldn't have entered that cavern at all." Mendel led him off the boulevard into a series of turns down slimmer streets.

"That quest was reported to be resolved several times by cowards who said nothing of a cavern. Think on that."

Mendel stopped in front of a humble magic shop that advertised training and items. "Where'd you get the amulets, son?"

The question surprised Aven. His hand felt for the rune on the Mythrallum chain. Before he could answer, Mendel turned on him and pulled out a replica from under his shirt. It was bulkier and had an age-darkened patina.

"Take it off."

Aven complied without thought, handing it over.

"Ah, Elden-made. Is Raliel's the same?"

Aven nodded. "Identical."

"I'd thought...never mind that...do you know what this is?"

"I was told it's to stay aware of its partner's location."

"BWA-HA-HA-HAAA!" Mendel's eyes watered with joy. "Partner

indeed, well, no harm in that." But then, the twinkle in his eyes faded, "I'm going to link mine solely for location, Okay?"

"Sure."

"I could already sense yours; now you'll be able to sense mine. We'll speak more of these amulets when we have time." Mendel lightly touched his rune to Aven's, causing them to spark like flint, then handed it back.

Aven could now detect a faint recognition of Mendel's presence but without the sense of feeling or mental state, he sometimes could from Raliel's link. At the mere thought, he noted Raliel's direction, distance—at the training grounds—and a hint of her exertion.

Mendel broke his train of thought, "let's get inside; there's someone I want you to meet."

There was that insufferable twinkle again.

***

"Keep flowing, woman!"

Raliel whirled the weighted axe, keeping it fluid and trying hard not to break its momentum. If that happened, she might not get it moving again.

"Offensive retreat!"

She performed an up-thrusting figure eight, alternating left and right as she danced backward around Marcus in a continuous circle. Once she achieved the proper velocity, she had only to struggle to keep it up. Her shoulders tried to quit first.

"Faster! Deflect with enough force to cut! You know this!"

She whirled faster, though wrenching more than 'flowing.' Sweat streaked her face, stinging her eyes.

"Sequence seven!"

Without faltering, Raliel shifted her swing into a violent spin, spiraling so that her weapon wheeled in an overhead chop to backhand swat. She repeated the sequence without pause, without the need to circle. Instead, she firmed her footing, focusing on the movement's ferocity.

"Good! Sequences one through four!"

She glared at Marcus before executing a flurry of forwarding thrusts, followed by a jab of her handle, two uppercuts, a spin, and a series of lethal chops that continued to widen as she held sequence four. It looked similar to a figure eight except that her arms remained fully extended. Every muscle in her body strained with effort. As she slowed, it threatened to steal her impetus and cause her collapse.

"Hold!"

As always, he'd caught her in the most strenuous position. She froze in full frontal extension, both hands holding the heavy training axe out, straining with all her might to hold steady. She expected to collapse any movement.

"At ease."

She choked up her grip close to the axe head and let her arms fall to her sides. She dripped sweat, taking large steady breaths. The lead feeling in her arms was beginning to fade, replaced by the easy swell of ready muscles. She'd noticed the feel of her more muscular body lately.

"Give me ten laps, and return for the next series."

Before she could commence, Marcus added, "Five laps holding sequence one; five laps holding sequence two."

Of course, she thought and loped off. Once on track, she began thrusting her way around the circuit.

She was well into her program before the center field filled with legion soldiers for their daily regimen. Of gaining interest to her were the growing ranks of a special force. She continued her laps, studying the group legionaries called the Death Corps. Their heavily mailed class was conducting formation drills, attuned to combating hordes of undead. They broke into a dozen small clusters of shields and sparkling mail. Bristling spears tipped with many implements—from blunt sledge heads to crescent scythes for crushing and cleaving bone to debris. She had to admit that they looked effective.

Leading their training and responsible for the force was a tall, dark-haired legion officer with bright new stripes. Rumor was that the group's formation had been on his proposal to Legion HQ in response to the call to purge the Witherwood. But, recruitment proved their biggest obstacle even with approval. Facing undead from atop a wall was one thing—widely known to be grueling in itself—but engaging them on their turf? She'd shudder if her attention weren't also on maintaining her forms.

The Death Corps consisted—so far—of UN-battle-tested youth fresh off the street. Rumor had it also straight from the gaols, a last-ditch option for those facing the gallows. Regardless, the young officer had already gotten his men to an impressive standard, earning the respect of his peers.

They were changing tentative sniffs to nods of approval, pride, and even hope. Raliel felt all those things as she observed the group.

She noticed Marcus nearing the young officer and focused harder on her thrusting. Raliel overheard that Marcus was assisting them with weapons fabrication. Both men had been brainstorming ways to solidify a more contemporary battle design. They'd been experimenting with various mining explosives, creating some that spread long-burning flame. So far, these had proven disastrous, equally lethal to the user.

The Death Corps was gaining attention, not only on the training field. Rumor had spread that they would lead the first excursions toward the Witherwood to establish fortifications ahead of a more significant force, footholds to push the undead back: the first to go in, clear, and the last to leave. No pressure—she thought. So, recruitment and training raced against the clock for orders that could come any day.

The military created similar forces on the other side of the gorge to leave the wall and begin a southward purge. Raliel wondered how that training went. Word was the forces from that side were thousands strong.

The notion was encouraging to all—the prospect of securing the wood, purging the evil. Settling outposts on land for the first time in centuries was invigorating. She supposed that was a drawing factor for most recruits. And why not? She also could feel the pull to be a part of something great. Historic.

As Raliel changed her stance for the following sequence, she suppressed a shiver at the thought of her night at the wall. Goosebumps spread in a wave down her back and limbs as the memory of howling undead beat at a superior force—relentlessly.

She didn't envy the Death Corps, who must be wondering what horrors they would face. She asked how many had the experience of a night at the Wall. Some? None? Suddenly, she could see it, the cold determination in their eyes, under burnished mail hoods, plenty of healthy fear too. They'd need that.

Shaking her head, she focused on finishing her laps.

CHAPTER FIFTEEN

Adam sat content on a bale of hay for his noon meal. Liz had—as usual—forced him to break by way of delicious food. Today, he held a slice of hot meat, cheese, and onion concoction, filling a small loaf of pale sour bread. Feet happily beating the side of the bale, Adam observed the comings and goings of the east gate. Mostly patrolling guards, speckled with swift armored carriages to transport people or smaller trade shipments.

Products could be, and were, teleported; however, the cost was high and commonly booked to capacity. Direct runs were the only option, attracting daring souls with speedy horses to avoid bandits and creatures alike. Another form of 'run' was pedestrian and merchant caravans, arriving and departing twice daily; one left at the crack of dawn while it was still dark within the walls. The noise of the torchlight procession often served as Adam's wake-up call—the second caravans left at noon. Any later would be too dangerous. At just before midday, Adam could usually catch the departure of the second caravan, with the gorge-side one arriving just before.

The incoming convoy was running late. So late that the outgoing one couldn't wait and had hastily wound out the gate, wagons, mules, oxen, guards, and all. After enjoying the spectacle, Adam wondered if he'd catch the incoming caravan in time. He dusted off the crumbs from his work clothes, procrastinating as much as he dared.

A growing racket piqued his interest just in time for him to catch a battered wagon exploding through guards and pedestrians. Adam's heart plunged, his senses dulled by the shock. The crowds' screams and scrambling seemed muted. Their movements slowed. Even colors seemed to be as drained as the blood from his face for a moment.

Adam struggled into his red robe and stood on the bale for a better look. The effort tickled his stomach and limbs. He fought through a precarious wobble, drawing his robe around him in the sudden chill.

The horses' harnesses snapped, freeing the heavily lathered and frothing beasts. Their eyes showed white all around as they stumbled in confusion. Two other horses lay in a crumpled heap—not stirring. A single wheel spun from the upended wagon. As guards edged forward, a single hand rose from the rubble of the ruined front end, then fell limp. Guards began searching the wreckage, retrieving three bodies, battered and bloody.

A few proactive citizens gathered the two panicked steeds, leading them away. A crowd was forming in earnest now. Adam was about to offer help when he spotted a second vehicle fly through the untended gate directly toward the unwary bunch. All he could do was mouth an empathic 'no' as he realized what would happen next. Adam shouted and waved, "LOOK OUT! MOVE!" but the crowd was too busy bustling from within itself.

There seemed to be a commotion at its center, and instead of moving away, people were struggling inward to see the cause.

The new team of horses collapsed, sending their armored carriage pivoting overhead and down onto the crowd in an explosion of screams and dust.

Adam's heart beat painfully. Plumes of dust obscured everything out but the cries of the injured.

"It bit me!"

Adam looked left, a man cradling a hand gestured at a fleeing horse.

"The damn thing bit me." He grumbled off.

Reinforcements arrived, secured the gate, and rushed into the dust to help.

Adam was in for another shock as the dust settled. The pedestrians, in groups, were brawling. Instead of helping the wounded, they attacked one another. People—crazed—leaped on each other at random, pummeling, only to rise together and jump another. As the crazy spread, so did their howls of anger. Soon, the guards were hard-pressed to contain a mob.

A bell tolled in the distance. At the signal, people around Adam, unnoticed, began running. Doors began slamming, windows shuttered and barred all in a flurry of panicked efficiency.

Adam looked back to the ring of armored guards struggling to restore order. Their ranks wavered and fell. A flood of bloodied and crazed bodies spilled over, shrieking and scattering. One fell upon a small fleeing dog, another one on a fallen guard.

'NO,' Adam mouthed again in disbelief. The squealing of the dog ended abruptly, and Adam was yanked from his perch by rough grasping hands.

"Hurry, Adam!" Liz and another lad, half dragged, half carried him. Another man, who worked the neighboring inn, was waving them to its cellar hatch. Heads, from its descending steps, bobbed out to look around.

Adam struggled to get his feet under him, and they'd just made near the cellar entrance when they were knocked down in a tangle of limbs. He lifted himself off his stomach, saw Liz silently screaming reaching toward him. A large man in a leather apron pulled her and the cellar door down with a clang and rattle of lock.

Adam's ears were ringing, his vision obscured by dust as he tried to get his bearings. He looked to a source of stirring dust to his right and found the other lad writhing. A blood-drenched attacker spooled ropes of the lad's intestines over a shoulder in a frenzy to extinguish life.

Beyond, a sputtering croak revealed a small mangled dog barking as it neared. Each croak sprayed a mist of bright red. One of its eyes dangled by the ligaments.

Everywhere pockets of tan dust billowed violence. Here and there, a break would show some gruesome scene of senseless butchery.

Adam's survival instincts kicked in, enough for him to dodge another tackle. The assailant disappeared into a tan cloud. Adam whirled around, suddenly very aware of his situation. The only visible landmark was the roof of the inn. He made for the cellar door. He stumbled into the fallen lad, who dragged himself toward the cellar, one arm raised to Adam for help. He reached into a pocket for a handkerchief to stop the lad's bleeding. He couldn't save him, but he could drag him to a safe place to die. Adam skid on his knees, grabbing the boy's shoulders and jerked back in time to avoid the snap of teeth.

What's wrong with these people? He thought.

The boy's fierce grip on his robe thwarted his attempt to rise. Instead, hand over hand brought snapping teeth—and vacant, gore-spewing eye-sockets—closer.

"Enough!" Adam pressed the ruby on his fist to a socket and gave the mental command to open the well of the ring's power. With a loud 'thwump,' the crazed lad was flung back, head an instant blazing torch. Adam stared at the crumpled body. As the heat caused a squeaking shriek, he listened as steam escaped the skull's boiling contents. Then, with a jarring 'POP,' the burning head sprayed its contents over the inn wall. Adam stared at his ring, sickened.

He decided to scramble for his loft. He ran through blinding plumes, not thinking or slowing until he slammed shut the stable door, dropping the heavy lock beam into place—nervous nickers. A quick inspection confirmed that the animals were restless but unharmed.

Footfalls sounded outside.

The only other opening in the building was above in his sanctuary. Nodding to himself, Adam raced up the ladder and flung wide the window hatch to a scene of utter pandemonium. The raving mob was scattered by now, beating on shuttered homes and barred shops. A dog or chicken ran desperately from a sprinting and spluttering lunatic here and there.

Adam shook his head in confusion. Any maniac that attempted to near the stables met a barrage of sparks and light flashes. It worked remarkably well. They feared light, and he didn't want to harm anyone that needed help once the insanity passed.

It was hard to tell who was victim or assailant, but his blinding flashes ended any scuffles within his range. He had to be satisfied with that and averted his eyes from any beyond. He spotted the remains of his lunch, for, upon the hay bale, he'd sat leisurely only minutes ago. How long would it take for order to be restored?

***

Ed and Mendel discussed Aven's great sword's design and potential attributes. Between them, they succeeded in uniting what the blacksmith could not, what Mendel called the 'essence' of the blade and hilt.

"The silver-steel alloy is undoubtedly Elden-wrought," Ed agreed with Mendel's earlier assessment, "a keener edge, strength, and effect on the fouler creatures." Then for Aven's benefit, Ed added, "Silver is a bane to evil and can harm things that normal weapons cannot."

Aven nodded.

"Good point." Mendel agreed. "But what about its main attributes?"

"It's still too weak to tell," Ed pursed his lips in thought.

Mendel offered, "But, as with most ancient enchantments, we can expect it to strengthen with use." He absently touched the handle of his hammer.

The peal of a distant bell penetrated the walls of the quiet shop. An even more distant tolling joined it.

"Alarm!" Ed rushed to the front window, "we're under attack!"

"Within the walls!" Mendel cursed, "Lock up the shop, Eddie, Aven, looks like we'll get to test your sword soon enough, eh?"

The shop door slammed behind them, instantly locked, shutters drawn. Aven jogged after Mendel, sword out. He felt no surge of power or speed from it, though its balance seemed improved since the joining.

The streets emptied fast. People scrambled to hide behind lock and latch.

"Is this common?" Aven asked, wondering at the speedy civilian response.

"Yes and no," Mendel responded, scanning the sky and walking to the empty boulevard's center. Aven followed, searching the open blue above, though for what he didn't know.

"Sometimes a wyveryn or two can cause alarm. Usually, only snatch a pet or two, but it's often enough to be wary."

So far, no wyveryn appeared. Aven had seen paintings of the beasts: pony-sized two-legged lizards with leathery wings and long barb-tipped tails. Believed to be intelligent, they often avoided civilization and could recognize ballistae.

"There! Come on!" Mendel pounded cobblestone east, where chaos

177

ensued. A wild horse ran awkwardly in their direction. "Keep away from it!" Mendel warned. The horse veered right for the massif, rolling its eyes. A mangled hind leg prevented it from rearing.

"Undead!" Mendel growled, even as he swung Attiel-garga, connecting with a clean 'clop,' felling the beast. Destroying the brain delayed the undead, but incineration was the only way to be sure. So Mendel torched the horse with his hammer, and in a flash, the creature was covered in white flame, producing black oily smoke.

They ran for the east gate. Once identified, the undead were easy to spot, and as the pair arrived, Mendel and Aven's life force drew the dead. Aven sighted pockets of city folk fighting right along with city guards. A dozen people rushed from the guildhall wielding weapons. A volley of tiny red fireballs stuttered from their midst. The scene became overloaded with activity.

True to Ed's word, the greatsword had a colossal effect on the undead. Each clang and ring of silversteel cleaved creatures in two. Whether through head, torso, or arm, the undead fell writhing— wounds smoldering. The blade's bite burned like acid to the abominations. If not a fatal strike, the effect offered plenty of opportunities to finish them off as they convulsed.

There was something else too. With each killing stroke, through hilt to Aven's heart, stomach, and body, Aven could feel an almost giddy tingle. An odd thing to feel in battle.

He could find Mendel always somewhere in his peripheral, sending bodies sliding in the dirt with swats of his heavy hammer. Attiel-garga made the air itself shudder with its passing.

Besides avoiding their scratch, fighting the undead seemed simple enough. The undead always came to you and didn't fight as much as run head-on into your blade. But Aven could see how, with numbers, this would turn deadly. This type of fighting suited a two-handed greatsword, and he was glad he'd chosen the style. If he'd worn his armor, he'd be nearly unbeatable.

It wasn't until the last body fell that Aven noticed he was laughing. His stomach was tight with delight, and he quickly suppressed the odd reaction. Probably shock. He met Mendel's grim, disapproving visage. Those were people they'd been destroying, innocent people, only moments ago. The number of bodies around them repulsed Aven, and more so by the gleeful tingle from his weapon.

Other pockets of fighters quieted as opponents thinned. Dozens of bodies littered the area in a bloody mess of split flesh and jutting bone.

"Are you cut?" an oddly clean and unruffled Sergeant Land demanded, looking them over to be sure.

"No," they said in unison.

"Okay. We're organizing to clear the city. You're free to come." A rumble of boots shook the ground from the west. Aven turned to see. There were legion reinforcements, some 300 heavily mailed soldiers with shields, and a wicked assortment of strangely tipped spears. Though it seemed like there should be, Aven found no pots or pans among the odd spear tips. Instead, dashing around them came Raliel, sans belt or armor, carrying an overlarge axe. It was painted with gore, just as much as the reinforcement's spears. Raliel took place between him and Mendel.

A tall raven-haired officer galloped up to Sergeant Land, "Sir. The Death Corps and I will begin securing the streets."

Land eyed the troops and locked eyes with the younger officer. A plethora of information seemed to pass through the stare. The officer nearly winced at understanding the trust involved in the task. Though the legion had broad jurisdiction, the city was Sgt. Land's and he would be in charge today. Satisfied, Land nodded. "Begin at the source and spread out."

Land joined his men to do the same.

"Aven!" Raliel pointed out a flash from the stables. The trio rushed over.

Several blinded undead ran shrieking into each other or other obstacles in circles. Finally, a small boy poked his head from a hatch above the stable's door. "You're not getting in here, creeps!" He was talking to the trio.

"You!" Aven said, recognizing the boy from the alley.

Mendel waved and hollered, "Hold your fire, boy! We're clearing the undead!"

The boy looked skeptical but let his remaining sparkles fizzle out. They fell upon the creatures still confused and blinded, eliminating them quickly and drawing out a few more before destroying those as well. The youth blanched at the violence but remained vigilant should anyone near his door.

Raliel appeared to handle the crude axe well enough, though it was undoubtedly heavy. At one point, she swung through the neck of a supine fiend, burying her whole blade in the hard-packed dirt. Then, forced to abandon it for a moment, she hopped back on the balls of her feet to check her surroundings.

As Raliel calmly walked over to free her weapon, a clatter and metallic groan raised everyone's hackles, busy finishing their tasks. Then, the stable door swung out, and a red-robed boy inched out warily.

"Adam!" a crowd formed from within a cellar door. A woman hurried ahead of a burly blacksmith wearing a scowl, "Liz, we really shouldn't be out until the 'all clear' bell." She ignored the man and approached Adam.

Aven noted others were spilling from the basement, agape at the carnage displayed. One, a young girl, shrieked and collapsed, causing all to tense, weapons bristling. They followed her line of sight to the headless ruins of a young man's body.

Liz roughly inspected Adam. "Are you hurt?"

To his credit, he endured the handling with a smile, "I kept the animals safe!" he exclaimed, oblivious to her concern over his wellbeing.

Screams erupted far off in the city. The companions searched for threat, and a fist of guards ran—weapons drawn—after a small dog.

"Let's go help," Aven suggested as Adam and the crowd headed back into the cellar.

CHAPTER SIXTEEN

Everyone had been too exhausted to talk during their evening meal last night. They'd spent the whole day helping the city guard—and guild—clean up the streets. So, after a silent dinner, everyone went straight to their beds.

This morning, Raliel had absolutely nothing to do. Marcus was nowhere in sight. Sgt. Land told her HQ summoned Marcus for a meeting, probably regarding yesterday's incident.

She returned to her room and donned her full gear for the first time in weeks. She thought of seeking out Aven or Mendel on one of the escort jobs currently supporting them. Even if Vic did the same, she felt a little guilty for spending so much time in training while they worked so hard. But, of course, it didn't help that she enjoyed it so much.

Aven had been training too and still found the time to join Mendel for jobs. So she put on her gleaming mail shirt, belting her axe over it, creating a skirt. She wore her steel boots, too, feeling much more accustomed to it all.

Now, following Aven's signal and Mendel's, she mentally applauded herself for all the hard work. Her axe felt weightless, and with her enhanced belt, she had a crazy spring to her step that she had to work to restrain. She was eager to test her capabilities, mentally cataloging all the forms and maneuvers she'd memorized. When her muscles twitched in response to these thoughts, she smiled.

The city boulevard was packed with armed guards and civilians today. It felt tense since yesterday's breach. Many blamed it on the increased traffic brought on by King Gershon's proclamation. Midhaven's caravans had never been so long, the gates never so busy. They grew larger every day. Wealthier groups arrived steadily, keeping the town portal flowing day and night.

A crowd—kept orderly by a compliment of stern guild veterans—formed a line of would-be adventurers seeking employment or membership at the guildhall. As Raliel walked past, she caught looks from the newbies. Her bright mail and gear weren't the shiniest—some ridiculously so—but she carried them like a true warrior. Some gawked. All showed deference. She felt respected and a little bit feared.

She was pleased to note clusters of women peppered throughout the group—women dressed in leathers, swords strapped to waists and backs, and steel in their eyes. Plenty also held crossbows, staves, and spears of all shapes and sizes.

The King's call to seize back the wilds had been responded to in force. Men and women of all ages filled the streets with packs on their backs and hope in their eyes. After weeks, she knew how that felt; her excitement electrified the air.

When she reached the entrance for the merchant district, Aven's signal moved farther west, while Mendel's led north into the district's huge square of shops. Raliel veered to intercept Mendel, who she knew would be handling today's job.

Mendel's reputation for dependability had preceded him. As a massif, the wealthy competed for his services to claim prestige. His skills attracted the best jobs available, which she suspected were created just to hire him. But, of course, he had no qualms about playing along with either, if only to see everyone up to pursue intense training. After all, their planned return to the ruins was near, and they needed to be ready.

Butterflies filled her stomach at the thought, but she relished the feel. She let it fortify her spirit with battle lust.

The small cobblestone lanes of the merchant district were flowing with customers purchasing weapons, equipment, and a plethora of products. Shops and street vendors sold everything from kitchen knives, pots, and pans to battle axes, helmets, and shields. Nothing was used or secondhand in the upscale merchant district.

The pleasing aromas of various foods wafted heavily from scattered vendors as well. Finishing up a meat pie, finger in mouth, she found Mendel. He was looking right at her as she rounded a corner building.

She guessed that his massif amulet must be more potent than hers because she caught him a fraction later, bright green eyes locking on molten red irises. Mendel's Massifae eyes could range from a warm brown to a vibrant crimson, betraying his mood. She'd never seen another massif, but the peculiarity was well known.

He gave her a nod and continued to watch over his wards: three wealthy youths. Mendel was strict while on the job, taking each very seriously. She imagined that was part of why he was in such high demand.

Mendel expected the same from his 'company associates' while on these 'campaigns.' She recognized he did this for their benefit and had assumed the teacher role of everything proper to running the company.

Adopting a professional demeanor, Raliel approached formally, taking her place next to Mendel. She analyzed the clients and the perimeter. "Need a break?"

"No." He maintained vigilance.

She noticed a familiar face among the lord-lings. Alicia? Drina? They all knew the girl's name from Aven's visit to the mansion, and she from the cave. Raliel examined the other two more closely. A brother and sister with dull dark hair, eyes wide, and faces beaming at Alicia. Though their clothes were new and expensive, their hair was mussed, and their hands and faces were not as meticulously clean as their host. Meanwhile, Alicia, resplendent in a white dress, forest green cape with white fur trim, and jewelry, talked up a storm. She showed the sister a pair of earrings, nodded, and paid a street vendor without collecting the change.

"Been at it all morning, she has," Mendel rumbled. A faint smile twitched at the corner of his mouth before he checked it. His eyes twinkled a warm brown.

Raliel pretended to adjust her belt and mail, hiding a silly grin.

"Since you're here, you could pick up this order for me." He produced a small ticket with an address on it.

"Sure thing," she said and headed off, glad for something to do.

The larger shops started farther north through a grid of booths and small stands. Cobblestone lanes became more intricate, cleaner, with multicolored stone. The crowds noticeably reduced where much more expensive specialty items and services were available. Raliel's boots knocked heavy with the weight of her gear; though she didn't feel burdened with her belt, she might as well be in a summer dress.

The thought tickled her as she envisioned just that-with axe strapped to her belt.

The address led her far north in the district. By the time she located it, she'd grown entranced by the change of environment. The scents of food were more elegant, and the eating establishments more refined. Crystal clear windows displayed the most fanciful products and wares, all glitter and gleam, on stands and velvet cushions. Everything was in a price range she'd never imagined. Just being among the shops was exhilarating.

It was here she found the shop. The immaculate black store building had no window or signs, just a single steel door with the address in bold silver numerals: 11500. No bell tinkled as she entered. The interior was illuminated only by a few displays, crystal cases small and large. The biggest held a man's gleaming suit of plate mail. Just within was a formally dressed young woman standing so still and quiet that Raliel's heart lurched to recognize the silhouette lived. The woman stood, hands clasped behind her back, in a sharp-cut dark gray dress.

"How may I assist you, miss?" her voice had a musical quality and sounded even younger than she looked.

Raliel handed over the ticket, and the woman, after a glance, instructed, "Follow me, please."

Beyond the crystal cases worked an older man in a suit, measuring a mannequin torso fitted with bright plate armor. He was intent on adjusting the buckles of the two-piece torso-encasing cuirass. Raliel looked for the woman but found her gone. Only darkness with display beacons remained visible.

"Miss Raliel, I presume? I'll need a few measurements from you;

please remove your mail."

She studied the cuirass. A shell of steel, sealing any breach and hiding the buckle releases, the front half made to overlap the back half; it was form-fitting, depicting artfully sculpted breasts and muscled torso, both elegant and robust. The top left a space for the neck, and from shoulders hung hinged pauldrons. Steel, polished to a shine, encased all until the swell of hip and thigh shone a delicate skirt of glittering mail draped below mid-thigh.

"Your measurements, miss?"

Raliel blinked and turned to the tailor of steel. The older man nodded, appreciating the pleasant reaction to his work. She scrambled to remove her mail and heavily quilted smock, carried away by unseen hands. The man finished the cuirass by attaching a fine red leather cape edged in steel studs. The image was so striking that she hardly noticed the final measurements taken.

***

There were five others in Aven's group today learning how to function under extreme weight, with only two others fully plated as him. Most others went for more simple mail or smaller pieces at a time.

Guildsman Malek seemed not to understand that a full suit was heavier. Much heavier. Aven was graded equally and had to keep pace if the group ran, jumped, or climbed. Full armor sounded glamorous, attracting many ambitious souls, but Aven learned almost no one stuck with it long. It was easier, if not more practical, to only wear what you needed.

Aven continued at a steady jog, careful not to lock his knees, keeping a rhythm. From neck, shoulders, calves to toes, he felt the weight. Every movement had to be compensated for and relearned. Malek provided tremendous insight for those who endured, such as pointers on how to pivot and swing, to not only handle the weight but add force to an attack.

Malek, a lifetime bearer of full armor, carried his with enthusiasm and an endless supply of commentary. "If you can dance in it, you can fight in it." To which he would often demonstrate.

The first few days of training were torture beyond anything Aven expected. At first, not the grueling exercise but the soreness of muscle and tendons in indescribable proportion. Aven would depart

185

trembling, fearing the inevitable cramping before he could soak in an ice-cold tub sipping the strange healing concoctions Malek provided for those who successfully climbed the daily 'mountain' of exercise circuits and challenges. The class strove hard for a limited amount of blessed potions. With their help, Aven quickly noticed the thickening of muscle, bone, and sinew in his body. After the first week, he began to relish the prospect of exhausting himself under the weight of heavy armor, a distinct ache that was becoming addictive.

Greater endurance brought the need for greater exertion. Malek responded with relays of rope climbing, sprinting, and leaping. No ordinary man could do much of either for very long, with, or without, aided recovery. Soon, though, what Aven could do so overshadowed where he'd been that he was amazed, then very proud.

His current group followed his pace stoically. Foreheads glistened and cowled with strain, his own hidden within a full helm. That got some getting used to also. Nobody wore their helmet everywhere; it wasn't practical because wearing a helmet reduced a person's vision. Aven was required to wear his though because during a fight was the wrong place to get used to one. Malek consistently tested his awareness with a thrown stick here and there.

Rounding a final corner, they trotted toward the guild's training grounds, which wasn't much more than a fifty-foot square of packed dirt. Upon arrival, everyone got in position for their assigned exercises. Most of these Aven already advanced beyond. Aven entered a small square of ankle-deep sand, where he was appointed to run circles. Not as easy as it sounded, and it quickly destroyed his first thoughts of increased personal adroitness.

"Aven!" Malek summoned from where he monitored his students. Aven approached. The veteran instructor was, as always, fully encased, minus the helmet, in plate armor aged with a dark green patina. It looked like bronze but couldn't be such a heavy metal. Not at his age and not with the ease he handled it. His eyes were pitch black, and his hair, once black, was now streaked with silver in a tightly combed ponytail.

The familiar scent of earth and oil of these grounds filled Aven's nostrils. He breathed deeply, "What's up, Malek, sir?"

Malek bristled at the 'sir,' making Aven grin wide beneath his helm.

"That's it, son," he fired back, "this concludes your final day of basic training. You can check back in from time to time, and I'll have some specialized lessons."

Aven involuntarily huffed a sigh of relief, heaving his chest and shoulder plates. "And here I thought it'd never end."

"Oh, it never does. If you stay busy, you shouldn't have much trouble staying conditioned. Just remember the simple routines you'll need during times of inaction."

"Yeah, of course."

"Well, Aven, you should get going then."

"Right. Thanks, Malek." Aven turned to go. He had nothing to gather. Everything he needed was on him.

"Oh, Aven?"

"Yeah?"

"Here are four recovery potions with a basic recipe most dealers can manage to follow. 'Course, if you want the best stuff, you'll have to see me."

"Thanks." Aven put the stone bottles in his pouch.

"And Aven?"

"Yes?"

"Uh, you can take your helmet off now," Malek smiled, extending a gauntlet. True to his word, he'd gotten Aven to forget it was even on. They shook gauntlets. Aven left it on as he left, sure that Malek was pleased by that. As he exited the grounds, Aven started when the veteran instructor barked at his students.

"Alright, you filthy boglins, who's up for some handstand press-ups!"

Aven merged with foot traffic on the main street. With his helmet under his left arm, he glanced over his right shoulder to the handle of his greatsword. The helmed visage on the pommel face, frozen mid-roar, watched his back.

It was just past midday, judging from the sun. Though training had been exhausting, he felt a little giddy by his graduation. A notable accomplishment considering the high rate of washouts: Aven felt like treating himself. He could always clean up later.

He veered away from his original course to Midways; instead, he headed to the farmer's market district with the fruit stands.

Midhaven was markedly more crowded than usual, but he'd finally, over the weeks, gotten hold of his 'city legs' and could weave and flow with the rest of them. The armor helped. He no longer received the looks from city folk he used to as a newbie. He felt natural among them.

Confident. He picked up the pace, flowing faster through the swarm.

There was a wider variety of people now that many were coming to heed the King's proclamation. Had he and his friends looked so aimless and awed?

No wonder they'd gotten looks. There were plenty of veterans about, most walking in smaller, disciplined groups if not solo. The inexperienced tended to group up in jovial clusters as if heading to a festival instead of danger.

The packed farmer's market caused a slight delay in acquiring fresh melons and assorted nuts. Instead, he found the park table and grass banks with messy picnics bordering campsites. It bothered him to see litter and trash marring the site of his and Raliel's first visit here. The breeze shifted just a breath and with it, a whiff of unwashed bodies and waste.

Their first visit here seemed so long ago. The trio had all grown much in such a short time. Battle experience, however small, had affected them greatly. He settled in an open spot near the river and wondered how much they'd be forever altered by what was to come because it was indeed coming. He felt it in his bones. In whatever this strange cavern would bring. He admitted the question—or fear—was, would they survive?

They'd ensured they were better prepared, but how prepared could they be for the unknown? How much could one—or ten!—do to ensure success if faced by another bogrock? Surely there could be more. What could they do if surrounded by a hundred bogrocks? Indeed, there existed worse things out there. Being unable to protect Raliel again paralyzed him with fear, but he couldn't show it. To suggest that she couldn't take care of herself would insult her. He knew better. He smiled at that.

If anyone could handle herself, it was Raliel. She'd made the most noticeable progress. It was increasingly evident in everything she did. She was radiant, with confidence, deadly grace, and lethal elegance. It had always been latent, but now it was a dominant feature.

Shaking the doubts and worries from his head, Aven produced his eating knife to begin his meal. The red melon was sweet and succulent. Careful to contain the mess, he became lost in the view across the water. Untouched by the encroaching visitors, like a completely different world.

Like a shade, Vic fluttered through the crowds. Because of the incredibly cheap cost of living, the slum district is highly populated, rivaling even the busy merchant district. Navigating the ebb and flow of bodies held no difficulty for the Hunter. Vic was in the mode most inherent to his calling.

Something was different about his instructions today. Usually, he'd be assigned a target to shadow while still at the base. Although today, Azure had said only to get to the location now just ahead. Something troubled him, and his instincts piqued. He sensed that something had changed in his world.

Nothing had tested his limits, so perhaps it was nothing more than nervous anticipation. Shadowing and spying—though at first exciting—were so easy. He wasn't sure, but it seemed to be all that Taberah's chapter did. After all this time, he wasn't sure about much.

His progress with Taberah? Now that was something real. The fluttering concept was simple, at least in theory, to reverse the technique Nazar had taught him. He'd just achieved his first flutter after much practice. He couldn't get enough, so he practiced now.

Even though he knew the effect to be within him, it was still fascinating to observe the seemingly altered state of the world around him. Before, through Nazar, he could 'speed' things around him. The ability to slow his heartbeat was functional when necessary to wait: the ability to slow his heartbeat and enter a state of lethargy without compromising mental acuity. He could slow bleeding and preserve life indefinitely with it. He'd gotten used to it. Fluttering was the opposite and much more dangerous for the same reasons. In a hyper state, one could bleed out in seconds. So it was something to be used sparingly and with the utmost caution. Not that he was that strong with it yet. That, like with his other skill, would take time.

He fluttered. He became more agile—quicker than an average person to those around him. From his perspective, those around him slowed down to an easily negotiable degree. Taberah claimed that a master could slow the world to a stop with time, at least from a perspective.

Another challenge was appearing normal in those situations and not attracting attention required subtlety. Possessing both abilities in regular use could atrophy standard muscle control, making movements seem odd, erratic, and suspicious. It wasn't as noticeable in the flurry of street traffic—a perfect training ground, allowing the Hunter to negotiate his route seamlessly.

Instinct led Vic to come fully equipped, more than usual. A nondescript rough-spun missionary's travel cloak concealed the array of throwing knives and spikes covering his stealth suit.

Cutting sharply into a narrow alley—between buildings—he used his newfound ability to kick off each opposing wall in a steady rise to the roof. Landing upon dilapidated clay tiles, puffing and sweating from the flutter, he searched for the described location in his instructions. There.

A few levels above, he could just barely discern the symbol. From up there, he could view the whole slums. Few buildings stood as high in the area. He could even make out the back of Midways.

Vic's dark cloak billowed in a sudden gust. Beneath the symbol was an opening to a gutter drain. Reaching in, he recovered a clay tube sealed with wax. His heart quickened involuntarily, and he resisted the urge to consciously slow it. He was checking his desire to rely too heavily upon his gifts. Nazar and Taberah had warned about that.

Cracking the seal, he poured out a tiny scroll inked with a micro script. He recognized the cipher and read it twice to ensure he understood. He'd been expecting this, a real mission and with it, real risk. He wasn't sure how he felt about killing a human but reached the crossroads where he had to trust it was justified, in Taberah's judgment. Surely Nazar knew this would be required eventually. He trusted Nazar. This logic restored his resolve.

The Hunter straightened and donned his custom helm. Then, somewhere, a nighthawk cried.

***

"Marcus!?" She'd hoped to find him in his workshop, but he was out. Raliel took a look around the room, now so familiar. Light from two high windows cast rays illuminating dust motes above a large work table. Golden particles ascended and descended like beings on a stairway to heaven.

An array of incendiary weapons she and Marcus had created lay on the table. She'd been staying to help him arm the D.C. troops in her free time. Instead of rushing off to work a company job, she'd stayed

190

and continued learning.

She inspected a few fist-sized clay pots used to hold a flammable liquid, a concoction they'd created themselves.

Marcus had become a friend, and it dawned on her that she'd never had many friends. She'd spent most of her life training or working in her father's stables, though by choice, always in her family's company or Aven, Vic, and Nazar. She'd preferred it over the average distractions girls her age shared.

Raliel had never enjoyed the company of other girls—her age or otherwise. While her mother encouraged her to, Fargar always supplied a way out. She supposed it was because of her affinity with him and that she was the only girl of the clan, his little girl. She smiled.

Gravel crunched underfoot outside as someone approached. She pretended she didn't notice. The steps paused at the threshold behind.

"Oh, Raliel, it's good you're here, though I'm afraid I canceled training."

She turned to face him. Today, her hair was loose, displaying her uniquely beautiful multi-colored locks of red, blond, and almost white tresses. The rays of light ignited them in a blaze.

"Hi, Marc; notice anything different?"

She posed valiantly in her new set of plate armor, which refracted light in flickers of silver and white.

"Ah! You've shaved your chin?"

Raliel rubbed her smooth chin with a mock scowl, "I'll give you one more guess before I shave YOUR chin Marc with my axe." She brushed her other hand over the hilt of her axe.

With a laugh, "Ha! You're getting better at that. We'll make a proper warrior out of you yet! Okay, so who'd you kill to get such fancy gear?" he closed the distance between them, inspecting the armor, tugging here, and rapping his knuckles there. It was a mark of their mutual amity that he was allowed to be so near. Raliel never trusted physical contact, especially with the opposite sex. A justified suspicion that clashed with her favored choice of company. With Marcus, she hardly noticed.

He stepped back. "Seems functional, well made, and solid."

She smiled, looking down to admire it herself.

"How does it feel," he asked, "not too heavy?"

"No, it's light, a steel alloy, strong and thin. So I can move well," Raliel said, stretching her arms and bending to demonstrate.

She silently challenged him to comment on the artfully and tastefully designed chest plate. But, fortunate for him, he seemed not to notice.

He turned his back, changing the subject, "There's something to discuss."

"Yeah, there is. So what do you mean you canceled training today?"

"Not just today. It's over."

Her face screwed up in irritation, "But I've paid…."

"You've paid for training in the use of the axe, and I've provided you that as agreed, even more than required, I might add, and it's been a privilege."

"But I've so much to learn!" Raliel's face was a mask of pain and confusion.

"Of course you do; we all must continue to learn, Raliel, but to be honest, you've surpassed my ability to teach. Can't you see how much I struggle to keep you challenged?"

She didn't reply because she didn't want to admit it was true. Training had ceased to become increasingly complex, as it used to, but it had become comfortable—a fixture in her life.

"What will I do…?"

"Oh, Raliel." He hopped up to sit on the table next to her. "There's more…."

She looked at him in wonder as he uncharacteristically struggled for the right words.

"I've just got back from a legion briefing. I've been reassigned."

"What do you mean? You can't get reassigned; you're retired, aren't you?"

"Well, yeah, but I'm still on legion payroll." He shook his head firmly, "I've agreed to fill the post."

"What is it?"

"A command position when the coalition forces push back the wilds."

Raliel stood up with force, knocking aside the comforting arm Marcus had attempted to place around her shoulder. "But it's suicide. You said it yourself!"

"I said that it would be next to impossible to hold any ground unless the proper numbers and order were present." He raised his hand to prevent her from interrupting, "I'd never thought it likely; the report is that the numbers are more than sufficient, but it'll still be a massacre without proper leadership." He took a deep breath, sitting up straighter, smoothing his tan uniform, its crisp pressed creases she only now noticed. Quite a few stripes and ribbons adorned it. "I couldn't live in peace knowing I refused to participate or allowed our first major offensive in centuries to fail. I have to help; we all do."

He studied her as she absorbed his words. She was lovely—distractingly so at times. His mind wandered a bit, entertaining thought of what could've been had he been a few decades younger. Finally, he shook the thoughts away and sighed. "Whether I go or not, this offensive will proceed. If there's any chance I can help make it a success, I have to take it," he paused, "while I still can; I'm not getting any younger, and if my training you has proven anything, I'm slowing down.

"So, that's it then. Bye." Raliel's face hardened, and she strode to the door, stopping to place a hand on the threshold. Marcus stood up from the table. He thought, here it is, a deciding moment. "You could come. We could use your skill and flaming axe; surely you know that."

She didn't turn to respond, "No. My place is with my friends."

Silence filled the space between them, knowing that their friendship had somehow altered.

He tried to think of something he could say, something profound or soothing, but couldn't find the words. He scowled at Raliel's back. No words would come; they knew each other's thoughts regarding this excursion too well to try and fool one another about the risk. His last words to her wouldn't be a lie. So silence won out, as painful as the struggle was to know she was waiting, "I gotta go, Marc."

And that was it; she was gone—the very best thing going on in his worthless life—gone.

Outside, Raliel combated rage and tears and rage *at* her tears. She refused to wipe her face and admit there was cause to do so.

Thankfully the grounds were clear; everyone must be preparing for the impending offensive into the wilds.

Why she was acting like such an infant, she didn't know. It only embarrassed her to think of how much a fool she'd seemed to Marcus. "Idiot!" she screamed, not caring if anyone heard. Men could be so reckless and foolish. So why should she care? Marcus had been fighting long before she was born and would be able to take care of himself. She needed to push this from her mind and focus on what was important. Tonight was the moment they'd been planning. Aven expected everyone to be ready to venture back into the cavern. Nothing could be allowed to distract her—today or tonight—she wouldn't allow it. But first, she'd need to blow off some steam.

***

"No, as far as I can tell, they don't plan to participate in the wilds campaign." Arman waited patiently for his words to relay across the gorge to the receiver location. And back: "As long as you're sure. Our benefactor would be most unhappy if anything happened to the friends."

"I assure you that they're in good hands. We've done everything possible to ensure their stay has been safe and profitable." Arman stretched, sitting back from the communication crystal on the table. The only piece of furniture within the secret room. "I have an agent on them at all times and am working on something…more permanent."

"That would be helpful."

"Indeed. I hope to keep the Bright Company employed and thoroughly distracted with any luck until things die down." Arman paused in thought before adding, "Or until the master shows."

"He intends on coming to Midhaven? Remarkable."

"Yes, it's been quite a while. Ten years. Another indication of how important this matter is to the Esteemed One."

"Yes."

Arman waited again for the message to clear before concluding, "If I can, I'll continue fortifying the friends with enhanced equipment, although it hasn't been easy—or cheap—to do so without raising their suspicion. That sword of Aven's," he searched for the right word, "an heirloom! Please extend my deepest respects to our brethren on that side and Raphu?"

"Yes?"

"Don't worry; I've got the situation well in hand."

"Very well, goodbye for now."

The crystal's connection was severed, diminishing its blue illumination and leaving Arman in the dark. Nevertheless, he could navigate the room by rote even without sight.

So far, Aven's company had managed to stay clear of lasting harm, but these were dangerous times. Arman was no fool. Eventually, the

194

kids would bite off more than they could chew and get killed. Any amount of covert assistance couldn't prevent it indefinitely. He needed someone inside, perhaps with enough influence to guide them in a more controlled direction. He'd have to look into that.

He didn't know his brethren's interest in the three friends, but his task was to keep them safe. At least for now. He sighed, hoping things stayed manageable.

He couldn't help but like this young adventurer, Aven. It was fortunate that the boy's team happened to be the group to rescue his other charge. Most fortunate. And yet, there was something familiar about him. Something that Arman couldn't quite place.

The muffled sound of grating stone segued into the backside of a vast tapestry concealing the secret room. He waited for it to close behind before producing a giant feather duster and resuming his daily inspection within the Lumin manor.

***

"It was like—I dunno—a giddy feeling each time I connected a blow, and the feeling intensified the more devastating it was." Aven had decided to consult Ed regarding the enchanted blade. He certainly wanted to avoid any surprises on their excursion tonight.

"What else? Remember, two enchantments are working on this weapon."

"Well, I think it's too weak to tell for sure, but I want to say that I never feel as tired when handling this blade. Nothing compared with my old broadsword. But it could just as easily be that giddy feeling distracting me." Unsheathing the weapon, Aven placed it on the counter for inspection; the long broad blade never lost its mirror-like polish or razor edge. The cross guard and hilt attracted admiration equally and resembled some silver-fanged beast's open maw. The pommel capped by that snarling helmed warrior, a snarl that appeared on the verge of lunacy. It was amazingly intricate and so well-crafted that, at times, it looked alive.

"Hmmm..." Ed studied the sword intently. He'd cast several detection spells. Still, the problem—for now—was already well stated and understood: because of the severing and rejoining that the pieces had endured, the magical enchantments were greatly diminished. The good news was that both were rare and valuable, the type that could gain strength—and affinity with the owner—with time and use. Not so great was the chance that they wouldn't discover the effects until it was too late. The unpredictability of combined enchantments was even more dire, which could have possible dangerous reactions.

"Well, so far, what you're experiencing sounds like nothing more than enhancing attributes. Which aren't as volatile as, say, explosive or elemental strikes." At Aven's crinkled brow, Ed explained, "for instance, imagine if you could join water affinity with a lightning strike. It'd shock the user just as much as their opponent—in theory anyway.

"Anyhow, there's no immediate danger because of the weakness of the magic. Just be sure to pay close attention to each use. If you feel any pain or weakness, discontinue use on the spot. Some artifacts are cursed, just as much as otherwise. It shouldn't take—at the rate you're goin'—more than a few more fights to proliferate. These tend to grow faster when they're weak. Especially when they've possessed greater strength."

Aven nodded somberly. Thoroughly tempered with a healthy respect for the weapon, as he should. "Thanks, Ed. How's business?"

"Improved, with this sudden wave of adventurers. With thanks to Bright Company, of course. I wouldn't have survived the last slump if it wasn't for your patronage."

Since meeting Ed, Aven and the team had worked to promote his business at every opportunity. To clients, fellow adventurers, and dealing exclusively with him themselves.

"Business has been good enough to consider hiring someone to run the shop for a day or two out of the month," Ed said, though his eyes still studied the blade.

"Great to hear. After tonight, perhaps we'll be able to contribute to your selection here."

Ed looked startled, "Whattaya mean, 'after tonight'? You're not planning anything too dangerous, are you?"

Aven grinned at the genuine concern in Ed's eyes. "Not to worry. Nothing out of the ordinary for a guild company."

Ed still looked concerned but nodded. "I hope you're taking Mendel, at least."

"Not much choice. I don't think anything could stop Mendel from joining this particular venture." Aven grinned as his sword clicked home in the sheath on his back. "We'll be fine and back before you know it."

"Oh, alright, so it's in town? For a moment, I thought you were leaving the safety of the wall."

"No, we're not leaving these walls, not yet anyway." Aven couldn't resist implying that the notion wasn't far off. Another look of concern rewarded him. Then, feeling a little guilty for tormenting poor ol' Ed, he concluded, "Well, thanks for the help," and set a coin on the counter for the service.

"That's not necessary; we're friends, Aven."

"Nonsense, the fee is advertised on the door, and a true friend doesn't take advantage."

Ed exclaimed, "You're every bit as bad as Mendel!"

When had the coin disappeared? With another grin, Aven bid goodbye, explaining he had to catch up with the rest of the crew for an early meal.

At the tinkling of the doorbell, left in an empty shop, Ed wondered what kind of adventure Aven could be getting into within the city and if it necessitated action on his part. He'd recently received some exciting instructions regarding the Bright Company, and he couldn't agree with them more.

CHAPTER SEVENTEEN

Today, Adam rushed to finish his chores. The novelty of working in the stables had long worn away for him. But that wasn't why he was leaving. Instead, it suddenly came upon him this morning while going through his meditation exercises. It felt right, and now he knew what he wanted to do. And that was that.

So he'd packed up his meager belongings and got set to go. He couldn't bear the thought of disappointing Liz, especially after all she'd done for him, but he didn't want her to worry, so he'd spent the last ten minutes composing a letter. He planned on leaving it where she'd find it. First, however, he had to hurry before she called him for supper, so he finished his duties hastily. Dressed in a new pair of muslin slacks and shirt, beneath his ruddy robe, he slung a leather satchel that was an old re-purposed saddlebag over his shoulder. It contained a change of clothes, personal effects, and a pouch with all the coin he'd saved from tips and such since working the stables. Liz had also gifted him a pair of sturdy leather boots.

Adam experienced another pang of loss at the thought of leaving such a good place. Liz had been the kindest in his life, next to Ed, and he already missed her. Initially, Adam planned to stop by Ed's to let him know of his plans, yet he wasn't sure how that would go. It wasn't like they could stop him; he was, after all, his own man, but…facing them he might lose his resolve. He finished wrapping a cloth filled with bread and cheese. He had a habit of stashing the stuff since he was little, just one of his many quirks. He'd need to buy a water skin, as well, before leaving town.

He stood, looking at the loft for the last time, nodded, and descended the ladder.

He fixed his letter to a nail on the first beam inside near the stable door so she'd see it there.

"Adam!?" Liz called from the other building. It was now or never.

Without looking back, Adam hurried out the stable door, careful to latch it, and scampered off as fast as possible; his unexpected exhilaration helped suppress the sadness.

Adam headed for a supply merchant, hoping he didn't run into anyone he knew before he could catch up with the others.

After encountering the undead, he wanted to be a part of the solution—eradicating evil. Empowered, he felt like this was the beginning of one of the stories he'd loved as a kid. He felt like his talents wouldn't be wasted on a silly family legacy for the first time.

The crowds had diminished somewhat now that people were heading out to the place of meeting, in some old ruins beyond the east gate. He continued to the nearest supply shop.

He wanted his life to mean something, so he decided to leave home. Everyone wanted him to do what they thought best, all in preparation for a life they wanted him to live. They had all sorts of fancy titles for it if you chose to embrace it, all kinds of terms, but it all amounted to the same. Call it 'duty,' or 'slavery,' it didn't matter.

The heroes in the stories never allowed anyone to tell them what to do. It was often the case, even the moral of the story that they knew better. Contrary to the majority. Now, he intended to make his story and follow his heart.

He was born with the talent, and if it were as strong or would become strong as they suspected, he'd need to work with it in the real world. What better way than to eradicate evil? He was, after all, doing the king's will.

"Maybe I'll even get some land of my own," he thought aloud. Getting a water skin was simple: in and out. He stepped to the side of the shop outside, trying to figure out the capping mechanism to get it filled.

The majority of traffic flowed toward the east gate. There were many different colors as several flamboyantly garbed nobles with an abundance of matching attendants paraded past. Here and there, units of ten to twenty heavily armed legionnaires marched, breastplates gleaming. Most others looked to be no more than ordinary farmers and village folk, out to try their luck and seek a fortune. Their weapons were sometimes crude or the look of being dug out of an attic. Picks and wood axes outnumbered swords and spears.

Adam knew of a public well he could fill his skin. There was a long line when he got there. People were thinking, like him, to fill up and depart while the sun was still early in the sky. In front of his spot were four young men, hardly adults, with money, judging from their gear. He couldn't help but overhear their conversation.

"We should make Deragard by nightfall if we hurry," one said.

"I still don't know why we don't just buy horses?" said another.

"It'd be so much faster." Another agreed.

"And do what with them," the first growled, "when we get near the Witherwood?"

"Sell them, of course."

"We'd hardly get our money's worth. Are you forgetting the restrictions on keeping any animals?"

"No, but it's gonna be such a long walk."

Adam interjected, "Excuse me?" the group turned to him with looks of annoyance. He continued, "Why are animals restricted?"

The first guy answered, "You hear about what happened at the gate?"

"I was there!"

"Sure, kid." They looked as if they expected him to retract his claim. When he didn't, their leader continued, "Well, you'd remember the animals." He looked at his friends, pleased at how he'd out-reasoned the lying kid.

"Oh yeah, that's right, they went crazy too," Adam confirmed.

"Not crazy, undead." Their leader looked Adam over, "Hey kid, you're not planning on going where we're going, are you?" they emoted disbelief in unison.

Adam didn't respond to it. Instead, he looked ahead to where a portly man and son filled a large bucket; city folk trying to negotiate their day around irregulars.

"Are you?"

Adam returned his eyes to the leader, unfazed, "Yeah."

"Look, kid," and it was said with genuine concern, "you tryin' to get yourself killed?"

"It's not like he'll get far, Clint," a member assured, "they'll turn him back as soon as they see how young he is."

"What do you mean?" Adam asked, not so serene anymore.

'Clint' sighed before answering, "You're way over your head, kid. Jake is saying that not only is there an age requirement, but everyone heading out needs to register at the guildhall." He pulled out a slip of thick parchment. "Everyone's got one of these, kid." His crew laughed at this.

Adam's face grew hot with embarrassment.

"Looks like someone's getting upset," one of them teased, but the comment was ignored by Adam as he turned his back on them.

He stalked off, empty water skin in hand. He needed to reassess his plan, to get to the ruins and get accepted. It was his best option to avoid having to return home.

He could sense that time was running out here, and he knew he'd have to establish himself soon or risk discovery. Sooner or later, someone would come looking or recognize him and turn him in for a reward. Sure, he took this risk, even in the Ruins, but he had to keep moving.

Adam walked for a long while, thinking, daydreaming, and something in between. He couldn't register with the guild. There would probably be a picture of him there soon, if not already. He could always go and take his chances.

"Hey there, Adam…goin' somewhere?"

Adam started; he hadn't noticed the massif approach. Though he liked the older warrior, he couldn't stop to chat, "Just running some errands."

Mendel fell in step with him. Adam said nothing; just kept walking, "hmmm," Mendel continued, "Errands, you say? Pretty far errands to be needin' a water skin and pack."

Adam didn't have the patience for deception, "I'm going to join the forces in the wilds." From the corner of his eye, he watched Mendel expecting him to do something. To what? Grab him? Throttle him?

Yell? It never came. What did come surprised him even more.

"Oh? Going to battle evil, eh? A noble quest indeed." There was no sarcasm in Mendel's voice. No mocking. If anything, his voice became grave.

"You're not going to try and stop me?" Adam asked, still wary.

"Why would I? I'm no friend of the undead. I've seen a little of what you can do. Your ability will be needed."

They'd wandered off the main boulevard and were leisurely striding through a residential area. Adam noticed a small park in the distance. On the green, small children chased a playful bounding kitten.

"So what's bothering you then, Adam?"

"I found out they won't accept me. I can't even register; I'm too young."

"Oh, there is that. So what do you plan to do?"

"I don't know Mendel, but I can't keep staying with Liz. I wish I could, but…" tears threatened to spill, but Mendel's big hand rested on his shoulder. It comforted him, and to his relief, the tears never came.

"Listen, son, whatever you're running from is your business." His big hand squeezed his shoulder, warm and surprisingly gentle, "let me finish. I'm sure you'll tell me when you're ready if you need, and you're free to go anywhere you want. I purposefully came looking for you. To offer you a job, son, when I found this." Mendel produced the letter Adam had left for Liz.

Again Mendel squeezed to forestall any needless interruption, "I'm offering you a position with me and some friends, who'll need your skills just as much. I've already talked to Liz, and she's agreed to relieve you of your duties for a while. You can still work there between jobs; we can hire you as a privateer without registering you at the guild."

"A guild company?" The idea was a bit overwhelming, more than he could've hoped. So much like the stories that it made him incredibly nervous.

"But don't think it's gonna be easy. No walk in the park." As Adam noticed that that was what they'd been doing for the past few minutes, Mendel chuckled. "We need your light magic, but I intend to see you trained during your off-time. As a privateer in training, you'll not be entitled to full hirelings share, understand? Nor a full treasure share…."

Adam's mind had long drifted off, daydreaming that he strode through the city in the company of grand adventurers, people all around agape with admiration. "...Adam?"

"Uh, yeah?"

"So, what's it gonna be?"

"Um," Adam cleared his throat and put on his best adult impression, "I'm in, sir."

"Good then. We've got a meeting to attend. Oh, and Adam?"

"Y-yes?"

"What should I do with this?" Mendel still held the 'goodbye' letter. Adam took it, and it bloomed in a puff of flame and ash.

Mendel's eyebrow raised, "We better get going before we're late."

***

"If you say so, Mendel, but I don't know how I feel about taking a kid down there." Aven felt nervous enough to take himself back there.

"We'll need light, and that kid is one of the most promising casters I've seen in a hundred years. I take full responsibility for him; he won't be any trouble."

Aven looked over to where Adam sat with Raliel in their usual booth.

Raliel was more withdrawn than usual; something was on her mind. Vic was nowhere to be found. It was like him to show up when you least expected, but not to be this late. Maybe it was just Aven's nerves, but everything seemed on the verge of going wrong. He scowled away the dark thought. He couldn't allow his resolve to falter, even in possible setbacks. His team needed to see confidence.

"I trust your judgment, Mendel. Any news on his story? I can't imagine a kid like him, with obvious education and nobody there for him."

"Orphans come in all shades, Aven."

"You're right, of course. I guess it's fortunate Adam found a crowd like ours."

"Seems Raliel is taking a liking to the boy," Mendel gestured, and when Aven saw, he grinned. Raliel was laughing aloud, ruffling Adam's hair. He shied away, frowning, making her laugh harder.

"Well, we might as well eat while we wait." Aven led the way to the booth, suppressing his worries well enough, or so he thought.

"He'll show, Aven," Mendel assured him.

"Well, if he doesn't soon, we're leaving without him."

"As you say, lad."

***

Vic located the building described by his instructions. Behind the Temple of Light were dormitories, the living quarters of its resident clergy, scholars, and workers. The temple itself was impressive; one of the largest single buildings in the city.

Whatever reason the brotherhood had, for him to recover an item from here, was none of his concern. All that mattered was a success. The mission, a more complex one than his usual, was evident by the authorization of lethal force. He couldn't fail and wouldn't. Not if he wanted to continue to excel at an accelerated rate.

He could almost feel the eyes on him, watching and weighing his every move. The brotherhood was nothing if not prepared, and he didn't doubt there were others out here ready to take his place or offer support from the shadows. That's how it worked.

The living quarters were two wings, separate rectangular structures running parallel from the back of the temple. Each branch was at least five floors. Inner windows faced each other over a garden set with paths and benches.

Grasping the lip of the overhang, he balanced himself to enable himself to peer over into the room below. A glance revealed nobody waiting nearby. He flipped forward over his hands, landing silently on leather-padded feet, instantly seeking the cover of a heavy curtain.

The room was much more elegant than he expected. The balcony opened to the backside of a foyer with a burbling fountain in the middle, beyond lie double doors of heavily constructed polished ironwood. To the right and left were arched walkways leading to, he assumed, the rest of the apartment.

He crept to the left, discovering the bath, a monstrous white marble room with a tub that could fit a group! Focus, he scolded himself.

The other arch revealed an equally expansive bed chamber and the glass case. *The* glass case! Vic continued to creep silently, painfully aware that his attire was conspicuous in the rose and cream-colored decor. A woman's room? A massive bed stood between him and the case, which glowed through the bed's gauzy curtains, illuminated by an unseen light source. It was the only light, a beacon.

Vic's night vision was sharp enough to study every detail of the room. A lady's. He couldn't imagine what the brotherhood wanted from here. Maybe this was nothing more than another test.

"Is someone there?" Vic froze at the woman's voice.

How could he be such a rookie? To make a sound in a situation like this was inexcusable. He couldn't even recall making a sound. Was he that distracted?

Movement on the bed. He quickly and silently wriggled under the bed to reevaluate his next move. Then, safely hidden, he heard a loud thump out in the foyer area. So it hadn't been him. Still, he'd missed the woman on the bed, and if she'd heard the noise, he should have first.

Another thump, followed by the splintering of wood, "Who's there!" the woman called. He heard a rustling above, the rattle of a drawer, and the unmistakable rasp of a drawn blade.

He'd wait to see what happened. Then, if he were lucky, the woman would investigate, leaving him alone to steal the item and flee into the night with none the wiser. However, if she raised the alarm, he could be discovered by guards and forced to fight his way out with a genuine possibility of capture or death. Temple guards were renowned for being well trained and well-armed, but worse: they were all casters and spell-swords. His only chance against them would be to hit hard and run harder.

"Whoever's there, I've got a weapon, and I'm ready to summon the temple guard on the count of three!"

Vic's heart sank, and he mouthed an expletive rough enough to make a soldier cringe.

"There, Lady Cassandra, it's only I, dear, your humble servant."

"Razael? You weasel, why have you, of all people, forced entry into my quarters at this hour? If your words don't satisfy me, I warn you, I'll scream!"

"Oh, my dear, I thought I heard you call out and found your door open. So, of course, I came in to investigate to ensure your safety." The bed creaked as she stood. Vic's gut warned that something was wrong and about to get worse. His instructions never said anything about harming this woman. Could he manage to smash the case, retrieve the item, and flee with them in the room? He might have to find out.

As the lady weighed the answer, a new, more menacing voice

introduced itself, "Just drop the slag and kill the witch already."

Uh-oh, Vic thought.

"You!" the female hissed.

"Yes, me, what of it?" Another louder and heavier rasping blade followed. "Razael, grab the relic and let's go."

"You'll do no such thing, GUARDS!"

"Go ahead and scream, wench, no one will hear you; we've seen too that. Go on, Razael."

The stifled thump of footsteps angled around the glass case, followed by a crash. Glass tinkled on the plush carpet next to Vic's right foot.

"I've got it, Jack."

"No names you imbecile! It seems we'll have to do something about her now."

"You said no harm would come to my lady."

"SILENCE! Now, Cassandra, why don't you put that dagger down? Don't make this messier than it need be."

Her voice sounded stronger than Vic expected. "If you think you're leaving here with my property, you're mistaken, and if you think I'm scared of you, that'll be a fatal mistake on your part."

"Have it your way. Razael, take the relic and go NOW!"

It was now or never. Vic wriggled to make his move even as the action began. From his view under the bed, he caught sight of a figure disappearing through the archway. Razael, he thought. A struggle ensued from Cassandra's side. When Vic made to chase Razael, he froze at her scream of rage.

Vic looked back, seeing her, "you!" he uttered, distracting her for the first time. They shared a look of confusion. Jack's sword plunged past her defenses, aimed at her heart.

Without thought, Vic sped his essence dangerously fast. Time seemed to slow. In one motion, Vic let fly a heavy knife at Jack's sword arm, even as he drew his sword, springing forward to strike the wild-haired thug down. The blade darted at almost natural speed, piercing straight through Jack's wrist before Vic realized his mistake: he became entangled in the near-transparent bed canopy. He lost focus, and time resumed to average speed around him.

"AHH!" Jack yelled, his sword rattled, Cassandra gasped.

As Vic fought to free himself, he heard a body tumble and the muffled thumps of fleeing feet. Free of the gauze, he looked for and tapped a 'light' rune on the headboard. Light bloomed above. His heart sank.

Cassandra lay back against the far wall, blood spurting weakly from a hole in her chest. He rushed to her side, skidding on his knees. Her silver-white hair was just as Vic remembered, flowing beautifully over her shoulders. He attempted to staunch the bleeding just above her left breast. It soaked the fabric in his hands, spattering her gown.

She began to make squeaking animal-like gasps, struggling to retain consciousness. She was slipping into a panic, causing her pulse to quicken. Her blood flowed freely, and Vic knew there was nothing he could do.

Her eyes were wide as saucers. From terror? He quickly removed his helmet, revealing his all-too-human gray eyes and black ponytail.

"Just relax; I'd never hurt you." Was the bleeding slowing? Vic asked himself; was she running low? Did it make a difference? She looked so pale. Her gasping eased, but he wasn't sure if that was good; he wasn't a physician! Finally, he pleaded, "Please try to hold on." For what?

Her right arm rose, pointing weakly to her nightstand.

"Do you want something from there?"

No response. No gasping. The woman's eyelids drooped. Reluctantly removing his hands, he saw blood oozing from a tiny hole. He crawled to the stand and found, among other things, a small golden bottle. He wasted no time, uncapped the cork with his teeth, and poured a small amount directly on the wound, hoping it contained what he thought it did. The surface wound sealed quickly and he poured the rest into her mouth, tilting her head back, even pinching her nose.

A clanging bell sounded through the walls; alarm. He had to go. She breathed faintly, but she lived. Donning his helm, he fled to the balcony, pulling himself up over the lip of the roof's overhang just as a BOOM rocked the heavy doors.

As Vic escaped into the night, the distant clanging alarm haunted him. He'd failed his first mission. So far, anyway. He didn't have to report until the morning, and not only did he get a look at 'Jack,' but he had two names.

The Elden girl would make it too, he assured himself. Within the Temple of Light, she was in the best position to receive help quickly.

There was no moon tonight, helping Vic remain unseen, as he sprinted on light feet to his next destination. It was time to focus on his next mission without letting the recent failure distract him. He cleared his mind and concentrated on his flight; he was already running late.

CHAPTER EIGHTEEN

The Town Portal was abnormally empty, even for nighttime. Aven stood, talking with a portal clerk, while the rest of his party waited behind. With Mendel's hammer and shield strapped to his back, he spoke with Adam, who looked like a half-ling compared to the massif's broad build. Just one of Mendel's fingers was as thick as Adam's wrist, an odd pair to look on.

Raliel stood stoically, flame-like hair braided tight. Every once in a while, she would look around to the front entrance expectantly.

They had to leave without Vic. Aven didn't like that he was late, but they'd all known he could only serve part-time from the beginning. So it hadn't been too much of a problem up until now.

Aven stood two feet over the clerk as the latter inspected the tattered scroll. Aven was also fully armed, in his steel plate suit, sword fastened to back, and full helm under the left arm, as he waited with forced patience.

"You do know that these don't last so long? Their magic does deteriorate."

"As you've said," Aven grumbled, "but it will work, won't it?"

"Yes, I can make it work this time, but you'll have to enter swiftly. I can't be sure how long it'll hold. Just let me know when you're ready."

"We're ready."

The clerk sighed, "Very well, please gather your companions to the side." The clerk indicated one of three circle patterns colored into the ancient marble floor.

They'd decided to travel light. The excursion wouldn't last long, just a quick inspection of the ruins. This time, Aven had two scrolls of the town portal, and every member carried a very expensive potion of healing, even Mendel, just in case. Aven had tried to account for every eventuality.

Everyone checked their gear once more as the clerk placed the scroll's remains into a marble bowl on a pillar before their circle.

On top of the healing potions and scrolls in his pouch, Aven had two recovery potions made, also just in case. He couldn't imagine needing more than one per day, but having two made him feel better.

A shadow near the entrance caught Aven's eye. Raliel confirmed it, "Vic's here."

Vic jogged up to Aven and explained that he'd been delayed in that hollow sounding voice. "I wouldn't miss this for the world," he assured, "can't let you guys have all the fun or take all the loot." He could be grinning, though all Aven could see was the fierce facade of his hawkish helm.

The clerk didn't try to hide his irritation, "Are you sure this is everyone?"

Aven, greatly relieved, nodded. "Yes, we're ready."

"Because once I open this, you'll have to head straight through, no delay."

"Got it, everyone, into position!"

They'd planned how this would go: the portal was made from

within a cell in the raider's camp, so Mendel would take the lead. Then Aven, Raliel, Adam, and Vic.

The clerk fiddled with the bowl's contents, gathered his pale blue robes, and concentrated. Suddenly, blueish-green electric currents crackled from the bowl, lighting the clerk's face, growing in intensity. In went his hand. Straight into electrifire. He deftly tossed a smoldering ball of energy at Mendel's feet. Blue-green flared furiously, almost violently. Then, just as suddenly, winked out. Still concentrating, the clerk waited, hands raised.

With an unnatural whirring sound, up spawned a silvery liquid mirror. It continued to vibrate with that strange whirring as it took form.

"GO!"

They rushed through in a rapid stream of bodies. Aven lurched, with momentary disorientation, finding Mendel at the cell door, hammer glowing just enough to show that there was no one else within the small cave.

Aven quickly cleared the cell as well. It was empty, of life anyway. He ignored the tiny remains—no time for that.

Raliel had already taken place opposite the cell door from Mendel. She waited for everyone else to take theirs.

Adam hung to the very back, preparing for his part, even as Vic shot through.

The portal stuttered and began to shrink with that odd whirring, causing too much noise for Aven's liking. Except for Raliel and Mendel, everyone uncomfortably watched as it sputtered and died fitfully. The only remaining light came from the blue foxfire of wispy lichen, hanging like spider webs outside the cell.

Aven motioned for everyone to hold silently. Beyond, out in the much larger cavern, dripping water echoed. The longer they waited, the louder it appeared to get.

Aven nodded to Adam, who held out his palm. Adam's whole hand began to glow. Faintly, at first, then gradually brighter until Aven could see Adam's feature clearly: red robe, it's hood up, and the boy's ruby ring sparkling on his other hand.

Mendel bent to examine the crude lock on the cell door. He tapped it lightly with his hammer. It instantly began to glow red, orange-yellow, and then a bright white before melting down the bars like molten wax. Mendel eased the iron door open carefully. It emitted a muffled groan that was torture on their nerves.

Once through, Vic darted out of the smaller cave, as quick and silent as a cat. Mendel had explained that his dark sight was naturally better than a human's though not as pronounced as some of the older mountain clans.

"No movement," he informed them, "looks deserted."

Aven took a look for himself, peering out into the greater cavern. At first, it looked like complete darkness until he began to discern points and accents of blue foxfire. Unfortunately, the distance was impossible for him to determine.

"Can't see anything," Aven whispered.

The party held patiently, waiting in the deafening silence, with some occasional shuffling from Adam. Their smallest member remained out of sight within the prisoner cave. Finally, after what felt like an eternity, Vic returned.

"It's clear. Abandoned."

Aven retrieved Adam as the boy's palm lit the way forward. Vic disappeared again, scouting. Finally, their party entered the campsite.

"Looks like more have come through here." Raliel observed aloud.

Further investigation showed evidence supporting that: a mess of indecipherable tracks covered everything, obliterating the camp; not a single structure remained.

"Good riddance," Aven remarked later, "not sure about you, but I wasn't exactly looking forward to meeting the bogrock's kin."

Raliel responded with a half-hearted chuckle. She had her axe at ready held in both hands. No matter the indications here, she didn't lower her guard.

It served as a reminder for Aven. He studied their surroundings with renewed suspicion. At their first stop, they found Vic, hands resting on the handles of his knives, standing motionless before the spot where they'd discovered Alicia's guardian.

"Gone," he stated.

"Adam, a little light, please," Aven instructed.

"Oh! Yeah, sure." His palm brightened, already more than any torch ever could. Pure white light allowed them to see much more than they could before. The stone floor had a dark green sheen to it.

"Looks like scavengers got to the remains," Mendel observed.

"Scavengers?" Aven asked, studying the scene.

"Yeah, don't be lulled by the serene environment; the chthonic world holds just as much life as anywhere else." As if in punctuation to his statement, a far-off screech echoed faintly. Raliel turned about, wary as ever.

Adam scanned the surrounding dark, eyes wide, his palm held high. Vic bent, examining the torn rags and bloodstains that marked the site.

"Not much we can do here." Aven nodded to Mendel and then to Vic to lead the way.

This part of the cavern, they'd discovered that the ridge rose to the right of the larger chamber with the camp and cell. A cliff dropped off at the back of the camp, showing the ruins down below. They had to head back, searching for a way through. With the proper light, it wasn't long before they discovered the entrance to a massive tunnel that veered off from the vast and uncharted cavern.

Within the tunnel, finally away from the forest of stalagmite and looming dark, visibility was unimpeded. The corridor was broad enough to walk ten abreast, and gravel spread across the ground. Stalactites still obscured the ceiling fifty feet above, differing in size and shape, hiding areas and casting strange shadows that moved eerily with their passing light.

Vic had gone far ahead out of sight, and Mendel led with Adam. So Aven found himself alone with Raliel. The atmosphere was more relaxed with better visibility, although Raliel still was not. She was intent on watching the growing darkness that stalked them from behind.

"Seems empty, doesn't it?" Aven said.

"It seems," was her taciturn response.

"Your new armor looks incredible." He tried again.

"It fits well," she said, "by the way, thank you."

"Oh, no problem. Mendel knew a place that specialized in it."

They continued walking backward, facing the dark. The walls here were a gray sculpted stone. This tunnel long predated the bogkind camp.

"This tunnel is ancient; what do you think, Rali?"

"Probably; what of it?"

"Nothing."

More silence but for the sound of the crunching gravel. Among the sound of dripping water, another screech pierced the dark, barely audible in the far distance, faint enough to leave one questioning whether they heard it. Moments later, another shriek answered, much closer. Raliel cast a stern look Aven's way—glaring.

"Oh." He reached back, drawing his greatsword. They continued backward. Careful to stay well within their light, allowing it and the crunching of Mendel's heavy tread to guide them. Aven sneaked a peek at Raliel, whose face showed only vigilance, eyes never straying from the blinding dark. Every time he looked at her, he couldn't help but feel glad she was with him. Also, to witness her growing into quite the adventurer filled his heart with admiration. That was it. He admired her for so many reasons. From the way she looked to the way she moved. Everything about her intrigued him.

"You should try to keep your eyes out there, Aven," she scolded, never averting her own. He spotted the hint of a smirk before he followed her advice and tried to suppress a blush. He was considering donning his helm to hide it when an odd chittering sounded just beyond their sight.

"What the hell was that, Aven!?"

"Not sure, but it sounds small."

"There!" A shadow, about the size of a small dog, shot out from the dark and froze. It chittered curiosity, but it was too dark for the two to see it even as Adam's light continued to retreat.

"It's just some small scavenger, probably harmless." Aven tried to soothe.

"And what do you think a scavenger eats in a place like this, Aven?"

"Good point. Hey, Mendel, we've got company."

"Oh, aye, we've had company for a while now. When's the last time you took a look above?" a strangled shriek came for Adam before Aven could do so.

"Holy Light, what the…" deathly silent, and just keeping pace inside the barrier of darkness was a veritable tide of spindly many-legged creatures.

"What are they, spiders?" Raliel hissed while struggling to watch above and behind.

Seeing Mendel's apparent ease, Aven tried to maintain a steady pace, though every instinct told him to flee. He also observed that the stalactites had thickened and began to offer the creatures enough cover to follow much closer than on the ground. Some were already scrambling for purchase directly above their heads.

"There's gotta be hundreds of them. Mendel, how can you be so calm?" Raliel sounded annoyed.

"Am I? Well, the best we can do is ignore them. They're not exactly 'spiders,' no venom to concern you. They're called crawlers and aren't too aggressive, to the living anyway."

A crawler lost its hold above, landing right in front of Raliel. Her axe thrust out to jab back the creature. But, instead, it latched on the blade with two powerful claws. The thing was covered in hard black shell with no visible eyes, yet still appeared wary of light. "Ahhh, get off, you disgusting…Thing!" Raliel swung her weapon, launching the creature into the dark; its chittering trailed almost comically if the thing wasn't so gross. Then, out beyond visibility, a satisfying solid 'clunk' sounded.

"Just keep moving and try not to engage; we can't afford to provoke them," Mendel growled, "I said they should leave us alone, but let's not test the theory."

They continued with the occasional crawler dropping, only to skitter off in a strange sideways scramble back into cover. Sometimes right up a wall with complete disregard for natural laws. Finally—and to Raliel and Aven's great relief—they reached the end of the corridor, capped in a smooth-cut chamber. The ceiling was much lower and cleared of stalactites, no crawlers either. A breach showed the rising cliff.

"Okay, let's brighten up that light a bit, Adam. Could you create another orb here at the entrance?" Aven asked.

"Yeah, no problem." Adam extended his free hand, sending a firefly of light into the mouth of the tunnel, exposing and driving back a wall of black carapace crawlers. The orb stopped right inside and brightened brilliantly. Crawlers fled far back out of sight.

"That should do it. Thanks, Adam."

"No problem."

"This way, everyone," Vic's hollow voice called.

Inside the new chamber wide stone steps were cut out of a natural incline. On each side sat the strange pots they'd noticed from far above and a succession of unlit pairs leading up. As soon as Mendel neared, the first two flared green fire, igniting the rest in a series of 'thwumps.' A jade-colored path ascended. As they climbed, Mendel explained, "Old Massifae magic. I wonder how long they've remained unlit. Only a massif's presence can activate their light." With each step, Mendel had become more and more eager. As Aven took note of this—as discretely as possible—he could see that Mendel's eyes were alight with more than just the green fire of the pots.

As they continued, the ceiling neared, much more distant than it had initially appeared, and the floor dropped further out of sight. The light from Adam's orb below grew faint with distance. The distance was one of the things Mendel had warned could be tricky down here. Finally, Aven caught up to Mendel, leaving Raliel to hold rearguard right behind Adam.

"Mendel, do you have any idea what this leads to?"

"Could be any number of things, really," his eyes met Aven's with unexpected measuring quality, never seen before, "Most are known and recognized. There are only a few within the human realms that are not."

"Like what exactly?"

"Well, Aven, it doesn't make much sense guessing about it when it's right up ahead now, don't you agree?"

At the top of the steps, two massive pots ignited green blazes illuminating a grand arched entrance on a landing. Their party entered in total awe, studying a large chamber. The room was cut in a great circle, green fire exposing every detail without hurting their eyes. As astonished as the rest, Adam dismissed his light spell, now unneeded.

Two dozen statues circled the chamber, displaying a variety of Massifae warriors and leaders. Each held a weapon and towered over the friends in majestic splendor. All were carved in smooth white stone, and each weapon—whether staff, axe, spear, or hammer—glowed a mystical green, including some they couldn't identify.

"The chamber's been looted," Mendel growled, "desecrated."

Aven noticed the broken stone doors hanging askew from destroyed hinges within the arch. Vic was inspecting the debris from broken chests and containers scattered around the chamber.

"Nothing but old supplies," Vic crushed a shriveled loaf of bread in his fist, rendering it to gray dust, "if the chamber is looted, it happened a very long time ago," he added tactfully, perceiving Mendel's discomfort.

"What is, or was this place?" Raliel asked, leaning back to examine an incredible carving of a robed massif heroine. The statue brandished one of the unidentifiable weapons over its cowled head.

"A redoubt," Mendel said quietly.

"What's a redoubt?" Adam asked in his squeaky adolescent voice.

"A place of safety. To rest and resupply."

"From the war?" Adam asked with reverence.

"Yes," Mendel sounded distracted, "from the war; nothing of value left, looted long, long ago...."

"Well," Aven encouraged, "it's not a wasted discovery. Historically, this place could provide answers that are invaluable to scholars."

"Yes, 'answers,'" Mendel drifted away to the rear of the chamber, intent once again on something unknown to everyone else.

"What's up with him?" Raliel asked Aven, abandoning one sculpture for another.

"Don't know. I expect it has something to do with the war." He guessed.

"You sure we can trust him?" Vic's hollow speech joined the queries.

"Yeah, sure, remember he did save our lives."

"I dunno," Vic continued, "something's been off with him ever since you mentioned this place. It's like this has been the plan all along."

"Seriously?" Aven took a calming breath. "What exactly are you implying?" Aven was open to speculation, just as long as there was some rational reason. When no one spoke it, he said, "Let's just drop this line of thinking; it's not going to accomplish any good for us down here."

"Yeah, Vic, try not to let this place get to you, Okay?" Raliel, playfully yet painfully, punched him in the arm.

Aven laughed. Vic did not. "All I'm saying is be careful, guys."

Aven and Raliel nodded, shrugged, and said in unison, "Okay."

"Hey, where's Adam?" Aven asked. The trio became very aware of how alone they were in the silent center of the redoubt.

***

They found Adam with Mendel in a corridor beyond the rear wall and a previously hidden exit breached long ago. They entered behind a giant statue through a dusty broken slab of foot-thick stone.

Mendel was farther in with Adam's lit palm, studying their surroundings as they continued down the narrow rough-cut tunnel. As Aven neared, he could hear Mendel's quiet narrative: "They sacrificed their lives to hold this chamber." He seemed to be speaking more to himself, though Adam listened intently. All around them lay countless long-dead Massifae defenders.

It was a battle site, but all Aven could see were bones and detritus. Anything of value was likely looted by marauders, leaving bodies where they'd fallen—clusters. The bones were picked clean, some stained with blood, blackened with age. Picked at by hungry crawlers, most likely. Aven shuddered at the image.

Again, somehow, Vic called unseen from beyond them all, "You guys might wanna take a look at this."

Aven and Raliel left Mendel to his thoughts and hurried to Vic. Lighting was dim this far from Adam, but the foxfire lichen illuminated everything in a blue film. It was thick, almost like growing hair, from the dead. Luminous bones filled the crudely cut tunnel. They could just see Vic standing at the very end, in front of a giant stone door.

Up close, they could see it was sealed, unbreached. It was covered by intricately carved Massifae runes. Two more fire pots framed the door unlit. Vic said, "If it's anything like the first doors, we'll probably need Mendel to open it."

The pots erupted in green flame as Mendel approached. Then he, quite uncharacteristically, gasped, "We've found it. Finally."

All looked to Mendel in question, even suspicion.

"What have we found, Mendel?" Aven asked.

"I think it's time you let us in on whatever you're hiding," Vic echoed through his helm.

Raliel watched him with narrowed eyes. Oblivious to the tension, Adam's face never left the carvings on the door. Mendel waved a hand at the trio, dismissing their unwarranted concern.

He wandered to an outcropping of rock left uncut next to a fire pot and took a seat. His broad figure strained leather and mail, creaking as he settled. Mendel looked up at them, face cast in green firelight, "About 40 years ago, give or take, I was part of a group much like this one. They've all long passed from this life, being humans an' all. One of the curses of being massif in this new age is that your friends tend to die around you.

"My group started much like yours, building up what we could to make this a better world by restoring its past glory. One of the biggest obstacles was that the world before the war was vast. With the unchecked hordes of wild creatures, it's impossible to traverse meaningfully.

"In an attempt to solve this dilemma, we got it in our heads to start seeking out ruins and their long-dormant portals. To reactivate them, fix them, and discover new ones. We found a few, opening up other gate-cities, leading to a few more portals and ruins, but we eventually hit dead ends. What we found were considered merely standard travel portals, pre-war.

"We knew that if we were to make any real headway, we'd need to find some more ancient networks like royal portals. The military later secretly used portals to move supplies during the war. Ones made before the building of the oldest cities. Ancient ones like Midhaven."

"So what you're saying is that beyond this door lies a portal, perhaps used in constructing this city?" Aven asked, eyes wide.

"But Midhaven is ancient!" Raliel scoffed.

"Yeah, but that's not the point, friends. Many of the portals created by pre-war civilization were destroyed. Mostly on purpose to prevent the other side from using them during the war. The portals were hotly contested over, as you can see…"

"What makes you think this isn't a destroyed portal like the others?"

"Won't know till we look." Mendel proffered a sad smile. "What's missing from this scene?"

They looked around at the remains of the long-past battle. Vic spoke first, "There are no Elden bodies."

"Exactly," Mendel agreed, "meaning?"

Adam answered, "They gathered their dead!"

"Then…?" Mendel continued to prod.

"Just tell us already," Raliel yelled in frustration.

"It implies, Rali, that they returned to where they came from, to move so much, would require a primary portal, like the one in Midhaven. Right?" Aven reasoned.

"You said it." Mendel grinned.

"Wait a minute here," Aven said, "What if they destroyed the portal on their side?"

"Not a problem. Through these portals, multiple sites connect," Mendel paused and sighed, "At the very least, *one* should be reachable, hopefully more. Locations unvisited by anyone for hundreds of years."

"Not visited by humans, you mean," Vic thought aloud, in a hushed tone.

"What are we waiting for then?" Raliel asked, "Isn't this what we came for?" She became increasingly agitated. Anxiety threatened to infect them all if they continued to sit still.

Aven took charge, "We'll secure the area around the portal, set up a town portal, and return with supplies for an expedition before venturing on."

"Very wise, Aven, these prime portals have a very long-range, and we can't be sure where they'll lead," Mendel agreed.

"I've got something to take care of early in the morning," Vic added.

"It's settled then, set up, leave, and return later. After you, Mendel…." Aven gestured to the door with one gauntlet. Mendel stood, motioned for everyone to give him space, and raised his hands. Nothing happened. He tried again. No effect.

"Hmmm…" Mendel inched closer to inspect the door. "Ah, I see, truly ancient indeed." He placed a hand on one of the runes, closing his eyes in concentration. Deep within the walls, they could hear and feel stone grating and rumbling. Then, the rune inscribed door was quickly pulled up into a recess in the ceiling, revealing another room filled with statues—Elden statues in a row down the middle. Dust, cobwebs, and lichen trailed with the gust of newly introduced air.

They moved in, studying the room under an eerie green glow. Something was different, Aven noticed; instead of the statues' weaponry lighting the way, green fire came from their eyes.

"Wait," Aven hissed, "something's not right."

Just then, the rune inscribed door slammed down, sealing them inside.

"A trap!" Mendel bellowed. The 'statues' trained green orbs on Aven and his friends.

"Undead," Aven cursed.

Exactly what Aven had feared, a threat much more dangerous than any of them expected, yet he didn't feel afraid. Instead, time seemed to freeze as they absorbed the full gravity of the situation--not ordinary undead, nor fresh but twenty powerful old ones, ones left in the room since the war which waited centuries, hungering to extinguish life.

The companions spread out, giving one another room to maneuver while keeping their backs safely to the wall.

"One scratch is death; make every hit count!" Raliel screamed axe held out in front of her, glowing red, ready to ignite whichever foe came first. "Why haven't they attacked us?" she growled. Mendel didn't answer—nobody did—he kept his eyes focused on the threat, hammer shining with white accents.

The pause allowed Aven to get a good look at the undead, who began to snarl and jerk within their dust-encrusted carcasses. They were Elden, tall and angular; pale flesh withered tight over decrepit skulls. Snarls became howls as their burning green sockets locked on hated life.

"Watch out!" Adam squeaked.

"Wha—" Aven tried to ask as the boy shoved between him and Mendel, taking a knee in front.

"Adam," Mendel grumbled, but no one made a move to interfere.

Holding out his ruby ring, he aimed and began concentrating.

"If you're gonna do something, do it fast, Adam!" Vic hissed.

Howling undead rushed, some leaping through the air, clawing and biting maniacally.

"Hurry, Adam!" Raliel raged.

Aven started when he saw a roiling ball of molten fire bloom unnaturally fast, boiling out from Adam's ring.

"HA! Better let go soon, or you'll kill us all, boy!" Mendel roared jovially.

The fireball lurched off toward the undead. Lazily at first, still growing. Then, frustratingly slow, it seemed it would miss the bulk of the creatures.

Mendel laughed aloud as he raised his brightening hammer high. Then, his other hand forward, fingers spread, casting, "Hold on to your helmets, kids!"

The fireball struck the floor just short of the monsters, missing all.

Then it exploded.

Aven had never imagined anything as powerful as this eruption of intense heat, splattering everything in liquid fire. The flash blinded him entirely for a moment. Then, when it receded, he saw that everything—except for the space around them—was covered in blazing yellow fire.

"Not bad, boy, but next time give ol' Mendel a heads up so I can have a better shield spell prepared." Mendel reached over to ruffle Adam's hair, but he shied away. "Sorry, I've never tried to use so much at once."

Aven continued scanning for threat, but the fire had utterly incinerated the undead. Reading his thoughts, Mendel explained, "Those ol' ones burn real easy; the boy couldn't have cast a better spell."

The fire burned hot, refusing to expire. When it finally died, the air was noticeably thinner.

"Back there," Raliel pointed to the far wall, "that must be the portal," where a platform loomed out of reach of Adam's newly lit palm. Then, however, the portal began producing light of its own.

"What's it doing?" Aven asked, concerned.

"The undead was a diversion." Mendel scowled as he assessed the situation, "that's why they stalled. Damn. If that's what I think it is, we're in worse shape than before."

The platform holding the portal was waist high, a ramp centering it. It had already activated but wasn't like any Aven had seen: a vertical circle of rune-etched stone, three feet tall. Inside, flashing electric currents swirled violently.

"Can we get this door opened?" Aven asked Mendel, though he was sure he already knew. Mendel's expression made Aven's heart drop. There was something very final about seeing it on the massif; it was a look of grief, like someone was about to die.

"Look for something to hold onto, Aven," Mendel instructed calmly, "and try and stay together."

The room shuddered. Aven's ears popped painfully, and the portal opened to infinite darkness. Aven felt he could swoon. The portal became a powerful vacuum. It was all he could do to grab hold of the runes protruding from the sealed door. He sought Vic and Raliel, his heart wrenching with remorse. Was this it? He asked himself. "RALIII!" She didn't hear him; the wind was much stronger now, tugging at everything he had on. The power was enormous.

"OUR BEST SHOT IS TO HOLD ON AND HOPE IT RUNS ITS COURSE!" Mendel's voice supernaturally boomed. Everyone seemed to hear it.

Aven tried again, "RALIII!" She looked to him, gripping a ledge even as the vacuum lifted her feet into the air.

Mendel had a hold on a boulder, and Adam held him with all his might, eyes scrunched tight, robe billowing.

They were indeed dead, Aven thought. His heart lurched again at the thought of anything happening to Raliel. But, when he looked her way, she appeared to be hanging on with ease. Vic was farther along the wall, body straight as an arrow, feet pointing directly for the portal.

Aven's gauntlets slipped, unsuitable for gripping stone. He knew he couldn't hold much longer. Intuitively, the vacuum intensified, ripping Aven from the door and dragging him across the floor to the portal. Scrambling, he found another handhold, though his helmet made it impossible to see the others. His world was reduced to roaring wind, shrieking all around him. In his mind, he allowed himself to imagine he could hear Raliel calling his name, which meant she still survived. Aven was still smiling with relief when darkness took him.

***

"AVEN!" Raliel couldn't be sure he heard her in the storm. As she watched him holding, tiles from the floor near Mendel broke free. The largest of the group bounded Aven's way, connecting dead-on with the top of his helm. And he was gone. Gone. She couldn't sense him through her amulet, and the shock of its emptiness almost caused her grip to falter. She held, angry.

To her left, Mendel was lashing Adam's robe to a piece of jutting rock. That done, he looked to her and roared, "WHATEVER YOU DO, JUST HOLD ON!" Then he let go.

The vortex was so big and powerful that Mendel never even touched the ground. Raliel looked down her body—dizzying as it was—just in time to see him disappear into the void.

Vic yelled, "RALIEELL! I DON'T KNOW HOW MUCH LONGER I CA—"

She tried irrationally to reach out, nearly losing herself; he was too far. His limbs seemed to blur for a moment, and he almost recovered. But, then, Vic, another lifelong friend, as close as any of her brothers, was gone too.

She couldn't even tell if Adam was conscious at this point. His slight frame whipped around like a rag doll, but his robe didn't rip. If it wasn't for Adam, she might have let go. She'd never contemplated ending her life, and she didn't want to die, but it was as if something inside her had broken. A pain in her heart real enough to weaken her grip. It whispered to her, seducing her to just let go.

"NO!" She squeezed tighter. If she had nothing else to live for, she should still help this boy survive. She still had family back home. Firm grip and resolve, she again looked to her left and kept Adam within sight. She left it all to his miraculous robe because if it didn't hold—then neither could she.

She felt the sheer force of the vacuum drained the blood from her head to feet. After that, it became a battle to keep hold of her ledge and consciousness. Then, when things couldn't worsen, gravel and dust blinded her, and there was no longer anything to hold with her right.

So, Raliel held on with everything she had. By one hand. There was no energy for thought, and she couldn't remember why she held, just that she had to. She imagined she heard a rip somewhere, and whether it was in her head or not, the perceived distraction was all it took for her hand to slip finally.

With bone-jarring impact, consciousness and all its worries and responsibilities mercifully winked out.

EPILOGUE

From a dozen feet above the sickly canopy, Horace watched the sun continue its ascent. He judged it to be almost noon. A good thing, too, because had he not found what he'd been searching for, it would force Horace to return to where he'd left his pack with Jenny.

His levitation amulet was potent and very rare. Likely the only one left of its kind. A Donivian relic from incalculable prehistory. Even it had limits.

The air seemed to smack his soles with the necessary force to keep him aloft with each step. Ripples of displaced air dissipated around each shoe as he went. To lower, all he had to do was stop stepping or disengage his amulet.

A sea of tainted leaves shimmered oily all around. It was still amazing to think there could be a remnant, a pure seed, still tenaciously clinging to this world below.

Under the sun's warmth, the befouled Witherwood's canopy releases a noxious vapor. Greasy fumes evaporate in brownish clouds.

Horace shook his head in disgust. The consequences of the broken Oath angered him. Infuriated by the pollution and lengths both sides had been willing to go to win the war. They had destroyed so much good to claim righteousness, including themselves.

"What you compromise to keep, you will eventually lose." He shook his head in profound sadness.

He began his descent in a downward spiral of slapping soles by reducing the number of footfalls. He led with the knotted tip of his staff, "Olam Or." The tainted foliage parted from its blessed touch, retreating as he passed.

Once his old eyes adjusted to the darkness, he could discern the murky depths below. With a flick of his wrist, an ember of pure white light shot out, growing and brightening as it scouted. Not a few hidden darkspawn fled noisily into the surrounding brush. Below, the entire surface of the cloudy waters shuddered and seemed to retreat a foot into the earth.

"Ah, I see you, vile wyrm," he said, sending the ember to rest over the center with a warning flare before dimming to a more natural luminosity.

"If you promise not to bother me, I'll not bother you."

The waters shuddered in response, then stilled.

Horace's eyes darted about, searching for anything that could be responsible for this visit. Everywhere he looked, he found it gnarled and tainted. His feet smacked in a broader circuit, one eye warily flicking back to check his warding ember. When he discovered a massive ancient tree, his soul leaped in recognition.

He shut down his levitation amulet not too far above the great tree's base, landing in a shock-absorbing squat. He used his staff to help him rise.

"So," he thought aloud, "here you are. Well, no time to waste." He reached into a fold of his dark robe, retrieving a green emerald, uncut and naturally shaped like a seed.

Approaching the tree's trunk, he muttered, "Hope this ain't goin' ta waste. If any part of ya can hear me, know that now's the time to try."

Horace touched the emerald to the tree's bark. It opened, receiving the gem and sealing over.

"Well, the rest's up to you, lil' one. Light be with ya."

From an alternate plane of awareness, he distinctly heard a little girl scream. His part completed, he nodded. He'd done the 'natural.' Now it was up to the supernatural.

As he slapped shoes in ascent, the waters bucked violently, sending dirty spray to spatter his legs.

"Oh, do be patient; I keep my word."

As he entered the upper reaches of foliage, leaves, and branches once again making way before Olam Or, he gestured for his ember to follow, dissipating to nothingness as it did.

Back above the canopy, free hand shading his eyes, Horace skipped merrily off. Muffled splashes below, coupled with throaty roars of gargantuan fury, only encouraged his glee, "Hee-heee!"

End of Part I

The adventure continues!

Turn the page for exciting excerpts from Book 2 of the Bright Heritage Chronicles, Nightswarm!

Mendelonius No Name shot through a tumult of branches and pine needles, trying to curl himself into a ball against the sheer force of his flight.

He met his first tree trunk in an explosion of bark. The blow was stunning but the shield on his back took the brunt. Chips of wood joined him as he bounced off more branches face-first into another tree. At the point of contact, he dug into the tree's bark with all his might. His gauntlets tore free, rending nail and flesh, doing little to slow his fall. His boots struck wood, sending him tumbling backward, flipping head over heels wildly. A thick branch relieved him of his helmet, another his left boot, another his breath, and finally, his consciousness as he careened off of rough bark, leaving bits of hair and scalp behind.

The darkness deepened, enveloping Mendel in a dizzying lurch into oblivion...

***

Vic spun and rolled, whipping his head around to face the weird sights. It was useless to try and control his flight. There was no wind resistance, only a sense of utter void, but it was far from dark...

***

Raliel stirred, gaining consciousness to the sound of quiet weeping. She continued lying there—eyes closed—until her memories barged back into her mind, painfully clear. Her heart ached and her will to get up and face reality was nonexistent.

The sniffling resumed. From Adam, she thought. She could hardly muster the energy to pay it much mind. Exhausted from the effort, she slowly began to doze. She welcomed oblivion despite her throbbing head.

"Miss Raliel?" Adam interrupted her reprieve, jolting her uncomfortably back to reality. One in which all was lost. She ignored

him. Sleep crept mercifully back.
   "Raliel!"

***

Aven awoke, gasping for air in a panic. The feeling of alarm was stifled by dread, as he became aware of his surroundings. 'Where am I?'
   His body hurt all over. He struggled to rise, settling for a crouch on all fours. It was dark here but he could still see well enough to make out the red pentagram he was now centered in. The floor was cobblestone, but flat and even. The work of intelligent beings.
   Light came from interspersed torches along the surrounding walls. There were wood doors too, bound in iron, with rings to twist and open.
   "Where am I?" Aven cringed at how loud his voice sounded. It echoed...